What the Cat Knew

Also by this Author

YOUR ADULT FICTION:

Tamara's Teardrops:
Tattooed Teardrops
Two Teardrops
Tortured Teardrops
Vanishing Teardrops

Between the Cracks:
Ruby, Between the Cracks
June and Justin
Michelle
Chloe
Ronnie
June, Into the Light (Coming Soon)

Medical Kidnap Files:
Mito
EDS
Proxy
Toxo

Breaking the Pattern:
Deviation
Diversion
By-Pass

Stand Alone
Don't Forget Steven
Those Who Believe
Cynthia has a Secret
Questing for a Dream
Once Brothers
Intersexion
Making Her Mark
Endless Change

What the Cat Knew

REG RAWLINS, PSYCHIC
INVESTIGATOR #1

P.D. WORKMAN

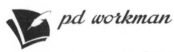

ISBN: 9781989080580

For those who see with more than their eyes.

★ Chapter One ★

R EG RAWLINS CLIMBED OUT of the car and stretched, her muscles cramped after being in the car all day. According to the dashboard readout, it was a few degrees warmer than it had been in Tennessee. Added to that, it was humid and the air felt muggy. She could smell the ocean. She'd heard that all points in Florida were within sixty miles of the ocean as the crow flies. She was looking forward to spending some time swimming and looking for seashells. She'd always wanted to live near a real beach. A warm, sandy beach.

"Witch!" accused a homeless man sitting on the sidewalk with a cardboard sign. He had long, scraggly hair and a beard, streaked with gray, and he was missing several teeth. His clothes were ragged, and even though he was a few feet away, Reg could smell his unwashed body.

She gave him a scowl, but didn't turn away. His reaction interested her. She was dressed for the part she intended to play—headscarf, heavy jewelry and hoop earrings, a long, flowing peasant dress—so it was not unexpected that he would notice her and comment on her getup. But he had gone with *witch* rather than a fortune-teller or medium, which she thought was an odd choice. She wasn't wearing a pointed hat or black robe.

"What makes you think I'm a witch?" she demanded.

"All redheads are witches!" he informed her.

"Ah." Reg's red hair was all done in cornrow braids, which hung free around her face rather than being wound up under her headscarf. She liked the effect. And she liked the way the braids felt when she turned her head and they all swished back and forth. She ignored the homeless man and looked up and down the boardwalk.

She liked the atmosphere of Florida. Laid back and relaxed, not like in Tennessee where she had visited Erin. There had certainly been some uptight ladies there. She didn't regret leaving, though she was sad things hadn't worked out with Erin. Erin had been a lot more fun when they were kids. She'd grown up too much and become a stuffy old woman instead of the lost child she'd been when they had lived with the Harrises and then again when they had both aged out of foster care and had run a few cons together. Now she was grown up and mature and responsible, no longer interested in Reg's ideas.

"You don't know what you're missing, Erin," Reg murmured, looking around at the blue sky and the green vegetation, the tang of salt hanging in the air. Swimming in Florida was going to be nothing like a dip in the ocean in Maine. Miles of sandy beaches, warm water, and not a care in the world.

She gathered up her braids with both hands and pulled them back behind her shoulders, letting them fall again.

"There somewhere good to eat around here?" she asked the bum.

People looked at her oddly as they passed, and Reg didn't know if it was because of her outfit or the fact that she was talking to a non-person.

"Only if you like seafood!" the man cackled.

Luckily, Reg did.

"You should go to The Crystal Bowl," he told her. "That's where the witches gather."

Reg pursed her lips, considering him. "The Crystal Ball?"

"The Crystal *Bowl*. Get it?"

"Where is The Crystal Bowl?"

He gestured down the boardwalk. "Yonder about two blocks. Big sign. Can't miss it."

Reg had been told that Florida, and Black Sands in particular, was *the place* for psychics and mediums but she hadn't expected there to actually be enough of a community to warrant a restaurant of their own. She was glad she'd picked Florida over Massachusetts; she'd had enough of New England to last her a lifetime.

The Crystal Bowl had satisfyingly dramatic decor and furnishings. Blacks, reds, and golds combined into a rich tapestry of mysticism, lit by flickering candles which were actually tiny electric lights. East met West in a sort of a cross between an opium den and a carnival fortune-teller set. They worked together in harmony rather than clashing.

The patrons of the restaurant, however, were disappointingly normal. Shorts with t-shirts or light blouses, sunglasses propped on foreheads, everybody looking at their phones or calling across the room to greet each other. No sense of mystical decorum.

The sign said 'please wait to be seated,' but Reg walked across to the bar counter and selected a stool.

The bartender was spare, his skin too pale for a Floridian. He obviously spent too much time in the restaurant out of the sun. Either that or he was a vampire.

"Afternoon," he greeted, adjusting the spacing between the various bottles on the counter and turning their labels out.

"Hi."

"Don't think I've seen you here before."

"No, just flew in on my broomstick."

He eyed her. "Wrong costume."

Reg grinned. "Good. The old bum down the street said that I was a witch, and I was afraid I'd gotten it wrong."

"It's the red hair."

"So I hear. Mediums can't have red hair?"

"Mediums can have whatever they want. So what will it be?" He gestured to the neat rows of bottles behind the bar and the chalkboard on the wall behind them.

Reg looked over the options. Should she establish herself as someone with exacting and eclectic tastes? A connoisseur? Someone who was obviously unique and memorable?

But she wanted the bar to be somewhere she could let her hair down, not where she had to always be playing a part.

"Just a draft," she sighed. "Whatever is on tap."

He nodded and grabbed a beer stein. He filled it and placed it neatly on a coaster in front of her, pushing a bowl of pretzels closer to her. Something nice and salty to encourage thirst.

"So, Miss Medium, your name is…?"

"Reg Rawlins." She figured she was okay using the name, even though that was what she had used in Bald Eagle Falls. She didn't think any charges would follow her all the way to Florida. It wasn't like she was going to be filing taxes under the name.

He gave a nod. "Bill Johnson."

Reg took a pull on her beer. It had been a long drive and she was glad to be able to relax and recharge her batteries. Thinking of figurative batteries, she decided she'd better check her actual battery. Reg pulled out her phone and checked the charge. Not too bad. It would last her a couple more hours, and maybe by that time, she would have settled somewhere. She launched her browser and tapped in a search for lodgings. There were plenty of hits for short-term rentals. Lots of vacationers. Finding somewhere permanent might take a bit longer, but at least she'd have a place to hang her hat. Or her headscarf. And plug in her phone.

"You need a place to stay?" Bill asked, obviously recognizing the website.

"Looks like there are lots of options."

"Sarah Bishop is looking for a tenant. She's easy to get along with. You two would probably hit it off."

"Oh?"

Bill looked around the room. "She's not here yet. She often shows up for supper. If she doesn't, I can give her a call and let her know you're interested."

Reg raised an eyebrow. "You don't know me from Adam. What makes you think I would hit it off with Sarah Bishop or that you can recommend me to her?"

"Let's just say… I'm good at reading people. And I would know you from Adam, given that Adam was of the male persuasion."

Reg considered pointing out that there were plenty of men who could pass as women or had transitioned from one to the other, but decided that antagonizing him wouldn't be the wisest thing for her to do. So she took a sip of her beer and didn't challenge him.

"Okay. Well, I'd appreciate that. Being able to move in somewhere long-term right away would be a real plus. Thanks."

"No problem." He moved away to help another patron.

Reg continued to browse through the lodging listings to get a sense of what costs to expect for rent and what her options were if she didn't like Sarah Bishop's place. It could be a dump. Sarah Bishop could be Bill's sister or ex and he just wanted her off of his back. He had been pretty quick to offer his help and judge Reg worthy as a tenant for his friend.

Someone took the stool next to Reg's, and she looked up to see who it was. A strikingly handsome man. Thirty-something, short hair slicked back from his face to show off a widow's peak, a stubbly beard that at first glance made it look like he had forgotten to shave for a couple of days, but on a more careful examination was painstakingly trimmed. His eyes were dark but glowed almost red in the dim lighting of the restaurant, reflecting the red furnishings and wall coverings. Add a cape, and he'd be perfect to cast as a vampire.

He gave her an enigmatic look. Almost smiling, but not quite. A smirk. She thought he was going to greet her as Bill had, recognizing her as a stranger and asking who she was. But he merely inclined his head slightly and waited for his drink, which Bill brought over without being asked. Obviously his 'usual.'

"Reg Rawlins, Uriel Hawthorne," Bill said, making a gesture from one to the other by way of introduction.

Great choice of name. Reg was impressed. Still, Uriel said nothing, just threw back his shot and watched her.

"Nice to meet you," Reg said, thrusting her hand out to shake his, forcing him to acknowledge her presence.

He left her hanging for a moment, not moving to take her hand, and then finally responded, taking her hand in his in a soft, caressing gesture that made her immediately want to pull back. But she set her teeth and gave him a warm smile. She gave him one more squeeze before letting go and pulling back again.

"A pleasure to meet you," Uriel returned. "Are you thinking of joining our little community?"

"Well, we'll see how it goes," Reg said with a shrug. "I'm new in town and I've never been part of... this kind of community before. I've always just been on my own."

"There is something to be said for that."

Reg raised her eyebrows in query.

"Setting your own rules, doing your own thing," Uriel said. "No one with preconceptions as to how things should be done."

"Right." Reg nodded. Rules, in her opinion, were made to be broken. She wasn't about to buy into a social construct that tried to control her activities.

"Ah, here's Sarah," Bill said, hovering near Reg.

It took her a moment to remember who Sarah was and why she should care. Sarah was the landlord looking for a tenant.

Reg turned, following Bill's gaze. She was looking for a woman of around her age, since Bill had said that he thought she and Sarah would hit it off. But she didn't see anyone who fit her preconception.

Bill gave a little wave, and a woman nodded to him and corrected her course to join him at the bar.

She was an older woman, at least in her sixties, with a round face, bottle blond hair that curved around her face, and wire frame glasses. She looked like a friendly grandmother, lips pink with freshly-applied lipstick, a flowered shirt, pink slacks, and flat white sandals. She smiled at Bill.

"Good evening, Bill. How are you today?"

He nodded and didn't bother to answer the greeting. "Sarah, meet Reg Rawlins. She has just arrived in town and is looking for accommodations."

"Oh!" Sarah's face lit up. "Well, my dear, isn't that wonderful! I just happen to have a cottage that I am trying to rent out! Would you join me for dinner?" She motioned to the tables in the dining area. "I'm afraid I can't manage bar stools these days."

"Sure," Reg agreed, sliding down from hers and taking her drink with her. "That would be nice."

She didn't bother saying goodbye to Uriel, irritated with his distant, disinterested manner. Sarah led her to a table which was probably her regular, as there didn't seem to be any problem with her seating herself instead of waiting to be seated. She smiled and chatted with some of the other patrons as she made her way to her seat.

"Sit down, sit down," she encouraged Reg, as if Reg had somehow been holding her back. "Reg? Is that short for something? Where did you come from?"

"Regina. I've lived all over."

"Well, that's a pretty name. Did you pick it, or was it already yours?"

Reg laughed at the question. "I was saddled with Regina, but I picked Reg."

"Very nice. I like it. And what do you do?" She made a little gesture to indicate Reg's costume. "You read palms? Tarot?"

"A little of everything. Mostly, I talk to the dead."

"Oh." Sarah nodded wisely. "That's a good gig. Have you been doing it for long?"

Reg studied the woman, not sure how honest to be. She wasn't sure whether she should be open about being a medium or a con. Both paths seemed equally treacherous.

"I've always had... certain tendencies... gifts, if you like..." she said obliquely. "I'm just testing the waters now... seeing whether this is something I should pursue..."

Sarah nodded. A waitress came over and handed them menus, introducing herself and showing off a couple of rather long canine teeth when she smiled. Sarah took no note, and barely gave the menu a glance. She'd obviously been there enough times to know what she wanted.

"What's good?" Reg asked, glancing over the offerings.

"The seafood is fresh. Other than that… burger and fries… I wouldn't try anything too adventurous."

"Good to know."

After placing her order, Reg leaned back in her seat, looking Sarah over.

"How about you? Did you retire to Florida, or have you always lived here?"

"I've lived lots of places, dear. Florida is good for my old bones. As for retiring… maybe someday, but not yet."

"What is it you do?"

Sarah raised her brows, as if surprised that Reg didn't know. Was she supposed to have guessed? Did Sarah think that Bill had told her?

"Well, I'm a witch," Sarah said, as if it should have been obvious.

"Oh." Reg sat like a lump, with no idea what to say or how to respond. Sarah had turned the tables on her. Reg was used to provoking a reaction from other people. She liked to dress up and to say extravagant things to see how people reacted to her different personas. This time she was in the hot seat. "Oh. I guess I should have guessed." Reg threw her hands up in what was both a shrug and indicating their surroundings. "After all, we are in the Magic Cauldron."

Sarah blinked. "The Crystal Bowl."

"Whatever. This is a witch hangout, right? So of course that's what you are."

"I thought you knew. You didn't just wander in here of your own accord, did you?"

"There was an old bum down the boardwalk… he called me a witch, and he pointed me this way. So, yes… I knew… It's all just a bit much." Reg looked around the restaurant. "I mean, *everyone* here can't be a witch."

"Of course not," Sarah agreed. "We have people of all different spiritual and paranormal persuasions. Witches, warlocks, wizards, mediums," she gave Reg a nod, "fortune-tellers, healers… people who are gifted and people who are seekers."

"Okay, then." Reg looked around at the patrons and shook her head, having a hard time believing that they were all running the same con. "And there isn't too much competition for the same… customers?"

"Some people think Black Sands has gotten too commercial, and some people complain it has gotten too crowded. But for the most part… people are willing to live and let live. We are peaceful people."

"Uh-huh."

Sarah launched into a lyrical description of the town and its more interesting citizens. Reg tried not to sit with her mouth open as she listened. The waitress eventually came over with their meals. Reg hadn't realized how hungry she was getting, but when the platter was placed in front of her, she suddenly realized she was famished.

"This looks lovely," she told the waitress, not expecting to be getting a beautifully plated fish at the offbeat witches' diner. She dug in immediately, taking several delicious bites before looking at Sarah to ask her if she was enjoying her food.

Sarah's eyes were closed and her hands hovered over her plate as if she were warming them in the steam rising from the food. Reg turned to look at the waitress, but she was already gone. Reg looked uncomfortably at Sarah, wondering if she should follow suit.

Sarah's eyes opened, catching Reg staring at her.

"Uh…" Reg fumbled. "Amen?"

Sarah nodded slightly. Then she started to eat.

"It really is good," Reg said. "Really nice."

"I wouldn't eat here all the time if it wasn't," Sarah agreed. She patted her stomach. "I wouldn't have to worry so much about my waistline if I was cooking for myself!"

She was plump, but in a grandmotherly sort of way. Reg couldn't imagine her skinny; it just wouldn't have fit. Adele,

Erin's witch friend back in Tennessee was tall and slender, and that worked for her, but it just wouldn't work for Sarah.

"So why don't you tell me about this cottage of yours?" she asked. "Bill seemed to think that we'd be able to come to terms."

"He's very empathic," Sarah said. "He reads people."

"Ah. Of course." It made sense for a bartender. Reg had known her share of good and bad barkeeps.

"It's just a little two-bedroom," Sarah said, answering Reg's question. "But it's just you…?"

"Yes. No dependents."

"So you could use one room as your bedroom and the other as an office, and still have space for entertaining in the living room."

"Right," Reg agreed. She hadn't thought about seeing clients in her home. She wasn't sure she wanted anyone to know where she lived. If they didn't like what she had to say, they wouldn't know where she lived to confront her. She had thought she would go to them, do readings in their own spaces. She could read a client a lot better if surrounded by their own things. People gave a lot away by the way they lived.

"It's separate from the main house, so we wouldn't be on top of each other. We can each keep our own hours. That can be a problem with night people and day people mixing. The kitchen is small, really just a prep area. You could come use the big kitchen if you needed to do any major baking or entertaining. I really don't use it that much."

"I don't expect I would either. I don't do a lot of my own cooking."

"You see? You'd be perfect. You wouldn't be complaining to me that there's no oven. It really does have everything you really need."

"Well, maybe we could go see it after dinner, and talk business."

"You're going to like it just fine. I can tell."

As Reg wasn't that picky, Sarah was probably right. If Reg didn't like it after a month or two, she'd have a good idea by that point of where to look for somewhere better. It wasn't a long-term commitment.

Which was good, because Reg Rawlins didn't like long commitments.

★ Chapter Two ★

*C*OLD, CLAMMY FINGERS TRACED across Reg's face, awakening her in the wee hours of the morning. She sat bolt upright, her heart racing. She looked quickly around her, trying to remember where she was and who was there with her. A chaotic childhood had conditioned her to be instantly awake and ready to fight. Strike fast to protect herself and escape to somewhere safe. But there was no one else in the room. Maybe the roof leaked and a drop of cold water had traced its way across her cheek.

She touched it, but it was dry, with only the memory of those icy fingers lingering behind.

Reg listened for a long time, hearing the lap of the waves in the distance. It was a restful, peaceful noise, and gradually the slamming of her heart slowed to its normal rate, though it was still pounding too hard to get back to sleep.

"There's no one here," Reg said aloud, very quietly. "You're perfectly safe, Reg. No one is going to hurt you."

It was comforting to hear those words.

When she was a kid, therapists had told her social worker and foster parents she had PTSD, and that was the reason for much of her unwanted behavior. It was nonsense, of course. Reg had never been in a war or terrorist attack. She'd never been kidnapped. Sure, she'd grown up rough, but a lot of kids had. And Reg was good at adapting. You couldn't call a few nightmares PTSD just because it was the fashion.

She listened to the waves for a long time. It was growing light as she drifted off to sleep again, still not sure what had awakened her in the night.

When she got up in the morning, it was with the clear plan to get a cat. She needed a cat. It would be a good prop. Witches had cats or other familiars. People instinctively felt that people who owned pets were kinder and more trustworthy than those who didn't. And it would give her a little company, without having to resort to having another person around the house. Reg liked company, but she liked having her own space.

A cat was the perfect idea.

Reg giggled to herself at the pun. A purrfect idea.

She checked addresses on her phone, thinking about what else she would need to buy in order to settle into her new living space. The fact that it came furnished was a bonus. She packed and traveled light and was used to operating on a shoestring. A fully-furnished cottage was a level of luxury she wasn't used to.

She picked up groceries and the basics she would need to care for a cat before going to the pound, patting herself on the back for thinking ahead and realizing that she wouldn't be able to do the other shopping once she had the cat in the car. She'd have to go straight home, and she wouldn't want to just abandon the poor critter there to go run errands.

At the animal shelter, self-styled as a pet sanctuary, before she was even allowed to look at the animals, Reg had to fill in a bunch of paperwork indicating her willingness to take care of a pet for the rest of its natural life and to follow all of the rules that the shelter set forth, such as not declawing a cat.

The place was noisy and smelly. Every effort had been made to make it a nice place, comfortable and humane for the animals, but it still stank. Reg thought about Erin. She probably would have run out of there puking, she was so sensitive to bad smells. Reg wasn't sure how she even managed to keep pets of her own, what with having to change litter and clean up after any accidents. They hadn't been allowed pets when they had lived with the Harrises, but Reg had seen enough examples of Erin reacting to human smells and accidents that she had no doubt she'd have difficulty cleaning up after animals.

There were old cats and tiny kittens and everything in between. Orange cats and tabbies and calicos. Short hair and long. Unlike the dogs, most of the cats didn't interact with the people walking by their cages, but simply slept, curled up in the corners of the cages. Occasionally, one of them would open its eyes or lift its head for a moment, but mostly they just continued to sleep.

She had thought she would be tempted by the playful younger kitties, but she thought of them keeping her up all night and wasn't sure that was what she wanted.

Maybe getting a cat had just been an impulse. Buying a pet was one of those things you were never supposed to do on impulse.

There were good reasons for getting a cat, but there were reasons not to as well. It might be noisy and wake her up nights. Have hairballs. Scatter litter and shed all over the house. It might jump up on the counter and get into things. Get out of the house and run out into the street.

It was probably a bad idea.

Reg looked into the next cage. The black and white cat raised his head, then climbed out of the nest of blankets in the corner, stretched, and walked up to the front of the enclosure.

"Hey, cat," Reg murmured.

He sat up tall and gazed at her, serious and still. Reg poked her finger through the bars at him, hearing a voice in the back of her head warning her never to poke her finger into an animal's cage. Even a hamster would bite you if you stuck your fingers through the bars. But just like she had ignored the foster mothers who had warned her not to do dangerous things, Reg ignored the voice in her head.

The cat's nose twitched as he caught her scent. For a minute, he just sat there. Then he leaned forward and took a step closer, touching his nose to her finger, and then rubbing his cheek against it. She felt his teeth brush over her finger as he rubbed. She scratched under his chin.

"Hey, you like that? Does that feel good?"

He rubbed against her and started purring a deep, satisfied rumble.

One of the shelter workers walked up.

"Wow, you connected with the tux!"

Reg looked at her. The girl was a teenager, maybe sixteen or seventeen, blond, with round cheeks. "The tux?"

"See, he's black with a white chest. Like he's wearing a black tuxedo and white shirt. So we call him a tuxedo cat."

"Oh, that's cool."

"And he has two different colors of eyes, too. I love that."

Reg looked at him and realized he had one green eye and one blue. "I guess that means he's special."

"I think he is." The girl poked her finger through the bars to try to scratch the tuxedo cat as well, but he only rubbed against Reg's finger. "He's been pretty depressed since he was brought in. His owner died and he hasn't really clicked with anyone. We've tried to play with him and to get him interested in things, but he's been so sad, pretty much all he'll do is sleep. He barely even eats."

In direct contradiction to her words, the cat stopped rubbing against Reg's finger and went over to his food bowl. He sniffed at the food, then began to eat, crunching the kibble.

Reg laughed.

"Well, he wouldn't!" the girl protested. "It must be you. Maybe you remind him of his owner."

Reg watched the cat. "What do you know about her?"

"Her? He's a he. A boy."

"No, I mean his owner. What do you know about her?"

"Oh. Well, he's also a he. A man. Don't really know much about him, just that Tux must have really been attached to him."

If she were going to get a cat, then it was obviously going to have to be that one. None of the other cats had shown Reg any interest at all, and she hadn't been particularly attracted to them. She clicked her tongue, thinking about it, and the noise made the cat turn his head to look at her again. He left his food bowl and again walked to the front of the cage, purring.

"I guess… this is the one," Reg said.

At least he was a short-hair, so he wouldn't get too much fur scattered around the cottage. And he seemed very quiet and sedate, not like a kitten that was going to jump on her face in the middle of the night and keep her awake.

"Oh, good!" the girl exclaimed. "I'll go get Marion, and she can help you with the adoption."

"Okay. Sure."

Reg waited there, scratching and quietly communing with her cat until the older supervisor approached to talk to her about the process.

If Reg had been expecting to just walk in and get a cat and walk out ten minutes later, she was sadly mistaken. Even the intake had taken longer than ten minutes. Apparently she needed counseling, needed to be walked through how to care for a cat, all of the things that could go wrong, budgeting for food and vets, what to do for behavioral issues, and on and on.

Reg had a headache by the time they were done and was ready to just pack it in and go home without a cat. But that would make the hours that she had been there wasted time, and she wasn't going to waste her first full day in Florida. Half of her groceries were already sitting spoiling in the car, and she wasn't going to walk out of there empty-handed.

Marion finally decided that Reg was ready to go and took the tuxedo cat out of his cage and settled him into a cardboard box, transferring the furry blanket he had been sleeping on into the box as well.

"That will help him transition, having something that already smells like home with him. Now you be sure to call if you have any questions about his care. Normally I would recommend that a first-time pet owner start out with a smaller animal, like a hamster, but… that tux needs a home badly, and he seems to like you."

Reg watched Marion close the box securely, and then took it from her. She didn't want to stand there discussing it any further. She wanted her cat home.

★ Chapter Three ★

WHEN REG RETURNED TO the cottage, Sarah had obviously been watching for her and immediately came out to talk to her. She grabbed a couple of bags of groceries to help Reg carry them into the house and eyed the cat box.

"We didn't talk about pets," she commented.

Reg had never had a pet before, so it hadn't even occurred to her that it was something she should clear with her landlord.

"Oh… you're right. I just assumed that it would be okay. I mean… witches use familiars, don't they? You don't have a cat?"

"I've never actually hit it off with cats," Sarah said with a sigh. "There just isn't any connection there. I'm more in tune with birds."

"Oh. Do you have birds?"

"I have an old Amazon gray parrot that has been in the family for years. I guess having it around for so many years is what probably encouraged my affinity for birds and antipathy for cats. If you're going to keep a cat here, it needs to be kept indoors. I don't want it stalking the bird feeders and birdbath in the yard."

Reg nodded. "Sure. That's fair. And I'm sorry for not talking to you about it first. I just got up this morning with the clear idea that I needed to get a cat. So… here he is."

They carried their respective loads into the cottage. Reg put the cat box down carefully and went back to the car to get the last couple of bags of supplies. When she was inside and had closed the door, the tuxedo cat let out a demanding yowl. Reg and Sarah both looked at the box.

"I guess he wants out. Do you want to meet him?"

Sarah bit her lip, taking a step back. "Oh, I don't know. Is he trained?"

"Trained? You mean not to bite people? I don't think you can do that. But they don't usually go around attacking people anyway, do they? It's not like he's going to come after you."

"Well, okay…"

Reg went back to the box and pulled open the flaps, moving slowly and carefully so as not to scare the animal.

The black and white cat stared up out of the box at her, with an imperious look that seemed to say, "Well, pick me up and get me out of here!"

Reg leaned down and slid her hands around the cat's body, and she lifted him up. His body draped heavily around her hands, and she put one hand under his back feet to support him. She turned to face Sarah, showing the cat off.

"He is pretty cute," Sarah admitted. "He looks very dapper in his little tuxedo."

It surprised Reg that someone who didn't like cats would immediately know the common name for his markings.

"What's his name?" Sarah asked.

"I haven't decided yet. They were calling him Tux at the animal shelter, but I imagine half the cats in the world with his markings are probably called Tux. I'd like something a little more imaginative."

The cat gave a squirm and a kick, and Reg put him down on the floor. He turned and licked his back fur down, then began to clean his front socks, ignoring the two of them.

"He has a third eye," Sarah said.

"What?" Reg had expected her to comment on his mismatched eyes, and didn't understand what Sarah meant.

Sarah pointed to the cat's head. "That white marking on his forehead. That's where the third eye is. It's the locus of the sixth sense. Psychic intuition."

"Oh. Yeah, I've heard about that."

"As a medium, I would expect you to know about the third eye."

"Of course. I just didn't know that cats could have it too."

Sarah looked down at the cat, nodding. "Like you said, witches can use familiars. Animals who help them to focus their powers. With a third eye, this cat probably has advanced psychic powers."

"Ah." Reg nodded. "That's probably why I was attracted to him, then. Or why he was attracted to me. Maybe he could sense my calling."

Sarah nodded her agreement. "I have a client for you."

"What?"

Sarah gave her a cheerful smile. "I have a lady who is looking for someone to contact her dead mother. I told her to come by to see you." She looked at her watch. "I wasn't sure what time you would be back, she should be here in about half an hour."

Reg couldn't believe that Sarah would just go ahead and schedule a client for her. But she couldn't find a reason to complain about it. First, the woman had given her a great deal on a living space—and not just an apartment or basement suite, but a sweet little stand-alone cottage—and now she was sending work Reg's way. The kind of work that Reg was actually looking for.

"Oh, well thank you for that. I guess it's good to know people with connections!"

"That's the beauty of having the close-knit community we have here in Black Sands. We know who does what and can refer work to each other."

"You must have other mediums who could have done this job. You really don't know anything about me yet."

Sarah laughed. "Amy Calvert has already seen every other medium in a hundred-mile radius. She needs someone new."

"Oh. Hasn't anyone else been able to contact her mother?" Amy sounded like she might be a tough nut to crack. If she'd seen that many different mediums and hadn't been satisfied that any of them had been able to reach her mother…

"Oh, yes. Certainly. But she's always looking for something more." Sarah straightened and smoothed her flowered shirt. "Just the kind of client you need. If she's happy with your services, she'll give you lots of repeat business."

"But apparently she'll still go shopping for another medium…"

"Eventually. But you can make a lot of business from her in the meantime. Good when you're just getting established. Once you've got a good clientele, you can send her on her way."

It sounded like a reasonable approach. Reg looked at herself. She'd just dressed in shorts and a t-shirt for her errands. "I'd better get ready, then."

"You go ahead, I'll get these groceries put away for you." Sarah opened a bag and started pulling out boxes and jars. "These are warm. You can't leave things in the car around here. They'll spoil."

"Yeah, I figured that out."

"You go ahead. I'll deal with these."

Reg retreated to her bedroom to get changed. Her hair was in cornrows and didn't really need any attention, so it was just a matter of putting on the right clothes and some makeup. She took her time, wanting to keep calm and focused for her appointment. If she got flustered, she wouldn't be able to pick up on all of the infinitesimal tells and microexpressions that she would need to read in order to keep on the right track during the session.

When she left her bedroom, she could hear Sarah talking, and gathered that the client was there already. Amy. When she got back to the front of the cottage, the groceries were all put away, but Amy wasn't there yet. Instead, Sarah stood with her arms at her side, looking down at the cat. He looked up at Sarah.

"That looks very nice," she approved. "Gives a client confidence."

Reg nodded and smoothed the glittery green skirt. First impressions were important. Clients wanted to believe, and she had to give them something to believe in. The show was what people came for. They didn't want an unemotional, logical answer to their problems. They could get that from their bankers and lawyers. They wanted drama and passion, something *moving*.

The doorbell rang, and Sarah went to answer it, greeting her acquaintance at the door and then bringing her in.

"Reg Rawlins, I'd like to introduce you to Amy Calvert."

Reg held herself still as she gave Amy a thorough look up and down, heightening the tension. Then she gave a nod and extended her hand.

"I'm so glad you came, Ms. Calvert."

Amy Calvert was around Sarah's age, as spare and uncomfortable-looking as Sarah was plump and grandmotherly. She gave a nervous giggle as she shook Reg's hand, a reaction so thoroughly unexpected and incongruous that Reg almost dropped her hand in shock.

"I suppose Sarah has told you all about me?" Amy asked in a breathy, little girl voice.

Reg held Amy's hand in both of hers, evaluating her for a moment before releasing her and answering.

"She told me that you wanted to talk to your mother. Is that right?"

"Yes," Amy squeaked. She looked around the room and caught sight of the black and white cat. "Oh—you have a kitty!"

Before Reg could do anything to stop her, Amy dove at the cat, apparently planning on making friends and picking him up. The cat shrank back, all of his fur fluffing out on end as he hissed at her. Amy jerked back her hand just in time to avoid being bitten or scratched, and held it to her breast.

"The cat is not a pet," Reg said sternly. "He is my helper and he deserves to be treated with respect. You need to give him his space and let him work. He enhances the psychic energy of the room, but it won't work if you upset him."

"Oh." Amy's voice was small. "I'm sorry, Kitty."

The cat drew himself up into a tall sitting position and started his bathing ritual once more. Reg nodded.

"He's meditating and cleansing the room of contrary spirits. It's very important to have a clean room to make a good connection."

Amy nodded, her eyes wide.

"Why don't we have a seat while he does his job," Reg suggested. She motioned to the grouping of light, upholstered wicker furniture in the living room conversation area.

"I'll leave you two to it," Sarah advised, giving Reg a smile. "I put the kettle on to boil and it should be ready—"

The teapot began to whistle noisily at that instant. Sarah gave a little wave and left the cottage.

Reg took the kettle off of the hot plate and turned the hot plate off. The tea things were arranged on a tray nearby, so Reg poured the boiling water into the teapot and took the tray over to the coffee table in the living room, and they both helped themselves. Reg wasn't much of a tea person, especially loose leaf tea, but with enough honey, it was palatable, and the leaves swirling in the bottom gave her something to ponder as she considered her new client.

"Tell me about your mother," she suggested.

Amy raised her eyebrows. "Aren't you supposed to tell me about her? Usually, you people try to tell me things about her to convince me that you've really made contact and it's not just a hoax."

"I assume since you came to me that you already believe in my gifts and don't need me to prove anything," Reg said with a shrug. "It's not an audition. It's much easier for me to get a good connection with your mother if I know things about her and can feel your connection with her. There is a thread that runs between the two of you, and it's much easier for me to follow the thread from you to her than it is for me to just reach out aimlessly and hope that I get her."

Amy apparently liked the analogy. She nodded sagely, and it was enough to open her up.

"This might surprise you... in fact, it's a little shocking... you would assume that I was very close to my mother, and that's why I'm still trying to talk to her after all these years. But actually... we were never close at all. She was very strict. Not a warm and friendly person. I feel like... we have a lot of unfinished business."

Reg nodded. It was not an uncommon scenario. Not everyone was best friends with their mothers, and deaths often left the survivors with feelings of guilt and loss that were difficult to come to terms with. Suddenly the opportunity to know the deceased was gone and all of the 'somedays' turned into 'nevers.'

"Was she an unhappy person in general?"

Amy nodded. "Yes. She didn't really get along with anyone. Didn't have any close friends. She and my father stayed together until she died, but they hadn't been happy for years, and he was like a different person once she was gone. He's been reinventing himself."

Reg noted the wistfulness of Amy's words. "Did you have siblings?"

"One other sister."

"You're the elder?"

Amy shook her head, surprised. "Yes. How did you guess."

Reg would recognize that firstborn's guilt and responsibility anywhere.

"Your sister didn't have as hard a time as you. She was more relaxed. Maybe even irresponsible. Your father spoiled her."

Amy was nodding along with all of these suggestions, getting more and more vigorous. Reg was confident she had the relationships and family dynamics worked out. She took one last sip of her tea and put the teacup down in the saucer.

"Did you bring something that belonged to your mother with you?"

"Yes." Amy opened her purse and found a locket in a clear plastic zip bag. Reg was afraid she was going to give it to her still in the bag and not let her touch it, but Amy apparently had been to enough psychics to know the drill. She opened the bag and handed Reg the large, somewhat tarnished locket.

Reg held the locket enclosed in both hands, warming it up and thinking about what she would say. She had some idea of what it was Amy needed, but Amy would have to lead her the rest of the way there.

"I feel cold," Reg said. "Do you feel that?"

It was a hot day, but Reg had the air conditioning turned up high enough that an errant shiver was not out of the question. Amy gave a little shudder.

"Yes, I feel it too," she agreed. "Does that mean she's here?"

"She's here," Reg agreed. "And she wants to talk to you."

Amy's expression wavered between eager and anxious. "Mom…? Are you there?"

Reg rolled her eyes back in her head, blacking out the room and giving herself an instant headache she knew from experience would last for several hours, but it was a very effective method for convincing people that she was channeling a ghost. Or having a seizure.

"Amy?" Reg imitated Amy's voice, but made it deeper, with strident overtones. "Is that you?"

"It's me, Mom. I just wanted to talk to you again… I miss you…"

"Why are you bothering me again? Haven't you interrupted my eternal slumber enough times?"

Reg lowered her eyelids so that it would look like her eyes were closed, but she could still see Amy's expression through a narrow slit. Amy's mouth dropped open, shocked. Reg was a little shocked herself. Where had that come from? She'd been planning to soft-pedal for the first little bit until she knew what it was that Amy needed to hear. But she had said the words that came into her mind as she tried to put on the persona of Amy's not-so-beloved mother.

"I'm… I didn't think I was bothering you…"

"You think I'm at your beck and call? It's not enough that I had to take care of you two and your father in life, you keep making demands on me in death as well?"

"No, I just wanted to visit. I just wanted to talk to you again. Because I miss you."

"Don't you have a life? You should be living your own life instead of disturbing my afterlife."

Reg had taken drama in high school. She had loved method acting and improvisation, and had been really good at both. But she had never gotten quite so carried away by a part. What was she doing telling Amy not to keep contacting her mother, when Sarah had just said she would be a repeat customer? Reg should have been encouraging Amy to visit even more often.

"I do have a life," Amy protested. "I just... wanted someone to talk to."

"Well, why don't you give your uncle a try? I'm getting tired of these constant demands to appear."

"Uncle Marvin?"

"I'm sure he'd love a visit from you. You should expand your social circle. Maybe start talking to some living people too."

"I do... sometimes... usually mediums..."

A wave of irritation washed over Reg. What an insipid milksop the girl was! "For heaven's sake, stop being such a mama's girl and stand on your own two feet. You spent your whole life trying to live up to my expectations, but I stopped having expectations years ago. It's time to grow up, Amy. You're a grown woman, not a ten-year-old girl. Isn't there anything you want out of life?"

Amy considered it, frowning. She brightened a little. "I always sort of wanted to take up gardening. I kept telling myself that once I retired, I was going to do that."

Finally, a clue to what Amy needed to hear, the guidance she needed in her life. "Then why aren't you doing it?" she demanded.

"You always said gardening is a waste of time when we have flower shops and grocery stores."

"I didn't need one more responsibility on my list. But if gardening is going to make you happy, then why would you care whether I enjoyed it or not? Go plant something. A flower pot. A border. A community garden. You want to still be sitting around talking to your dead mother when you're ninety-five?"

"Oh, I won't live to be ninety-five. I always figured I'd die young."

"Well, I hate to tell you, girl, but you missed that boat a long time ago. If you were to die next year, would you want to have spent that year gardening or talking to dead people? You'll have plenty of time to visit with dead people when you're dead yourself."

"Will I really? Will I be able to see you then?"

"Do you think that only the living can talk to the dead? What a ridiculous notion. Of course you'll be able to see me after you die. And you won't have to use a ridiculous-looking gypsy fortune-teller to do it!"

Reg felt like someone had shoved her forehead, making her rear back in her seat. A bit too much method in her acting. Maybe Sarah had put something weird in the tea. Catnip or some Chinese herb that was supposed to help her to open up her third eye.

"She's not ridiculous," Amy protested. "I thought she looked very lovely!"

"Ridiculous," her mother's voice repeated. "Go start your garden. Go make a real life for yourself instead of a pale shadow of mine. Do what your father has done and enjoy yourself. And while you're at it, tell that addled sister of yours that thirty cats will never make up for a mother's love, and it's time to clean house. Literally."

Amy nodded, her mouth open.

Reg's body slumped. She could normally carry on an act for longer than that, but Amy's mother had taken a lot out of her. She closed her eyes all the way, hoping that her headache would go away faster if she did. But she still felt like she was looking at Amy, who sat there with sort of a pink halo around her, trying to process the claptrap that Reg had just fed her.

They both sat there in silence for a long time. Eventually, the cat came over and rubbed against Reg's leg and gave her an irritated little meow like he was telling her to wake up.

"Well!" Reg bent down and petted the cat, then scratched his ears. "That was quite the session, wasn't it?" She offered Amy the locket.

Amy took it back, her eyes still far away.

"I've never heard anyone channel my mother so completely… usually they're all 'your mother wants you to know she loves you very much,' or 'she's trying to tell you something about a family member whose name starts with the letter M.' I've never had someone actually use her voice and facial expressions. That was scary."

"I'm sorry…"

"No, don't be. If my mother was here… that's just exactly what she would have said. I told you, she was never the lovey-dovey type. She was a hard, impatient woman who I could never satisfy. If I couldn't satisfy her in life, why on earth did I spend forty years trying to satisfy a dead woman? I should have just been happy she was gone. I should have done like my dad and gone after my own thing."

"I'm sure you've done some worthwhile things since she died. But now… maybe it is time to start living for yourself."

"Yeah, you're right. You're absolutely right. Wow. That was really something. How much do I owe you?" She dropped the locket carelessly into her purse and pulled out her wallet. "Do you take American Express?"

Reg shut the door behind Amy and looked around her living room. She was exhausted. It must have been all of the previous day's driving, because she wasn't normally the type of person who needed a nap. She didn't usually have any trouble going all day and half the night. After a few late nights, she'd spend a day catching up on her sleep and then be ready to go again.

"Well, Mr. Kitty, I think I'm going to have to have a cat nap," she told the tuxedo cat as he stared at her.

He gave his head a shake, making a noise that Reg thought was his ears flapping with the quick changes of direction. Then he just sat and stared at her.

"Okay. Night night."

Reg went to her room and practically fell into the bed. She crawled up to the pillows and laid herself down and was instantly asleep.

★ Chapter Four ★

S HE AWOKE LATER, NOT sure how much time had passed. When she moved, she found the cat curled up in a warm ball against her stomach. She gave him a nudge.

"Hey, no cats on the bed. What do you think this is?"

He stared at her with his mismatched gaze, as if he understood her perfectly, but wasn't going to budge. Who was the boss here, after all?

"I am," Reg insisted. "I am the boss. And the rule is, no cats in the bed. Or on the counters. Or in the bathroom. There have to be limits. We need boundaries."

He stared at her, unblinking. Reg stared back. Her eyes started to burn.

"How do you do that? Don't cats ever blink?"

He didn't answer and didn't blink.

"Off you get," Reg told him, and started to push him toward the edge of the bed. The cat twisted onto his back and grabbed onto Reg with all four paws, claws extended.

"Ouch! Ouch, that hurts, you cut it out!" Reg tore her hand free, which was probably not the right thing to do, since the cat hung on and Reg ended up with scratches from all of the claws all the way down her arm. They burned like the dickens and instantly welled up with blood.

"Holy crap. Ouch, ouch, ouch! That was a nasty thing to do!"

Reg climbed out of the bed and hurried to the bathroom, where she ran cold water over her arm to calm the burn of the scratches and examined them more closely. The cons of cat ownership? How about claws like a miniature cougar?

"I might have promised not to get you declawed," Reg growled at the cat when she re-entered the bedroom with her arms swathed in bandages, "but it isn't like anyone is going to be checking up on me. There's no excuse for this kind of attack. I was just getting you off the bed!"

The cat gave a snort, then rolled over on his back, showing off a beautiful white belly to be scratched.

"Hah, you think I'm going to fall for that? I'm not touching you without gloves until you're properly trained."

Reg's stomach growled. The cat rolled back over and glared at her as if she had done something offensive. Reg pulled out her phone to look at the time. It was late afternoon and she hadn't had anything since a meager breakfast before running errands. And tea.

"Time to eat."

The cat jumped down off of the bed and mewed a silent mew, looking up at her expectantly.

"Yes, I said food. I suppose you're hungry too."

She headed for the kitchen. He followed close at her heel.

Reg had intended to make her own meal first and feed the cat afterward, but he apparently had other ideas. He kept winding around her legs and tripping her up, until Reg finally gave in and got out the cat food so he would leave her alone. She filled one bowl with cold water and another with dry kibble and put them down on the floor. The cat immediately went over to them and started sniffing them. Reg went back to work on her own dinner. She was feeling better after her nap, but still didn't have a lot of energy, so she was thinking maybe just a tuna sandwich.

As soon as she put the can opener into the can, the cat was again underfoot, bumping up against her and meowing excitedly.

"Oh, no you don't. This is my dinner. You go eat your own."

She opened the can and started to scoop some out to mix with mayonnaise, and suddenly the cat on the counter in front of her, sticking his nose in to help himself.

"No, no, no!" Reg shouted. She picked him up and put him on the floor before he knew what was happening, with no time to fight back against her. He stood up on his hind legs, resting his front paws on the cupboards.

"No you don't. You want me to lock you up? Because if that's what I have to do to keep you out of my food, I will."

He dropped back to all fours and sat back.

Reg ignored his glare and continued to make her supper. In a few minutes, she was sitting down at her table to have a bite to eat. The cat followed her and sat on the floor beside her, staring up at her reproachfully. At least he didn't jump up on the table or try to snatch it away.

"Oh, alright," Reg grumbled. She used her finger to scoop out a little of the filling, and flicked it onto the floor. The cat went after it immediately, licking it up in two bites and then cleaning the floor where it had landed with his long, raspy tongue. Reg ate the rest of the sandwich without looking at him, not wanting to end up giving him the whole thing.

She had found Erin's cat both funny and annoying, but hadn't really seen the point of owning a cat in the time she had stayed there. But Orange Blossom wasn't anything like Reg's new little tux. Not even close.

After the food was cleared away, Reg sat down in front of the TV to relax and fill her mind with junk. But she couldn't seem to get into any of her regular shows. Everything was reruns, and even the shows that she could normally watch over and over again held no appeal.

She muted the TV during a commercial and looked at the black and white cat as he painstakingly cleaned his fur.

"You need a name. I can't just keep calling you the cat or Kitty, and I expect Tux is way too common. So, what's it going to be?"

The cat stopped washing and looked at her. Reg snapped her fingers for him, and he approached her and sniffed at her fingers before accepting an ear scratch.

"Mittens or Socks?" Reg suggested. She had looked up the cat's other markings, getting to know the lingo. "Puss in Boots?"

He gave his head a shake, rattling his ears again.

"No?"

He bumped his head against her hand, begging for more ear and chin scratches. Reg stroked his white chest.

"Oreo? Penguin?"

He rubbed his head against her, and Reg rubbed his "third eye" white spot with the tip of her finger.

"Spot? Snowflake? Star?"

He stopped rubbing her, staring. Reg frowned.

"Star?" she repeated.

He didn't move.

"Stardust? Starlight?"

He bumped her again.

"Starlight?"

He nipped playfully at her fingers and then danced away from her. Reg watched his antics for a minute, and nodded.

"Starlight it is, then."

It was evening when there was a knock on her door, and Reg opened it without looking out the peephole, assuming that it would be Sarah with some new gossip or another client booking.

But it certainly wasn't Sarah.

It was a man Reg had never seen before. She just about had to bite her tongue to keep from asking him "Where have you been all my life?" A handsome man in his thirties or forties with movie-star good looks. His hair was neatly moussed back, beard trimmed short, and gorgeous dark eyes that she could have climbed right into.

"Hello," the man greeted, his mouth quirking up in one corner in a slight smile.

Reg closed her mouth. She hoped she hadn't looked too much like an idiot with her mouth open wide enough to catch flies.

But he was probably used to women reacting like that to him. He probably expected it. His smile said it was nothing new.

"Hi."

"My name is Corvin Hunter. I heard that Sarah had a new tenant, and I thought I would come around and welcome you to our community."

Reg nodded, grinning. "Thank you, I'm glad you came."

He stood there for a moment waiting, then indicated the interior with his eyes and a slight nod of his head. "Do you think I could come in?"

Reg choked back a silly laugh and opened the door farther. "Yes, yes. Of course."

He entered and looked around. His glance was casual; he had, in all likelihood, been there before to see Sarah's previous tenants. Reg hadn't really added anything of her own, so there was nothing that would be of great interest to him.

He sat down on the wicker sofa. Reg picked up the cold tea service. "Sorry, this has been here for hours…"

"There are usually drinks in the cupboard nearest the window."

Reg hadn't even explored that far. Sarah had been the one to put away her groceries, and Reg had only opened enough of the cupboards and drawers to find what she needed to make her sandwich. Why in the name of all that was good had she decided to have a tuna sandwich for supper? She hoped her breath didn't still smell of it. When she opened the cupboard nearest the window, she found Corvin was right; there was a varied selection of bottles.

"What would you like?"

"Jack Daniels?"

Reg opened the next cupboard over and found the glasses. She poured Corvin a couple of fingers of Jack.

"Ice?"

"Just a bit. It's blasted hot out there today."

Reg complied. She poured the same for herself and sat down across from him, though she would have been happier snuggling with him on the couch. Corvin took a sip of his drink, smiled his approval, and set it down.

"So... tell me about yourself," he told Reg.

She shrugged. She'd never been good at talking about herself, and she hadn't invented much of a backstory for her medium persona yet.

"My name is Reg. Just moved here. Not really much to tell."

"Everybody has a story to tell. You're clairvoyant?"

"Word certainly spreads fast here."

"It does," Corvin nodded his agreement. "Word is you blew Amy Calvert away, and that's not easy to do. How long have you been doing this?"

"Not very long." She hadn't been doing the medium gig for very long, that was true. But running cons? All her life. The trouble she was having with meeting the members of the supernatural community in Black Sands was telling the difference between the people who really believed in their paranormal abilities, and those who were simply running scams like Reg. She couldn't exactly ask them, and every conversation ended up being a little dance as she tried to figure out whether they were like her or whether they were real loons.

"When did you discover you had psychic abilities?" Corvin asked.

Reg closed her eyes partway, examining him. *Con or crazy?* "I've always been different than everyone else. But it's taken time to... find my gifts."

"You don't actually believe in spiritual gifts."

Corvin's voice was flat. Not emotion-packed. Not accusatory. Just a statement, like he could see straight into her mind. He was brilliant at cold reading. She knew she had controlled her gaze and her breathing. He shouldn't have been able to detect any stress in her voice. Reg could fool even the most sensitive equipment. So how had Corvin figured it out in just a few words?

Reg sipped at her drink. She had an almost-immediate head rush, which she never experienced with alcohol. Had he managed to spike her drink right there in front of her? It would take incredible sleight of hand, but she hadn't been watching him for it. Maybe when he had leaned forward to pick up his own drink... Reg put her tumbler back down again. No point in helping him accomplish whatever he had in mind by finishing the drink. Should she call for help? Was there really something in the drink, or was she just fighting a head cold? She had needed a nap; maybe her body was fighting off some virus and she didn't even know it.

"What makes you think I don't believe in spiritual gifts?" she returned coolly.

"I have gifts of my own. You might not believe that, but that doesn't make it any less true."

"Oh, I believe you have gifts." The gift of good looks. The ability to read her. An animal magnetism like she had rarely experienced before. And maybe really good sleight of hand. "So what is it you do?"

"I'm a warlock."

At least he didn't say he was a vampire. It could have been worse.

"I see. So you're like Sarah. The male version of a witch."

He raised his eyebrows and didn't give her any further details. He had another sip of his Jack Daniels, watching her over the brim of the glass the whole time.

"The spiritual energy in this room is very high. And yet, you don't believe in yourself. How can that be?"

"Why don't you tell me? You seem to be the expert here."

Corvin's eyes went around the room. Starlight came out of one of the bedrooms and positioned himself directly in front of Reg, as if guarding her from Corvin. Corvin's eyes glittered.

"Well, well, well. Who do we have here?"

The cat and the warlock stared at each other. As usual, Starlight won the staring contest.

"This is Starlight."

"Sarah didn't mention that you had a familiar."

"It's a recent development."

"He's very protective of you."

"I feed him." Reg pointed out the obvious.

Corvin chuckled. "They *are* corporeal beings."

"So what is it *you* do for people?" Reg asked, turning the conversation back to him to get herself out of the spotlight. "Do you make potions?"

"Sometimes. I cast spells. Help to remove curses. Bless houses or other items."

"All good? You don't cast curses?"

"You have a lot to learn about the world you inhabit."

"I've read up. I'm no expert, but I know the basics. Obviously, if you can remove curses, then curses exist, and you must know something about casting them."

"Accusing someone of casting curses is tantamount to a slap in the face. I wouldn't recommend you start throwing suggestions like that around without some kind of proof."

"I didn't say that you did curse anyone. I asked you."

"And do you go around lying to old ladies and bilking them out of their money?"

Reg's face suffused with heat. "I'm not bilking anyone—"

"I just asked a question. I didn't accuse you."

Reg let her anger subside. Score one for the warlock. He'd gotten under her skin and definitely hit a nerve with that one.

"Hmph," she grunted. "Okay, I see your point. I apologize for the offense."

Corvin leaned forward, reaching toward her. For a split second, Reg thought he was going to take her drink or to grab her, but he was aiming for Starlight, extending his hand to scratch the cat behind the ears.

Starlight flattened his ears back and hunched down, puffing out his fur and hissing at Corvin.

"What are you worried about?" Corvin reproached. "I haven't done anything to hurt you.

But Reg thought the cat had the right idea. She'd been too quick to let the handsome warlock into her house, attracted by his astonishingly good looks and reassured by his mention of Sarah. She'd assumed that he meant her no harm.

But that hadn't been smart. He could read her, might have spiked her drink, and he was bigger and stronger than she was. Did she think that nothing could happen to her with Sarah being so close? The older woman was not within sight or earshot of the cottage. And even if she had been, what could she do to protect Reg other than call the police?

"It's been a tiring day," she told him. "I really hate to cut our conversation short—" that, at least, was true, "—but I think we're going to have to finish it some other time."

"How about setting a date and time?"

How about when pigs could fly?

"Saturday," Reg suggested. "Why don't we meet for dinner at The Crystal Ballroom?"

"The Crystal Bowl," Corvin corrected. "Okay, it's a date. Don't break it."

He drained his glass and stood. Reg rose as if attached to him by a string. He extended his hand and Reg grasped it to tell him goodbye.

An electric shock ran through her, tingling all the way from her fingertips to her heart and brain. Reg gaped at him. She'd thought that she could fall into those lovely dark eyes, and she did. Deep into the uncharted depths.

Then suddenly, Reg's leg was on fire.

"Ow! Oh!" She looked down, trying to shake off Starlight, who had inexplicably attached himself to her leg with all four paws, ripping into her tender skin with all of his claws.

Reg bent down to remove the cat.

"Bad cat! What was that for?"

Corvin was laughing. He headed for the door. "I'll see you Saturday. *Without* the cat."

★ Chapter Five ★

REG WAS ASSEMBLING HER breakfast of cold cereal when she saw Starlight's head go up, and he looked sharply at the door. She walked to the door and checked through the peephole to make sure she wasn't getting any unexpected visitors. She saw Sarah coming down the stone path to the cottage door. Reg opened the door, startling Sarah. Sarah put her hand over her heart, blowing and puffing dramatically.

"How did you know I was there?" she asked, as Reg allowed her in.

"I'm psychic," Reg said, tapping her temple.

Sarah laughed. "Yes, of course! I brought you a copy of our community calendar. There are some meetings and mixers you might want to attend. Get to know people and have a voice in how things are managed around here."

She handed Reg a photocopied green flyer. Reg turned to put it on the counter, and when she turned back around, Sarah was sniffing at the air, a frown on her face. Reg thought immediately of the cat litter, which she hadn't yet had a chance to deal with.

"What's that smell?" Sarah mused.

Reg took a tentative sniff herself. If it was obviously cat box or tuna fish, Sarah wouldn't be asking. Reg did smell a vaguely floral scent, very faint. Maybe flowers in the garden outside the cottage? But the flowers were in Sarah's own yard, so presumably she would know what they were.

"Roses," Sarah decided. Then her expression sharpened. "You didn't have Corvin Hunter here, did you?"

Reg blinked at her. "Yes, he was here last night. Didn't you send him?"

"Me send him. Why would I send Corvin here?"

Reg thought about it. "I thought he said… maybe he didn't say he had talked to you. Maybe he just said he heard I was renting from you. But I *thought* he said you had sent him."

"Don't let him glamour you," Sarah warned. "You let his good looks and roses get the better of you, and…" she trailed off. "You didn't let him stay the night, did you?"

"Not that it's any of your business, but no." Reg thought about the strong attraction she'd felt to Corvin the night before and the electricity that had seemed to flow between them when Corvin had touched her. If Starlight hadn't unaccountably attacked her leg, would they have ended up together? Corvin did have a strong "glamour" about him. Must be pheromones. Maybe something in his rose scented cologne.

Sarah breathed out. "You must have strong willpower to resist him. Even with how old I am, I still find him… tempting."

"You're not *that* old," Reg said with a laugh. There were plenty of seniors who still had healthy libidos.

Sarah gave a little smile. "Don't be fooled by my youthful good looks," she advised. "I'm older than I look."

Reg looked at Sarah critically. She couldn't see anything that would indicate that her original estimate of somewhere in her fifties or sixties was wrong. "How old are you?"

"A lady never tells."

Reg rolled her eyes. "Well, thank you for this." She fluttered the flyer at Sarah. "I'll take a look and see what I want to go to. You've been very helpful to me up until now, so I'm sure I can rely on you if I need anything."

"Of course," Sarah agreed. She looked around the cottage one last time, her eyes lingering for a moment on the hall to the bedrooms. "And you'll be careful of that Corvin. He's… a very dangerous man."

"Dangerous?" Reg laughed. "He puts on a good show, but he's probably as harmless as a kitten on the inside. These guys who like to role play villains… they rarely are. More likely geeks who never got a date in high school."

"This is not a game," Sarah warned. "Corvin is not playing a role. He is very serious about his craft, and he is very good at what he does."

"Which is…?"

Sarah averted her eyes. "He's a warlock," she said flatly. "A warlock who is only going to get stronger. Don't underestimate him, Reg. Don't be taken in."

Reg sat down with her bowl of cereal. Starlight had apparently been unimpressed with his kibble. He sniffed at it a little, crunched one or two bits, and trailed Reg around like he was waiting for the real food to show up.

She put the flyer from Sarah beside her and studied it for a moment, but it was so densely written that she pushed it aside, irritated. Sarah would tell her if there were things she should go to.

Sarah's words still rang in her ears. Corvin's powers were real. In spite of being absolutely sure that there was not really any such thing as magic or sorcery, Reg was a little shaken by Sarah's insistence that Corvin was dangerous.

Certainly he had an aura about him. He exuded confidence and charm. But those were carefully cultivated personality traits, not magical properties. She could feel the same thing from the president of a tech company, royalty, or the pope. People were intuitively drawn to those magnetic qualities of leadership and power. But that was all it was. Intuition. Unconsciously reading a person's body language and small details about them. Observable qualities, nothing magical about it.

Sarah might be right about Corvin being powerful and dangerous, but it wasn't because of any special magical powers.

She was just a foolish old woman.

Reg was just contemplating the joys of owning a cat, in relation to having to clean the kitty litter and deal with picky eaters and sharp claws, when there was a knock on her door. It was soft at first, and she wasn't sure she had really heard anything. Then the knock came again, louder. Reg eagerly left the kitty litter box and went to the front door of the cottage to see who was there.

Her visitor was a young Asian woman she'd never met before. She looked shy and sad and Reg was afraid that anything she said might send the girl skittering away in fear. Was she Sarah's maid, sent to the cottage to make sure that everything stayed clean and in order? In spite of Sarah's claim that Reg would have her own space and they would not always be running into each other, Reg was beginning to sense that Sarah intended to closely supervise the little cottage.

"Yes…?" Reg prompted her visitor.

The woman looked at her for a minute, wide-eyed, before finally opening her mouth.

"My name is Ling Lau." Her English was unaccented. Probably born and raised in the US, if not in Florida itself. "I am… I am looking for someone to talk to my husband…?"

"To talk to him about what?" Reg asked. Was her husband the gardener? Maintenance man? Why would Reg be needed to talk to him?

"Well, he's… just to make sure he's okay… to talk to him one more time." Reg suddenly realized that she had misjudged the situation. "I never got to say goodbye."

"Oh, of course. Come on in." Reg opened the door the rest of the way, hoping she wasn't blushing as furiously as her burning face suggested. "Can I get you some tea?"

That way, she'd have a minute to get rid of the flushed face and gather her wits before the session. Going into a reading flustered wasn't going to produce good results.

"Uh, yes. Tea would be fine."

Reg pointed Ling in the direction of the seating area in the living room, and retreated to the kitchen to put the kettle on. Starlight followed her, meowing loudly to tell her that he needed to be fed. Reg glanced over her shoulder at Ling. "There's food in your bowl," she told Starlight. "I'm not giving in and feeding you gourmet food because you're a picky eater. If you're hungry enough, you'll eat the kibble."

Starlight yowled and wound around her feet.

"No." Reg pushed Starlight away with her foot. "Be quiet and quit making such a fuss. We've got company."

Starlight sat down and stared at Reg.

"That's not going to work. You can stare as long as you like. Eat the food I got you."

She tapped her foot while waiting for the water to boil. She realized after the kettle started to whistle that she hadn't cleaned up any of what had been used the day before. She put the china carefully into the sink, and checked the cupboard for more. Luckily they were from a service of six, so there were still fresh cups and silver left over. Reg loaded up the tray, added a plate of store-bought cookies, and took everything over to the coffee table.

"How did you hear about me?" she asked Ling. "I just barely moved here. Did Sarah send you over?"

"No, I heard about you at The Crystal Bowl last night. Everybody was talking about what a wonderful reading you did for Amy Carver. She was so excited that someone had *really* made contact. So I was hoping…"

Reg sipped her tea. "Of course. That's what I'm here for. Why don't you tell me about your husband?"

"His plane went down over the ocean. They found the wreckage…" Ling's voice cracked. "Some of it. A lot washed ashore. But they didn't find his body."

Reg nodded. No wonder the young woman looked so sad. What a horrific way to lose her spouse.

"I'm so sorry."

"Not having his body… I can't help feeling like he isn't at rest. That he'll just have to keep wandering the earth until his body is discovered and properly laid to rest in consecrated ground."

It was good of Ling to give Reg the key to what she was looking for.

"Do you have a picture of him?"

Ling nodded and pulled a fat red wallet out of her purse. She had a small snapshot of her and her husband side-by-side. Maybe an engagement photo.

"He's very handsome, isn't he?" Reg commented. He had a young face, in spite of the mustache and beard. Pleasant looking. Ling's age or a tiny bit older.

"Very," Ling agreed, laying a hand over her heart. "I miss him so much. I thought we would have years and years together... and to suddenly have him taken away from me so soon... I just don't know what to do with myself. That whole life that we were going to build is just gone."

"What were your plans?"

"We wanted to build our own home. Have two or three children when we were ready. Warren flew, and wanted to start some kind of charter business. He was always talking..." Ling choked up again. "He was always talking about how safe flying is. So much safer than driving a car." She covered her mouth and sobbed.

Reg was sitting too far away from Ling to pat her hand or her shoulder without first going around the coffee table. She should have been more aware of her placement and not put the coffee table between them. Trying her best to be unobtrusive and not make Ling uncomfortable, Reg grabbed a couple of tissues from the box on one of the side tables and went around the coffee table to hand them to Ling and sit beside her on the couch. She tentatively put a hand on Ling's back.

"Focus on the good things," she said. "I know it's hard, but we want lots of good energy here. We want to make it a welcoming place for Warren to come back to."

Ling nodded and dabbed at her eyes. "Yes. Yes, of course."

"How did the two of you meet? And did you go on an airplane for your first date?"

Ling smiled through her tears. "We met at the restaurant where I was working, while I was home from school. He came in one night... and then he came back the next night... and the next..."

Reg grinned. "He knew what he wanted when he saw it, hey?"

"Our first date wasn't on a plane... just to a movie. But we talked about planes, and he told me all about his dreams to run his own charter."

"And you're not afraid of heights? Flying always makes me nervous," Reg confided. "I'd rather drive across the country than to have to fly."

"It's so different in a little plane, where you can see everything and you know the pilot. It's like... being on a big commercial jet is like taking the bus. But going on a private charter... you're sitting together in a Ferrari. It's so much nicer."

Reg imagined it. She closed her eyes and took deep breaths, getting herself into character. She tried to imagine all of the things Warren and Ling would have talked about, how it had felt for them to be close together, how much he would be missing her now if they had been forced to separate.

"What's his full name?"

"Warren Blake."

"Warren Blake," Reg spoke the name out loud, tasting it, trying to construct a full man from the little bits she had been given. "Are you here, Warren Blake?"

She took deep breaths and cleared her mind, letting herself fall into the character. She rolled her eyes back.

"Ling? Is that you, Ling?"

Ling covered her mouth, muffling her words. "It's me, Warren."

"Where am I?"

"This is... I came to a psychic, so that she could talk to you. I wanted to make sure you're okay."

"A psychic? Why would you go to a psychic?" Reg paused, searching for words in the void, feeling her way through the character. "Where am I?"

"You're dead, Warren. You're a spirit. On a different plane."

"I'm not on a plane."

Ling laughed. "A different plane of existence, not an airplane. You died."

"But they brought me back, right? Because I'm alive now."

"No," Ling's voice was infinitely sad. "You're dead."

Reg couldn't open her eyes widely enough to see Ling. Something was keeping her eyes shut, like tape over her lids. She explored the darkness there.

"I couldn't be dead."

"Is this normal?" Ling whispered. "How can he not know that he's dead?"

Reg was unable to answer to reassure her.

"If I was dead, I wouldn't be able to hear my heart beating. But I can."

"No. You're dead. They're looking for your body."

"My body is right here." Reg thumped her chest. "I can feel it. I'm not dead."

"I wanted to tell you that I love you." Ling had apparently decided to continue forward with the conversation even if Warren was being difficult. "I didn't get a chance to say goodbye, and I wanted you to know how much I love you and that I'll always miss you."

"Don't leave me, Ling. I love you too. Stay with me."

"I won't leave you, Warren… but I can't stay with you. We only have a few minutes to talk. We're using Reg as a channel… I can't come where you are, and you can't come with me."

Reg grasped Ling's hand, unable to open her eyes but still needing to connect directly with Ling. At least this time, she wasn't pushing the client away and telling her not to come back again. Ling would keep coming back for as long as she could, if Warren kept telling her to stay with him.

"Is that really you, Warren?" Ling squeezed Reg's hand.

"Who else would it be, Ding-a-Ling? Don't you know me?"

Ling gasped, and then was crying softly, her breathing ragged as she tried to contain herself.

"I love you so much, Warren. I don't know how I'm going to go on without you."

"Then don't leave me."

"I won't. I'm not going to leave you."

There was a sharp pain in Reg's ankle, as if someone had tried to shove a nail through her foot. Her eyes flew open, startled by the hot, sharp needle of pain. "Ouch!" She looked down and saw Starlight there. He'd crept up behind her, crawling under the couch to bite her from beneath the wicker couch. "Ouch, you evil beast!" She shoved him away from her and felt her injured ankle. She expected to see blood, and there it was, welling up from the fang marks. "Are you a cat or a vampire? Sheesh! Holy crap, that hurt!"

She became aware of Ling, watching her with wide, round eyes.

"What happened? Why did he bite you?"

"I don't know. Because he's perverse and wants to go back to the pound, I guess! Crap! Crap, crap, crap!" Reg grabbed a napkin from the tea service and pressed it over the bite marks. "I'm sorry. I'm being a baby, I know but I was not expecting that, and he bit me deep!"

"Do you need a tetanus shot?" Ling asked. "Should I take you to the hospital?"

Tetanus? How about rabies? Just how much did the shelter know about Starlight's medical history? Could he be rabid without them knowing it? They hadn't said that he was aggressive at the shelter, just that he had been depressed. Unless they were trying to cover it up. Could they cover up that they were caring for a rabid cat? And letting someone adopt it? Reg was pretty sure that if they knew the cat was sick, they'd have to put it in isolation. Wasn't that what they did with Old Yeller?

"I don't think it's that bad," she assured Ling. "I'm overreacting. It just surprised me so much. I wasn't aware of anything that was going on in the room..." She trailed off. "What about your husband? Did it help? I don't think I'm going to be able to reestablish the connection today."

"It was so good to hear his voice," Ling said.

Reg couldn't remember if she had done a special voice. That was pretty bad, because if she didn't remember how she did Warren Blake the first time, how was she going to get it right again?

"But it's so strange that he wouldn't believe he was dead. Is that... normal?"

"Sometimes spirits can be confused," Reg assured her. She'd seen enough Steven King movies and episodes of Ghost Whisperer to know that. "It might take a few sessions before he realizes the truth. Right now, he's unanchored, just floating around, trying to figure out the rules. He'll get stronger."

Ling nodded. She didn't argue that Reg had solved all of Amy's problems with just one session. Amy's mother had been dead a long time, and Amy had contacted her many times over the years. It wouldn't take long before Warren understood where he was and could tell Ling that he was okay.

"I'm so sorry that happened to you," Ling said, looking down at Starlight. "You are a bad kitty!"

Reg smiled and nodded her agreement. "Yes, he is!"

Ling settled up her bill. Reg limped to the door to see her out, and then went into her bathroom to doctor her injury. There was something very wrong with that cat. She was seriously considering taking him back.

★ Chapter Six ★

R EG DIDN'T GET MUCH else done that day. She didn't take Starlight back to the animal shelter, but she did give him a very stern talking-to. Halfway through the lecture, he started rubbing against her leg and purring so loudly that he drowned her out. Reg eventually bent down and picked him up. He snuggled in her arms and bumped the top of his head to the bottom of her chin, acting like she was his favorite person in the world. Why had he bitten her? Was he trying to play? Was he mad at her for not giving him what he wanted to eat? Jealous of her attention to her client? She hadn't introduced him to Ling and told her how he was her familiar, was it possible that he resented that?

She was anthropomorphizing him and that just wouldn't do. He had bitten her because of some cat instinct. Maybe a flea had bitten him and he was taking out his anger on whatever was closest to him. It was a lucky thing that he had chosen to bite her instead of Ling. That would have been disastrous. She couldn't have an animal that might injure her clientele. He'd have to be locked up during sessions. The whole point of getting him to begin with had been to use him as a prop. What good was he to her if she had to lock him up and hide him away from clients?

Reg put Starlight back down on the floor and they considered each other.

"Truce?" Reg asked.

Starlight rubbed against her leg.

She wasted a bunch of time on the internet figuring out all of the bad diseases she could catch from a cat bite. Who knew they could be so dangerous? It was probably a good thing she hadn't ever had a cat as a pet when she was a young girl, or she never would have made it to adulthood.

She didn't feel like making anything for dinner, but she didn't feel like going to The Witch's Cauldron again either, so she made another sandwich, sharing the filling with Starlight. She again looked at the community flyer as she was eating, narrowing her focus to just one paragraph. It was an advertisement for some kind of witches' gathering. Not quite Reg's wheelhouse. She knew she needed to keep her focus narrow, or her marketing would end up bringing in no one. She was doing well as a medium, she needed to just keep doing what she was doing. No witches' hoedown for her.

She tried to watch TV, but was too tired and headed to bed early. Hopefully, she would soon be able to adjust to a regular schedule and not be so tired after each reading. She needed to be able to do several a day to make good money; she couldn't just wimp out and have a nap after each session.

Reg was in a darkened room. She couldn't see anything around her. She could hear noises; people talking, a public address system, a rolling mail cart, televisions, crying… it was all a muddle of muffled sounds. She couldn't pick out any voices that she knew. Her head hurt and she was frozen, unable to move her body. Trapped inside of herself.

She tried to call out to get someone to help her. The cat moved restlessly near her, trying to find a comfortable place to curl up and go to sleep. She couldn't reach out and pet him or push him off the bed.

"You're dead," a voice told her.

Reg tried to answer. She could hear the protests in her head, but she couldn't voice them aloud.

I can't be dead. I'm right here.

"You died," the woman's voice told her with certainty. "I'm sorry."

Reg's heart rate increased. Her breathing sounded louder in her own ears. How could she be dead if she could hear her own heartbeat? She could hear the blood pumping through her veins. She could feel her chest rise and fall with each breath. But she couldn't get out any words or move her body. What had happened to her? Why couldn't she move?

I'm not dead.

"I'm sorry, you died in a plane crash. A plane of existence."

That didn't even make sense.

It must be a dream. That was the only thing that made sense. When nothing made sense, then the only sensible thing was that it was a dream.

"You're not asleep." Ling's voice was in her ear again. "If you were asleep, I'd just wake you up. You died days ago. You're not even here."

I am here, or I wouldn't be able to talk to you.

"But you're not talking to me. You're not here. I'm talking to another Reg in another existence. You are gone forever.

Panic flooded Reg's system, but she couldn't do anything about it. She couldn't move. She couldn't call for help. She couldn't even open her eyes to see whether she was having a dream, or whether Ling were really there. She couldn't see where she was.

A pain in Reg's arm dragged her from sleep. She opened her eyes to see the darkened interior of her bedroom in Sarah's cottage. It had just been a dream, but it left her with a heavy feeling of disorientation. Like the nights she dreamed she was looking for something, and when she woke up she still pushed the blankets around and searched under her pillow, looking for the object lost in her dream. Reg looked down at her arm, feeling where it hurt. Starlight was lying next to her, looking up at her in irritation. Wondering why she was thrashing and groaning in her sleep, probably.

"Did you bite me again?" She squinted and felt the painful spot in her arm. He hadn't drawn blood; she didn't think he'd even broken the skin; but it was still painful, like a hard pinch. "You need to stop doing that! Really!"

He gave his head a shake. Reg picked him up and pulled him into her lap. "What was all that about, huh? Why can't you just be a nice kitty?"

His purr started, and Reg closed her eyes, just enjoying the warm, furry bundle in her arms and the vibrating rumble of his purr.

"I'm glad you woke me up, though. That was a really freaky dream."

He continued to purr.

"You probably don't have any idea what I'm talking about, do you? Do cats have dreams?"

It was obviously her brain reprocessing the reading with Ling, reaching out and contacting her husband. The brain consolidated memories during the night, and Reg's brain was obviously trying to analyze and process the memories of the conversation between Ling and Warren. Figuring out how to categorize and store it.

"But all you have to remember is that you bit me. That's not so hard, is it?" Reg asked Starlight.

His droning purr was comforting. She often had trouble sleeping after a disturbing dream, but Starlight's throbbing purr was soothing and made her feel like going back to sleep. It was like he was purring her a lullaby.

Instead of throwing the cat off the bed, Reg rolled over, nestling him back against her body, and closed her eyes to go back to sleep.

Before she managed to drift off again, she heard the words of Erin's friend Adele, who professed to be a witch.

Are you aware of the power you are playing with? Do you really know what forces a medium employs?

The dreams she fell back into were more comfortable. The old days, remembering her time with Erin when they both lived with the Harrises.

"Are you sure about this, Reg?" Erin asked uncertainly. She was a skinny, diminutive teenager. She looked younger than she was, twelve rather than fifteen. Her hair was hacked short. Erin had been chewing on her hair, an anxious habit, completely forgetting the gum already in her mouth. Chewing gum was supposed to keep her from chewing on her hair or her fingernails. Instead, the hair and the gum had mixed in her mouth, and though Erin had desperately tried to bite it back out, she just ingrained the gum farther into her long, dark tresses. Mrs. Harris's solution had been simple and drastic, and Erin had cried for days over the loss of her hair.

"What's wrong with picking bottles?" Reg challenged. "We're cleaning up. We're recycling. Improving our environment. There's nothing wrong with that."

"But..." Erin twirled a lock of hair around her finger.

"But what? We're supposed to recycle, right?"

"Yeah."

"And this way, we actually get paid for it. The Harrises said they would pay us for chores, if they could afford it. That's all that we're doing. Cleaning up and getting paid for it."

Erin had been okay with picking cans and bottles up off of the street and the school field. She'd been less sure about picking them out of people's recycling bins in the alley.

"They threw them out," Reg had pointed out. "If they wanted to return them themselves, they wouldn't have done that. They're just throwing money away. We're helping."

"But if they threw them away..." Erin was still squeamish about taking things out of the trash and recycling bins.

Reg had known the final step would take a lot more finessing. Going into people's yards and filching the bins and bags of bottles that they were saving for themselves.

"They put them here for us," Reg told Erin firmly. "If they were going to keep them, they would keep them in their houses or garages. They're in the back yard. That means they're going to throw them out. But they don't want to put them in the bins in case the trash collectors don't see them and just take them to the dump. They don't want all of these cans and bottles being taken to the dump."

"No," Erin agreed, shaking her head. Her eyes were wide. She had such a naive, innocent way, Reg knew the Harrises wouldn't punish her too badly if they got caught. And sooner or later, Erin would get caught; she didn't have the same gift for lying that Reg had. "Cans and bottles won't break down. They need to be recycled."

"And that's what we're doing. These people don't want the cans and bottles to go to the dump. That's why they're in the yard instead of in the bins."

Erin nodded her understanding.

"So come on," Reg insisted.

She opened the gate and went in, waiting for Erin to follow her. Erin twirled her hair and bit on her thumbnail, then followed Reg into the yard, her eyes down.

Reg wanted to tell her to keep her eyes up and look around. To make sure that they didn't get caught. But that would ruin her whole argument. Erin would know that Reg was lying to her and the people who lived at the house hadn't just left the empties in the yard for Reg and Erin to pick up.

Reg picked up the two garbage bags full of bottles and motioned to Erin to pick up the bin. Erin did so, letting it rattle loudly. Reg looked toward the house for any sign they'd been heard.

Reg didn't have any other appointments and, as far as she knew, Sarah hadn't set anything up with anyone. There was no way to know whether someone would stop by during the day when she was not at home, but people would have to learn to make appointments with her ahead of time, or else she was going to have to set up regular office hours to give herself set times when she could run errands, socialize, or find other ways to relax.

She had designed some flyers for her services to be posted on bulletin boards, and started a slow exploration of the stores and other buildings around the neighborhood to see who had places where she could post them. A lot of little groceries and convenience stores had boards for community postings. Reg would get them up wherever she could. Of course, there were also the online postings and social networks, but she had to be careful that an internet search wouldn't bring Officer Terry Piper or another enterprising cop to her door. Old school still worked, especially with old people who had retired to Florida.

"You're a crook!" an angry voice grated from nearby as Reg pinned up a flyer in a coffee shop.

Reg turned her head to look at the old man leaning on a walker nearby. His face was flushed red, a stark contrast to his wispy white flyaway hair.

"I beg your pardon?"

"You're a crook! A charlatan! A hustler! Why are you trying to steal people's money away from them? They've earned that money through hard work, and you're trying to take it away with your make-believe nonsense! You're a fake!"

Reg turned away from him and finished tacking the flyer up. "I'm sorry you feel that way. I work hard to provide a service. If you don't like that service or don't see any need for it… that's your own business. But a lot of people find it valuable."

"A lot of people are idiots! People like you, going around, whispering all of this woo-woo ghost nonsense, trying to bilk good, honest, hardworking folks out of their money! It's unbelievable that people would even give you the time of day!"

Reg shrugged. "Some people cut their hair at home and some people go to the salon. That doesn't mean salons are rip-offs. People just choose what services they are willing to pay money for. If you ever want a free reading, just let me know. I'd be happy to help you out."

Predictably, the man's face got even redder. Reg knew she shouldn't provoke him. She didn't want him to have a heart attack right there in the entryway of the coffee shop. She didn't need that on her conscience.

"It's fraud!" the man shouted. As Reg moved away from the bulletin board to pass him and get out of the situation, he toddled closer to the poster. "People like you should be thrown in jail! I don't understand why everyone comes to Florida to bilk innocent people out of their life savings. You leave retirees destitute. They spend their whole lives trying to save money, and you just take it all away!"

"I'm sorry you feel that way." She inched past him and was almost to the door when she heard the paper tear. She turned and looked back. The old man had ripped the poster down. He turned to face her, sneering and laughing to himself.

"You're sorry, are you? I'll say you're sorry! Why don't you get your sorry butt out of here and never come back again?"

"Do you own this place?" Reg asked, feeling her eyes widen at the destruction of her sign.

"No, but that doesn't mean I can't have a say in what people like you are trying to get away with. Why don't you just get out of our town? Get out of Florida altogether. Take your show on the road, somewhere else!"

There wasn't any point in coming to blows with the gentleman, so Reg turned away, letting her breath out in a sigh. There were plenty of other bulletin boards for her to put her poster up on.

There would always be people who were not fooled by what she was doing. As strong as the human desire to believe was, there would always be cynics who wouldn't be convinced of the legitimacy of psychic phenomena. It was best to just not engage with them.

★ Chapter Seven ★

I T W A S S A T U R D A Y , A N D that meant she had a
date with Corvin Hunter.

Reg couldn't help the anticipatory acceleration of her
heart whenever she thought of it. Corvin was one of the
most desirable men she'd met, and the fact that he was
apparently interested in her sent her heart skittering like a
puppy on a slippery floor whenever she thought about it.

Sarah had warned Reg not to be taken in by him. She had
said that he was dangerous. But she hadn't said how he was
dangerous. What exactly did Sarah think Reg was going to get
herself into?

Was she worried that Reg would get her heart broken
when Corvin moved on to his next conquest? Was Corvin
into pain? Or was it his alleged magical powers that Sarah was
talking about? Maybe she thought that Corvin would put
some kind of spell on Reg that would… what? Make her his
slave? Make her give him wildly expensive gifts? She couldn't
think of any spell that Corvin would actually want to put on
her, even if he did have some kind of power.

Reg couldn't see anything dangerous about Corvin. He
was just another handsome man with a big ego. If he liked
her, why not take advantage of the opportunity? She'd been
on too many bad dates in recent memory.

She traveled light, so her wardrobe was not very
extensive. Now that she was settled down in Florida for a
while running the fortune-teller scheme, she should spend
some time shopping for a few new pieces. Living out of a
closet instead of a suitcase had its perks. She did her best to
assemble an elegant, mysterious costume suitable for the The

Crystal Bowl, and after checking the time once more, headed over.

Corvin had arrived there ahead of her, which was a good sign. He hadn't made her wait for him. Reg had arrived slightly ahead of schedule, so he would know that she respected his schedule as well. Reg believed in being prompt and making a good impression on people.

He was at the bar, so Reg headed to his side, ignoring the sign that said to wait to be seated. Reg wasn't sure she'd seen anyone actually wait to be seated yet. Maybe that only applied to newbies.

"Good evening, Regina," Corvin said in a low, husky voice. He said it the right way, *reh-jee-nah* rather than *ree-ji-nah* like the Canadian city. It sounded intimate and romantic and didn't irritate her the way it usually did when people presumed to use her full name. "You're looking lovely tonight."

"Thank you. You don't look so bad yourself," Reg said breathlessly. And he did look incredible, even better than he had when he had stopped in at the cottage to welcome her into the community.

When he'd come to the house, he'd been wearing casual clothing, nothing that really stuck out. Dark jeans, a t-shirt, and a black overcoat pulled over everything in spite of the heat. For their date, he had dressed in a top-quality tailored black suit, blindingly white shirt, and a tie loosely knotted, not quite snugged up to his throat. There was a corner of a kerchief poking out of his breast pocket, and she was quite sure it was a real, properly folded hankie rather than just a pocket insert for show.

Corvin knew how to dress. And he was no pauper.

"Why don't we grab a table?" Corvin suggested.

It was the same restaurant Reg had gone to earlier in the week, but she felt completely different. Then she had been a visitor, new in town, completely unfamiliar with the community and everyone in it. She didn't know a lot more people than she had, but she felt comfortable there, and she eagerly anticipated spending time with the gorgeous warlock.

They were seated, again without the assistance of a waitress, and Reg let out a slow sigh of satisfaction.

"So, how have your first few days been?" Corvin asked.

From what Reg had seen of the paranormal community, word spread pretty fast, so she had no doubt that Corvin probably already knew how her week had gone just as well as she did, if not better.

"It's been good. I've had a couple of good readings, and I think word of mouth is spreading nicely. I've put up some advertising around the neighborhood. I'm hoping to be able to get a pretty steady flow of clients… if the first few days are any indication."

"I've heard good things," he agreed with a nod. They sipped at their drinks. "So how is it that you didn't pursue a living as a psychic before now?" he asked. "Was it just not included in those 'what are you going to be when you grow up' coloring books you got at school?"

Reg chuckled. Those books had always frustrated her. She would leaf through them, looking for the type of job that she wanted, not finding anything but doctors, lawyers, teachers, and store clerks. Where were the fun jobs? Sure there were astronauts, actors, dancers, and artists, but no parent or teacher ever tried to persuade their kids to pursue those careers. All of the jobs seemed so dry and humdrum, even the ones that should have been fun. Reg had never had any desire to become a dentist or veterinarian. She wanted to do something exciting and dramatic and to make a lot of money doing it. She knew, even back then, that her academic scores were never going to be good enough to pursue a degree, and that she didn't want a job in an office or retail outlet.

"I've tried a lot of different things. I never really considered being a psychic until recently, but I am pretty good at it."

"What made you decide to do it when you didn't actually believe you had any psychic abilities?"

Reg stared down into her glass of wine. She probably shouldn't have too much to drink while she was with him.

She was influenced enough by his magnetism. And she remembered that at the house, she had thought he might have put something in her drink. She kept it in her hand, watching him carefully.

"I was down and out. One of those times when you scrape bottom and don't have anything or anyone to help you... I was on the street, not a cent to my name, nothing in my pockets but my own cold hands. So... I had to do something."

"Sometimes it takes a crisis like that to really recognize our latent powers."

"Uh... sure. So I read palms until I could buy a cup of tea... read tea leaves until I could buy a deck of tarot cards... and just kept building. Made myself look reputable. Got a car. Looked for a community where I could operate and there would be a lot of business..."

"And out of the various psychic methods you tried, being a channel to the dead was the one that resonated with you the most?"

His eyes were intense. Reg thought a staring contest with Starlight was difficult, but trying to keep eye contact with the warlock was incredibly uncomfortable.

"I guess so," she agreed. "It was... the most interesting and entertaining. And that was the one that really seemed to connect me with the most people."

"Communing with the dead is not just a method of entertainment," he reprimanded.

"No," Reg agreed smoothly. "It's also a way of making money."

He looked at her, then started to smile. "You are brazen, aren't you?"

Reg raised her eyebrows at him. "If you don't want the truth, I'm a very convincing liar."

"I'm sure you are."

The waitress brought their first course. Reg sipped a spoonful or two of soup, but wanted to save her appetite for the main course.

"Did you have imaginary friends as a child?"

The change of subject surprised Reg. Were they finished dueling over paranormal powers, then?

"Yeah, sure," she agreed. "Most kids do."

He waited for further information.

"I didn't have a lot of real friends," Reg said. "I got moved around a lot, and it's hard to establish friendships when you're only in a place for a few months. So I had imaginary friends. Lots of imaginary friends."

"And were they all children your own age?"

Reg frowned. "No. All kinds. Old, young, men, women, kids, pets... everyone I needed to stay entertained."

"And you don't think that's unusual?"

Reg raised her brows. "No."

"Did you talk about your friends to the grown-ups?"

Reg thought back. She could remember trying to tell her foster mother or teacher or psychologist about her friends, but they had quickly clamped down on that, telling her that she wasn't allowed to talk about her imaginary friends at the dinner table or during class. Sometimes she tried to whisper to her foster mother or sisters as she went to bed, telling them about what her friends had said or done that day, but they would just shake their heads at her and turn their faces away, clearly indicating that it was an unacceptable topic.

"Sometimes, but grown-ups really don't get imaginary friends. They think it's cute the first time or two, but then it's 'don't talk to me about them' or 'don't try to blame this on your imaginary friend.' They don't want to hear about it."

Corvin chuckled. He took a couple of spoonfuls of his soup and laid his spoon down. "You didn't have imaginary friends. You were talking to spirits."

Reg's mouth dropped open. She forced herself to close it again. "I was not! I just had an active imagination."

"That's what the psychologists said," Corvin intoned.

Reg was nodding before she realized that Corvin was just guessing. He couldn't know what the doctors had really said. More than one foster mother had taken her to the doctor, thinking that there must be something wrong with her. They thought she was hallucinating or schizophrenic or seriously disturbed. But the psychologists and therapists always just shook their heads and smiled. "She's just a little girl with an active imagination. If you don't want to encourage it, then don't give it a lot of attention. Keep her busy with other things, set up play dates, enroll her in some after-school clubs…"

But none of those things had banished Reg's imaginary friends. It was the other foster children who had set her straight, telling her that she needed to fly straight and not attract attention to herself if she wanted to stay. If she didn't want to end up locked in some psycho ward, she needed to blend in and act normal.

"You saw dead people," Corvin said with a smile. "I'd bet anything. Do you still see them? Or is it only when you are trying to make contact now?"

"I don't see dead people." Reg hadn't intended for her voice to be so loud. A couple of people turned and looked at her. Reg lowered her voice so that only Corvin could hear her. "You can believe what you like, but I don't believe in ghosts. I provide a service. I help people to reconcile with their pasts. I give them a tool to get closure. I do not actually see dead people."

"No. Of course not."

Reg shook her head. "Enough about me. Why don't you tell me about your week. What have you done? And I don't care whether it's witchy stuff or just mundane. I just want to talk about you."

"Witchy stuff?"

"Or warlocky stuff. What's it like being Corvin? Or what was it like this week?"

"I met a pretty new psychic this week," Corvin said teasingly, looking straight at Reg. "Someone I think is going to stir things up a little around here. Other than that… my car was in the shop, so I didn't really get anywhere. I won an award for some writing I did on witchcraft in early American history. I tossed and turned and didn't sleep well because there is something disrupting the spiritual atmosphere in Black Sands."

Reg blinked at Corvin. She started to laugh, but he appeared to be serious. All of his points were so unrelated, she didn't know which item to pursue a conversation on. "I have to take my car in for an oil change," did not seem like an empathetic response to his offering.

"I've been tired all the time," she tried instead. "I guess with the traveling, getting adjusted to a new home and routine… it just seems like I'm tired all the time. I was wondering whether I should see the doctor to get some blood tests done. Thyroid or mono or iron…"

"It could be," Corvin acknowledged. "Or it could be that you're sensitive to the disruptions in the magnetic fields as well. Not everybody is, but when I was in your house the other day… there was a very strong spiritual presence."

"You mean you think it's haunted?"

"No, no. I mean that you have a very strong magnetic field yourself, and in my experience, people who have that kind of aura tend to also be very sensitive to changes in their environment. You're already trying to rebalance yourself after having moved into a completely new location. Changes going on in that environment would make it very difficult to find your balance."

Reg had another bite of her soup and then pushed the bowl away. "Not to mention an unruly cat."

Corvin snorted. "Yes, the cat could be upsetting your balance as well."

"He definitely is. I tripped over him at least three times today. Just about found myself doing a face plant directly into the fridge."

Corvin smoothed the beard on his chin. "Did anyone ever point out that when you feel uncomfortable, you deflect with sass and sarcasm?"

"Is the pope Catholic? Or maybe I should translate that into pagan terms… do you have some kind of head warlock? Like a worldwide leader?"

"No. Leadership amongst practitioners of magic is quite localized. A coven has a leader, but there is no grand master of all witches and warlocks."

"Well, then, that doesn't work, does it? We'll have to go with: 'Is the pope Catholic?'"

He looked like he'd lost the thread of the conversation, which suited Reg perfectly. "What did you win the award for? That sounds very scholarly."

He didn't look like the professorial type. Far too ruggedly handsome for such a nerdy pursuit. The history of witchcraft in North America?

"Witchcraft is a much-misunderstood topic in American history. People have passing familiarity with the Salem witch trials. Or are at least aware that there was such a thing. But they have no idea what actually happened during the trials. Or about witchcraft in the rest of American history. It's like that's the only time we can acknowledge that there were witches—or suspected witches—in the country. Just that one little pocket, and then the hysteria went away, and that was the extent of the influence of witchcraft in America."

"So were the Salem witches actually witches?"

He pursed his lips and considered. The waitress attended to them to remove their soup bowls and bring them their dinners.

Reg had opted for the burgers and fries, in spite of the fact that it was a date. She just felt incredibly hungry for an all-American burger and greasy chips.

Maybe she was still channeling Warren Blake.

★ Chapter Eight ★

WHETHER OR NOT THERE were actually witches accused in the Salem witch trials is for you to decide," Corvin said, after eating a few minutes in silence. "The mainstream will tell you it was just mass hysteria. The community will tell you that some of them were witches. In fact, a number of the people in this community are descended from people who were tried as witches."

"You're not going to give me a yes or no? I thought you were the expert. You wrote a paper."

"You're welcome to read it."

Reg rolled her eyes. "I'm not much of a reader." She took another big bite of her juicy burger. She felt something brush past her ankles and looked down, startled, expecting to see Starlight. Of course her cat wasn't there. She thought maybe there would be another cat. Maybe the restaurant had a mascot or some witch had figured it was okay to bring her familiar along. But there was nothing there.

"Problem?" Corvin asked, looking under the table himself.

"No. Just... bumped into the table leg, I guess." Reg looked at her burger. "I should keep some of this for Starlight."

"Does he like burgers?"

"I'm guessing he does. He doesn't seem to like kibble, but anything I'm eating is fair game."

"Maybe he's a reincarnate and doesn't really believe he's a cat."

Reg shook her head. "Right. I don't know why I didn't think of that."

"Like I said before, he has a powerful presence."

"Sarah says he has a third eye. Because of his markings."

"She's very experienced."

"She said she's older than she looks," Reg said. "How old do you put her at?"

His expression was masked. "I know more of her history than you do, that wouldn't quite be fair."

"So how old is she?"

Corvin pondered for a moment. Then his eyes fixed back on her. "Older than you think."

Reg rolled her eyes. Figured. They were circling the wagons. Protecting each other. "She says you are dangerous."

He smirked. "Does she, now?"

"Why would she think that?"

Corvin's smile deepened. Even with his sardonic mien, Reg still felt a magnetic physical attraction. "I can't imagine why," he said in a low, melodious voice that pulled at Reg's heartstrings. She started to make a list in her head of reasons she shouldn't get involved with Corvin. Then she laughed at herself. Making lists like Erin? She certainly didn't need any of Erin's strait-laced habits rubbing off on her. Life was dreary enough without following a bunch of societal strictures.

"Where did you go?" Corvin asked.

Reg took another bite of her burger. It was absolutely delicious. "I was just thinking about... my sister."

"I thought we were talking about me," he reproached, looking like a disappointed schoolboy.

"We were." Reg leaned a little closer to him, which felt a little like opening the oven to check on supper. A wave of heat spread over her. "My sister is dating a cop. Much safer than having supper with a warlock."

He chuckled, looking pleased.

Reg looked away, feeling her cheeks flush. One of the curses of her pale complexion was a propensity to blush when she was embarrassed. While she could lie without any physical sign, she still had an emotional reaction to other circumstances. The dim, candlelit interior of the restaurant would help to hide some of the redness of her cheeks.

In looking away, she realized she was being watched from a nearby table. It was the man she had met at the bar when she'd previously been in the restaurant. He had an odd name, and she struggled to remember it. Uriel. Mayberry? Wolfsbane? Some kind of plant name. When she caught his eyes on her, Uriel didn't look away. He didn't smile or wink, he just continued to stare at her. Reg looked behind her to see if he might be watching or looking at something else of interest and she had just mistaken his gaze. But there was nothing behind her that might have captivated his attention.

"Do you see that man?" Reg asked Corvin.

"Uriel Hawthorne?"

"That was it. He's staring at me."

Corvin stared back at Uriel, his gaze hard and challenging. Eventually, Uriel stood up. He didn't walk away, but approached the table.

"Corvin," he greeted coldly. "Miss Rawlins."

"Reg," she corrected breathlessly.

Corvin just looked at Uriel, not offering his hand or returning the greeting.

"You two know each other?" Reg asked.

Corvin looked at Uriel and didn't explain. Uriel smiled thinly. "You get to know everybody in the community eventually."

They were obviously not friends.

"I'd appreciate you not staring at my date," Corvin growled.

Uriel looked at Reg again, a clear challenge to Corvin's territorial rights. "Of course. I understand." He gave Reg a nod, then moved away.

Reg gave a shudder. "That's kind of creepy. You don't think I need to worry about him, do I?"

"You're with me. He won't bother you."

"What about when I'm not with you?"

"If you tell him to back off, and he doesn't, feel free to complain to management." Corvin nodded toward Bill at the bar. "Or the police, of course."

That didn't give Reg much comfort. She ate a few more bites of her burger and then picked at the fries.

"You're done?" Corvin eyed her burger.

"I'll take the rest home. Starlight will enjoy it."

"Lucky cat."

When they had finished their dinners, shared a hot fudge brownie, and lingered over demitasse coffees, it was clearly time to adjourn their date. Reg looked at Corvin, not sure what to expect, as they waited for the waitress to come back with the doggie bag. Or rather, the kitty bag.

"Come back to my house for a nightcap?" Corvin suggested.

"Well…" She was certainly tempted. But she had already been warned how dangerous this man was, and her own instincts were fighting against her attraction, warning her not to jump into anything.

She knew very little about what kind of a man Corvin actually was. A con, for sure. His charms were too well-polished to be natural. They were a hook to be set in order to reel unsuspecting prey in. She wasn't sure what his motivation for pursuing her was. If he was after money, he was going to be sorely disappointed. It might just be the thrill of the hunt, the satisfaction of knowing he could have whatever woman he set his sights on.

"You know you want to," he urged, voice husky.

The waitress came back and handed Reg her take-home container. Reg focused on that.

"I'd better get home to Starlight," she said. "He'll need to be fed…"

"I'm sure he has food available if he gets hungry. You can leave him alone for another hour or two."

"I've been so tired lately. I'd better get to bed and get to sleep."

He took her hand in his. "Reg…"

She again felt the electric charge of his touch. Her stomach dropped like she was in an elevator. Her heart sped and pounded hard.

Without warning, she flashed back to the cottage. To Starlight clawing her leg when she'd been caught in Corvin's vortex before. She focused on that memory, of being completely aware and pulling away from him, and in doing so was able to release his hand and break the connection.

"You need to stop doing that," she told him.

"Doing what?"

Of course he knew exactly what he was doing to her, but he wasn't going to admit it, and Reg didn't want to acknowledge the powerful force she felt either. It was hormones, that was all. A handsome man, the scent of his rose-laced cologne, a warm human touch. It was just the perfect storm for a lonely woman who hadn't had a good relationship for a number of years. But a one-night stand would just lead to future awkwardness, and a long-term relationship with the mysterious man was an even scarier proposition.

Reg didn't touch him or look into his eyes again. "Thank you for a lovely evening."

"So that's it?" Anger grated in his voice. He wasn't a man who was accustomed to being turned down.

"I don't owe you anything," Reg asserted. "We planned for supper. We've had supper. I need to get home and get some sleep."

"Coming home with me would be a lot more fun," he coaxed.

"I barely know you. It's not going to happen. Not tonight."

"We could go back to your place, if you're more comfortable with that."

"Goodnight, Corvin."

The heat that rolled off of him then was not animal attraction, but fury. Reg braced herself. She was far more used to defending herself against anger than against physical attraction. *That* was something she'd dealt with all her life.

He didn't say goodbye. Reg turned her back on him and left. She did stop once she got outside the door and look back to make sure he wasn't pursuing her.

She got back home with the clear feeling that she had escaped something predatory. Starlight rubbed against her legs, yowling at her. It was probably just the smell of the leftover burger in Reg's takeout container, but she liked to think that he was relieved to see her and have her home again.

"I made it," she said. "I wasn't sure I was going to."

She put the container on the counter and bent down to pick Starlight up. "You helped me even though you weren't there," she confided, speaking with her lips pressed against the short, velvety fur of his head. "I just kept thinking of you biting my ankles."

He purred loudly, pressing his head against her. Reg had a sudden vision of Corvin, storming down the alley behind The Crystal Bowl, kicking over garbage cans in a fit of rage.

She shuddered and held her cat close.

★ Chapter Nine ★

S HE SLEPT RESTLESSLY, ALTERNATING between dreams of Warren's restless spirit bound somewhere and not believing that he was really dead and visions of Corvin, menacing in his long black coat, trying to pull her in with his magnetism, no matter how hard Reg fought back against the pull.

It was comforting having Starlight there, even though Reg had sworn she would never allow him to sleep on the bed. He purred and kneaded the blankets and managed to soothe Reg back to sleep several times before she finally gave up and got up for the day. It was much earlier than she would have chosen to get up. Not as early as Erin had to get up to bake bread and goodies before her bakery opened for the day, but earlier than Reg, normally a night owl, preferred. She was sitting on one of the stools beside her kitchen island, working on a large cup of coffee, when the doorbell rang.

Most people knocked first. But most people didn't come at seven o'clock in the morning. She needed to decide what her office hours were and post them on her door. She didn't want to be seeing people all hours of the day and night.

Disgruntled, Reg took her coffee mug with her to the door and looked out. She wasn't expecting to see a uniform. Meter reader? Courier delivery? Reg opened the door and looked out.

Not a meter reader. A police officer. A woman, skin a golden brown, with black hair. Reg wasn't sure whether she had Hispanic or native blood. Reg looked toward the street where she had parked her car, but she couldn't see it from the cottage.

"Is everything okay?" she asked.

"I need to talk with you, ma'am." The woman's voice was flat, almost robotic. Difficult for Reg to get a read on. She motioned the woman into her living room where she had done the last couple of readings.

"Do you want... coffee?"

"No, thank you," the policewoman responded sharply.

"Okay..." Reg sat down in the nearby chair. "What can I do for you, then, Officer..." Reg focused on the name bar. "Detective Jessup?"

"It has come to the attention of the police department that you are may be participating in fraudulent business practices."

Reg's stomach knotted, but she kept her cool demeanor. "Fraudulent? I'm not sure what you're talking about. Have you had a complaint?" She'd only done a couple of readings—how could anyone have filed a complaint against her already? As far as she knew, both Amy Calvert and Ling Lau had been more than satisfied with the readings she had provided.

"We try to keep pretty tight track of what is going on in the neighborhood," Jessup advised. "There are a lot of people who come here with schemes to defraud the citizens of Black Sands, and it's my job to keep that from happening."

"So there *hasn't* been a complaint?"

Jessup didn't acknowledge the question one way or the other. "I understand that you purport to offer psychic services?"

Reg swallowed. "Yes, certainly. And that's not against the law in Florida."

"Not specifically, no, but offering a service and then not providing what was advertised..."

"I've provided the services that I advertise."

"Except that psychic services are not legitimate services. You can't actually predict the future or talk to the dead, so what you are doing is fraudulent."

Reg pointed to the tent card on the coffee table in front of Office Jesssup. *Readings and other services are for entertainment only.*

Jessup's nostrils flared. "So you admit that you are not actually psychic."

"I'm intuitive. I notice things that other people don't, and provide clients with a performance that incorporates those elements. It feels very real to them. They put their own interpretation on it and go home happy."

"You're not psychic."

"I don't know of any objective test to find out whether someone is psychic or not. Do you?"

"There is no such thing. It's hogwash. Therefore, what you are offering is not a legitimate service."

"I've providing entertainment," Reg reiterated. "Surely you do believe in acting. Performance art. Those are legitimate services. You're not arresting all of the actors and artists, are you?"

"You've been advertising and putting up flyers."

"Yes. In places where they are allowed." Reg had been very careful to only post the flyers in places where community notices were allowed. No notices on telephone poles or windows.

"Do you have an example of what you have been posting?"

"Yeah, sure." Reg got up and went to the second bedroom, which she had set up as her office, and picked up the top sheet from a stack of flyers. She took it back out to Detective Jessup. She pointed to the disclaimer that repeated the line on the tent card. *Readings and other services are for entertainment only.* It was a good thing she'd done her research before beginning.

Jessup's lip curled into a sneer. "People like you give Black Sands a bad reputation. People don't come here to be cheated out of their money."

"If people want to be entertained, what's the harm in them hiring me to do it? Everything is on that flyer. They can see what it is that I'm providing, and as far as I can tell, you haven't had any complaints about me."

"There is no such thing as a true psychic, Ms. Rawlins."

"Prove it."

But Jessup already knew that she didn't have any basis to bring charges against Reg. She got to her feet scowling. "I've got my eye on you," she warned. "The first time you step out of line, I'm going to be there, ready to catch you."

"It seems to me that if the town is overrun with crooks, like you say it is, you've got your work cut out for you. Why don't you concentrate on the people who you know have been ripping citizens off instead of someone who just arrived in town?"

Jessup didn't answer the question. She went to the door.

"I'll have my eye on you," she repeated, and left.

"Well." Reg looked down at Starlight. "That was a fun experience, wasn't it? She's got her eye on me now." She went to the kitchen to refill her coffee mug, even though she knew she probably shouldn't have quite that much caffeine in one morning. "Have you got your eye on me as well? Or all three of them?"

Starlight paced around the kitchen, stopping for a moment to sniff his dishes and then resuming his restless circuit. "Hungry? You're going to have to wait until I've had a chance to shower and make myself decent if you want to share my breakfast. Although… there is still more of that burger left over from last night."

She went to the fridge to get it out. "You'll eat it cold, right? I don't have to heat it up for your majesty?"

She opened the clamshell and looked at the partially-consumed burger. She was suddenly famished. How long had it been since she'd had a really good meal? It seemed like forever, even though she knew with the logical part of her mind that she'd had plenty to eat just the day before. She picked up the burger and put it on a plate. The smell filled the air, making her salivate.

She put it into the microwave to warm it up. She felt a sudden chill in the air and glanced over at the air conditioner to see if it was on. The room was quiet, and she couldn't detect the hum of the air conditioner over the noise of the microwave. Starlight darted in and nipped at her leg, but Reg saw him coming and jumped out of the way before he could dig in with his claws or teeth.

"No, Starlight!" she shouted. She picked up a thick grocery flyer from the kitchen island and rolled it into a tube to smack him with. He danced back when she swung it, so that she only skimmed his fur. He yowled and put his ears back.

"Go eat your food," Reg told him. "This is mine! No attack cat, or I'll send you back!"

He sat down out of her reach, but didn't go back to his food bowl or try to close in on her. Reg waited until the microwave beeped, then pulled the dish out. She couldn't believe how hungry she was. It was like she hadn't eaten in a week. She jammed the food into her mouth, wolfing it down. She closed her eyes and tried to remember what she had seen and heard during her session with Ling. Visually, there was nothing, just like when she closed her eyes. But she could hear and smell. There were smells of cooking food, like the hamburger and french fries. There were people talking. Machines making regular noises and, of course the beating of her own heart. *I'm not dead. I can't be dead, I can still hear my heart beating.*

"Reg? Miss Rawlins? Are you okay?"

Reg was far away, and she didn't think she could get back to the voice. There was too great a distance to be traversed.

"Miss Rawlins?" A sharp pain in her arm. "Come on. Wake up."

"I… can't…"

"You need to. Come back."

Reg tried to withdraw from the poking and prodding, just focusing on the sensations in her memory. Where was he? He was closer than it seemed. She was getting closer to him.

There was a sharp, acrid smell that blocked out the smells of the hamburger and the other familiar smells of the memory. Reg coughed, choking on the evil stench. She put her hands up to her mouth and nose, trying to block the smell.

She opened her eyes. She was on the kitchen floor, Sarah hanging over her, face worried. Reg choked again. "What is that? Take it away."

Sarah withdrew whatever stinkweed she'd been holding under Reg's nose.

"It's a traditional—"

"It's foul!"

"You were in a trance. It was the only thing I could think of to pull you out."

"A trance?" Reg scoffed. "I was not in a trance."

"You wouldn't wake up."

Reg opened her mouth to say that she had just fallen asleep. But it was a pretty silly thing to say when she was lying on the kitchen floor. She hadn't just lain down there for a nap.

She sat up slowly, trying to keep her wobbly head under control so that she looked like she was okay, and not all wonky like she was.

"Tell me what happened," Sarah said, offering her hand to Reg to help her up. Reg ignored the hand and pushed herself up on her own. She didn't want to end up pulling Sarah over. Reg was healthy and fit and in her prime. She didn't need an older woman to step in and pull her up. Reg sat for a minute and then got shakily to her feet.

"I don't really know. I was eating. I was thinking of the hamburger and just about Ling's husband and then…" She shook her head. "I'm sure it's just jet lag. I'm just fatigued after all of the driving."

She remembered how Corvin had suggested that there was some kind of cosmic disruption that was keeping him from sleeping. Which was ridiculous, of course. There was nothing any of them could do to affect magnetic waves or energy fields of even a room, let alone an entire community.

"Think about it," Sarah insisted. "This isn't just about being tired. That was a trance. You were under a spell."

"No one could have put a spell on me."

Sarah laughed. "You're not very familiar with the magical world, are you?"

"Well... no," Reg admitted. If magic wasn't real, it couldn't harm her, and any time Reg spent in studying it was wasted.

"Someone has cast a spell," Sarah insisted. "But I'm not sure it's on you. I'm not sure you were meant to be caught by it. Sort of like a dolphin getting caught in a tuna net."

"What were they trying to cast a spell on, then? My house? Starlight? Was my food contaminated?"

Sarah looked around the house, her hands outstretched as if trying to catch the wisps of spells. She closed her eyes and swayed back and forth. Reg almost found herself believing it, even though she knew it was just an act. Sarah looked up toward heaven, staring beyond the ceiling.

"We should cleanse the room," she suggested. "Burn some sage to get rid of the spectral imprint... who did you have contact with last?"

"There was a policewoman this morning," Reg offered.

"You did a reading for her?"

"No, she was trying to warn me off. To keep me from offering my services."

"That's not what I mean. I mean what *spirit* did you contact last? Was there some influence that was very strong?"

Reg shrugged reluctantly. "That would be Ling's husband, I guess. I haven't been able to get him out of my mind."

"Because his imprint is still here. You should say a prayer. Do you have sage?"

At Reg's doubtful look, Sarah waved her hand. "Never mind. I do. Don't do anything before I get back. Understand? Don't try to contact him again."

"I wasn't..."

"Just don't. Don't even think of him."

Reg wasn't sure how she was supposed to stop herself from thinking about a particular thing. Because of course the first thing that happened when Sarah left the cottage was that Reg thought back to the contact she had made with Warren.

Starlight brushed against Reg, meowing.

"I know, I haven't fed you either. But you do have food in your dish."

Starlight turned to look at Reg, clearly communicating his displeasure. Reg looked around. There was no sign of the hamburger, which presumably meant she had finished eating it herself, or she had dropped it on the floor when she had fainted and Starlight had moved in and gobbled it up.

She looked in the cupboards and found a can of tuna. She opened it, Starlight purring and rubbing happily against her legs the whole time, put some in a bowl, and put it down on the floor for him. Starlight trotted over and started to gobble it down. The smell was sweet and meaty and a little nauseating to Reg. It helped to clear the residual cobwebs away.

Obviously, she was fighting some kind of virus. That was why she had been having such trouble sleeping, having such vivid dreams and memories, and had fainted in the middle of the kitchen. She was coming down with the flu. That's all there was to it.

Sarah returned. She smiled at Reg and nodded encouragingly. "We'll have this place fixed up in no time," she promised. She put some green leaves on a tray, then used a lighter to start them burning. She waved the tray up and down and back and forth, spreading the sweet-smelling smoke around. Like the tuna, it helped Reg to put aside her thoughts of Warren and focus on the present. Though the tuna might actually have helped more.

"Now, tell me about this spirit," Sarah said, putting the tray down in the middle of the counter as it continued to smolder.

"He was recently killed in a plane crash, but he didn't know he was dead. He kept saying that it was all a mistake. He could hear his heartbeat, so he couldn't be dead. And I keep having dreams of him... hearing that heartbeat, as well as the other things going on around him."

Reg realized after saying it that she had ascribed those feelings and words to the spirit, when she herself was the one who had come up with them. She was falling for her own con. The Warren she was dreaming about wasn't the real Warren, but someone she had invented. She frowned to herself, thinking about the irony of it.

"He could hear his heart beating?" Sarah repeated.

"Yes. That's what he said."

"That's very odd. A spirit wouldn't be able to hear his heart beating, because it wouldn't be beating."

"I think that was his point."

Sarah frowned. "You're sure that this fellow *is* dead, right? It's not a missing persons case?"

"Of course. He was killed in a plane crash."

"So they have his body."

"No. They've recovered some of the wreckage, but not his body. It might have been really torn up. Maybe sharks..." Reg trailed off. They both knew what predators could do to bodies. Luckily, neither of them had to see that. They both had professions that allowed them to sit in the comfort of their own homes, spinning their little tales.

"Then the answer is simple," Sarah said. "He isn't dead."

★ Chapter Ten ★

IF WARREN BLAKE WASN'T really dead, then Reg had made a big mistake contacting him spiritually. When Ling figured it out and came after her, Detective Jessup would have the information she needed for her fraud charges. Contacting a spirit who wasn't in the spirit world was a pretty dubious talent.

"I think if Warren wasn't dead, Ling would know it," Reg asserted. She turned away from Sarah to put the rest of the tuna into a sealed container and store it in the fridge. It was only an excuse to compose herself.

"Maybe Ling does know it in her heart, and that's why she came to see you," Sarah said. "She was looking for answers. She didn't believe what the police told her and thought he was still out there, somewhere."

"He couldn't still be alive. If he was still alive, I wouldn't be able to contact him, and the police would have been informed he was still alive. He couldn't survive out there in the ocean, which would mean he is on land, somewhere close by. Where the ocean washed him in like the rest of the debris from the crash."

"Not if no one knew who he was," Sarah said.

"He would know who he was."

"Maybe he's in a coma. Some spirits have been known to wander while their bodies were in an unconscious state."

Reg felt a rush of warmth. Like goosebumps, except calming instead of uncomfortable. Like her body had just confirmed what Sarah had told her.

"You really think he's still alive?"

"It sounds like it, my dear. There's only one way to find out. We need to contact him and get all of the information we can, and then track him down. Then he can be reunited with his wife."

"Sarah, I can't really—"

"You can and you will. You've been trying to shake him off ever since your session, so it shouldn't be hard to establish contact again. He's practically begging you to be his vessel again."

"This is ridiculous…"

"No, it's not. Now come and sit down and get comfortable. Do you have any rituals? Do you want a cup of tea or need some time for meditation…?"

"Well, the last couple of times I've had tea… but I don't really have anything special. I just talk to the person about their loved on, and then see if I can… channel them."

"I'll put the kettle on. It may take a little while, since we've just cleansed the cottage of his spiritual imprint. He might not be as amenable to coming back again…"

Reg sat in her living room as she was told. She didn't know for sure why she was doing what Sarah told her to, since she knew it was all just in her own head. There was no real spirit of Warren, just the voice Reg herself had made up. But Sarah was surprisingly convincing.

In spite of the amount of coffee and excitement that morning, she was already feeling drowsy by the time the kettle began to whistle. Sarah poured the water into the teapot, prepared their cups, and brought the tea service over. Reg poured water over the loose leaves and stared down at them. What if there was something more to reading tea leaves than just exercising a vivid imagination? What would it be like to have an actual vision or visitation?

Reg closed her eyes.

"It's cold."

"Are you reaching out, Reg? Can you feel him?"

"I'm here," Warren's voice answered.

"Well, you *are* strong, aren't you? Am I talking to Warren?"

"Yes. Who are you? I can't see you."

"I'm Sarah, a friend of Ling's. Tell me about where you are, Warren."

"I don't know. I can't see anything."

"What do you hear?"

"Voices. Beeping. Amplified voices."

"Are you in a train station?"

"No," the voice was dry. "It's not a train station!"

"Is it your house? Are you sleeping in your bed?"

"I'm not in my house..." Reg searched for the words when the voice petered out. But she couldn't find the words to put into Warren's voice. She had to wait for them. "I might be in a bed, though. Where am I?"

"Are you in a hospital?" Sarah suggested.

"A hospital? Yes!" There was growing excitement in the voice. "I think it might be. But why would I be in a hospital? What happened?"

"Don't worry about that. Those machines you hear, could it be a heart rate monitor? A respirator? Think about it."

"Yes... they could be."

"Do you know which hospital you're at?"

There was only blankness when Reg reached for an answer. She couldn't answer that question.

"Are you still there, Warren?"

"You said I was dead. But I'm not dead." There were a few seconds of silence. "Not unless they come back for me."

★ Chapter Eleven ★

REG REMEMBERED PLAYING ON the swings when she was little. She tended to be excluded from the groups playing tag and grounders and other group play, and instead had to find other ways to entertain herself. She loved to swing for hours. High and low, fast and slow. Turning to get the chain all twisted and deformed in a big knot, and then to let it go and spin, spin, spin back to her original position.

For a long time, she was back there, spinning contentedly, letting the swing wind down and down until it was back in its place. She opened her eyes and looked around, disoriented to find herself in the cottage.

"You'd better not do that again," Sarah said worriedly. "Something is happening to you when you communicate with Warren. I don't know what it is, but you keep getting stuck."

Reg looked around. She was dizzy and lightheaded. The position of the sun through the windows suggested that it was late afternoon.

"What happened?"

"It's too hard getting you out of those trances. I don't think you'd better do it again."

Reg rubbed her temples. Whatever had just happened, she didn't intend to go back there. "Did you find out what you needed to know?"

"Warren isn't dead. He's in hospital in a coma, and he might be in danger. I think our next step should be to call the police."

Reg really didn't want to have to deal with Detective Jessup or any of her contingent.

"We don't need to do that, do we?"

"There's no point in us calling the hospitals asking for Warren. They won't give us any information. But the police could cut through the red tape and find out."

"What about Ling? She's his next of kin, she could call the hospital." Reg was feeling slightly nauseated. She picked up her cold tea and sipped it, hoping to settle her stomach.

"You're going to call her and tell her that her dead husband is still alive? When you don't have proof? You really want to do that to her?"

Reg wished that the answer was yes. She was perfectly capable of putting that burden onto someone else. What did it hurt her if Ling had to experience that disappointment again? But if she wanted to build a business, she had to be trustworthy. People wouldn't hire her if they thought she didn't know what she was talking about and was only playing a game with them. She couldn't prove that Warren was in hospital. That was what she had imagined up under the influence of Sarah's suggestions, but it wasn't necessarily true. In fact, it probably wasn't. It might fit the set of known facts, but neither of them actually knew that Warren was in hospital.

That meant that not only could they not go to Ling with the information, they couldn't go to the police either.

"Letticia might have an idea," Sarah offered.

"Who is Letticia?"

"Letticia Williams. She's an old crone I know. Not many people have more experience than I do, but she's been around for a long time and is very smart."

"I don't think we need to bring anyone else in on this," Reg protested. "I'll just try calling the hospitals. If we don't have any success with that… then I don't know. I guess I'd rather go to your friend than to the police."

"I didn't say she was a friend," Sarah warned. "Letticia is… she doesn't have the same philosophical outlook as I do."

"Philosophical outlook?" Reg needed something for her headache. Normally good at reading people, she wasn't picking up on Sarah's facial cues. What philosophical outlook was Sarah talking about?

"Letticia is more… results oriented. In my opinion, it isn't just the end result that matters. It's how you go about it too. To me, it's important not to trifle with powers you don't have the proper control over or that may cause harm."

"Are you talking about dark magic? Letticia is a bad witch?"

"There is no good and bad the way you are thinking, no white magic and dark magic. This isn't television. There are many different ways to approach a problem…"

"And Letticia might have some ideas of things that you wouldn't do."

"Things that I wouldn't think about," Sarah amended.

"Spells or practical steps?"

"I don't know, if I haven't thought about them."

Reg had to admit that it had been an impossible question.

"Okay. Can I have some time to get myself together again?"

Sarah nodded. "Have a hot shower and a stiff drink and I'll call her to see if she can meet."

"Do we need to meet face-to-face?" Reg wasn't sure she wanted to meet a dark witch if she could avoid it. "Can't you just tell her on the phone and see if she has any ideas?"

"Letticia doesn't like phones, especially cell phones. She'll want to see you and evaluate the situation for herself."

"She doesn't have a phone?"

"She has a phone, an old wired set from decades ago. I'll call her and she'll come here."

Reg sighed. She was used to her apartment being a refuge from the world, somewhere she could go where it was just her and she could relax and let her hair down. The cottage felt more like Grand Central Station. She swept her corn rows back with both hands.

"I'm going to have that shower, then.

"I'll be back with Letticia if she can come over. You won't… contact Warren while I'm gone?"

Reg shook her head vigorously. "Definitely not."

★ Chapter Twelve ★

AFTER DUE CONSIDERATION, REG decided that Sarah's recommendation of a good stiff drink was a sound one, and she allowed herself a tot of the Jack Daniels she had shared with Corvin.

Why couldn't *he* be the one they consulted with? Even though Sarah said that he was dangerous, Reg felt that she had been able to stand up to him just fine on their first two encounters, and nothing was going to happen if Sarah were there to intervene on her behalf as well. She could bet that he would have some suggestions. Reg didn't like the sound of the new witch and would prefer not to have to meet her at all.

When she had gotten out of the shower, she had pretty much decided that there was no point to a meeting with Letticia. In fact, there was little point in their doing anything. Reg was not responsible for proving whether Warren Blake was dead or whether he was a missing person. That was the job of the police and coast guard and the FAA or whoever was involved with downed planes. If they weren't doing their job, then it was up to Ling to get them moving. She could go to the media and insist that something be done.

Reg, on the other hand, was just a psychic. It wasn't her job to find the missing man. If it turned out that he hadn't been dead during the reading Reg had done for Ling, then that called Reg's skills into question. Alternatively, saying that he was still alive and then having his dead body show up later would only compound the problem.

After a drink, she turned her mind to the opposite problem. What if she did nothing and it turned out that Warren was still alive?

If she and Sarah pushed for answers and they found Warren still alive, then Reg would be a hero and her reputation would be greatly improved. She could double her rates.

But the only evidence that they had that Warren was still alive were Reg's own imaginings and Sarah's interpretation of the odd events around Reg's readings. Reg's fainting, wild ramblings, and disorientation could be explained simply enough if she were fighting a flu bug or something else she had picked up while traveling.

Then there was the fact that Warren's body had not turned up.

But there were plenty of reasons for a body not to turn up. It could have been carried out to sea, consumed by sharks or other predators, caught on rocks, or cast up on some deserted shore where it was never found. Or he could have intentionally run away from his wife and his life. It would be dangerous to assume that because the body hadn't washed up where and when expected that he was still alive and in need of saving.

Reg sipped at the whiskey, closing her eyes and pondering the best plan of action. The best solution was probably to keep all options open until they either knew for sure that Warren was dead or that he was alive. He didn't think he was dead, so she was not passing judgment until she knew for sure. It was possible that she was communicating with a live person telepathically rather than channeling a dead one; there was no way to know until he either accepted that he was dead or they had proof one way or the other.

She put her empty tumbler into the sink, satisfied with this approach. Just like so many other con jobs, it was a delicate balance. Letting people believe what they wanted to and just adding some shading and color to provide definition. There were some complications, with Sarah and now this new witch being involved, but she could manage that, if she were careful.

Starlight had been sleeping on one of the wicker chairs and, hearing Reg in the kitchen, he got up to see if she was making anything good.

"Uh, sorry kitty, nothing going on here…" Reg apologized. She toed the bowl of cat food. "I do have this for you, you know. Other cats eat it."

He sat back on his haunches and stared at her, inscrutable.

"Do you really think you aren't a cat, like Corvin said? Do you think you're a person in a smaller, furrier package?"

He stretched tall, giving a little tail-to-head shiver, and then turned and walked toward the cottage door. Sarah knocked before he was halfway there, and opened the door. What Reg wouldn't have given for ears like a cat's.

"Reg? Oh, you are ready. Great."

She pushed the door open the rest of the way and let the other witch in behind her.

Like some slapstick comedy or comic book, the two witches were opposite in almost every way. Where Sarah was short and heavy, the other witch was tall and spare. Her hair was black in contrast to Sarah's soft blond. Rather than coming across as a soft, grandmotherly person as Sarah did, Letticia was not a person to be trifled with. She walked ramrod straight and did not smile. She looked around the cottage and sniffed. Reg could have been offended, but since it had only been her home for a few days and the decorating wasn't hers, she just let it go.

"Reg, this is Letticia. Letticia…?"

"You have a cat," Letticia observed.

"Uh, yes."

"Why don't we go sit down," Sarah suggested, gesturing toward the living room grouping. But Letticia didn't make any indication she had even heard.

"You didn't tell me she had a cat," Letticia told Sarah.

"Are you allergic?" Reg asked. "I'm sorry, I can put him in the bedroom, or we could go up to Sarah's house…"

But Letticia was apparently not allergic. She walked up to Starlight and looked down at him. Starlight looked up at Letticia. He didn't run away when she bent over to pick him up. Letticia didn't cuddle Starlight but held him as if she were a shelf, letting him sit on her arm, gazing at her, nose to nose.

"He has been here during the communications?" she demanded.

Reg looked over at Sarah, looking for an explanation of what was going on. "Yes. He's been here."

Letticia swiveled on the spot and walked over to the seating area. She sat herself, still ramrod straight, Starlight sitting on her lap like a king on his throne.

Reg sat down, waiting for Starlight to leave Letticia and join her instead.

"How has the cat behaved during these visions?"

"I don't know…" Reg was boggled that the woman would even ask. "He's been behaving really strangely since I got him, so I don't know what's normal and what's unusual. He's been biting or clawing me for no reason that I can tell. He won't eat the cat food I got for him."

"Did he bite you when you communicated with this man?"

"Uh… yes, really bad, actually." Reg showed off her ankle, bare under her capris, with a couple of bandages in place. "I was still channeling Warren when he did it. Pulled me right out of… right out of the experience."

"She fainted right there on the floor this morning," Sarah told Letticia, gesturing, "and I had a really hard time getting her out of her trance when she channeled Warren today. Something is wrong. That's just not normal."

Was there paranormal normality? Did one really expect things like fortune telling, spells, or speaking with the dead to follow certain rules? While Reg had tried to follow the patterns of mediums she had seen on TV so that her readings would resonate with her clients, she hadn't really thought of there being a right way and a wrong way to be a medium. Surely everybody had their own methods and what worked for one person wouldn't necessarily work for another.

Letticia stared hard at Reg, making her squirm in discomfort.

"She could just be a fake," Letticia pointed out, as if Reg weren't even there. "None of this makes a lot of sense."

"No," Sarah protested. "I've seen her in action. I would know if that was just put on. She definitely made contact with someone or something."

"Someone or something?" Reg repeated. The air conditioner was again blowing too cold. "What does that mean?"

"There are… other entities that you could have made contact with," Letticia said, as if Reg should know that. "Obviously there are spirits other than Warren Blake around here, and you could have contacted one of them. Or it might have been something other than a restless spirit."

"Like what?"

Letticia shrugged. She looked at Sarah. "You were quite sure that she was in contact with who she thought she was? There was no indication that it might not have been Warren?"

"We talked about Ling. We talked about the earlier contact. Of course it was Warren."

"He didn't say anything that only Warren would have known…?"

"We weren't trying to prove him; Reg had just invited him back. He'd been trying to get her to be his vessel again, and he was there as soon as she asked him. We have a harder time getting rid of him than getting him to come."

"So if we're to assume that it is him…"

"If it is him, then he's in hospital somewhere. He was quite clear."

"And he said he was in danger," Reg recalled. She'd felt suspended in air since her last encounter with Warren's spirit, unable to remember everything she had said for him to Sarah.

Sarah gave a little nod. "He indicated that he could be in danger."

"If someone came back looking for him," Reg said. "What does that mean? Who would be going back for him?

Does he mean the searchers? The police and rescuers who were looking for his body? That doesn't make any sense."

"If he nearly died," Letticia said, "then doesn't it make sense that someone was trying to kill him? He went down in a plane?"

"He was the pilot of a small aircraft. Yes."

"And was he any good?"

Reg lifted her hands in a shrug. "I never flew with him. His wife seemed to think so."

"Then how did his plane go down? It was a storm? He lost his way? Had an engine malfunction?"

"All I heard was that the plane went down."

"That's one of the two directions planes usually go. The problem is the speed they go down with. You don't know what caused the accident?"

"No."

"Maybe you should ask Ling that. Or ask Warren. He didn't tell you what happened to the plane?"

"I didn't think to ask," Sarah said, moving her hands nervously and looking flustered. "I should have asked, of course. It only makes sense. But I don't think Reg should call him again."

"That's a problem, since you and I don't speak with the dead."

Sarah nodded, looking down, as if she were a small child who had just been called out in front of the class. "I am sorry."

"So we need to find out where he is and who is trying to kill him and to stop them," Reg summarized, her voice rising with stress. "That doesn't sound too difficult!"

"Stay calm, child; have a drink of tea," Letticia advised.

Reg wanted to kick the old woman right in the knee. Who did she think she was, treating everybody else like they were two years old? She might be a free thinker, someone Sarah said could help, but that wasn't any reason to treat everyone else like they didn't matter and should bow down to her.

Sarah gave Reg a warning look. She probably sensed that Reg was ready to blow her top. It was all getting to be a bit much. She had planned to set up shop in Black Sands, do a few casual readings a day, and be able to make a living off of her craft that way. Instead, she was surrounded by crazy people who thought that they really were witches and warlocks and that everything she said was gospel. She'd been dumped right into the middle of—what?—a murder mystery? She was tired, she had a cat that bit, and she wasn't going to put up with any more nonsense.

"If you'll excuse me for a moment," she said sweetly to Letticia, rising to her feet. "I need a break." She remembered Erin and her little bakery in Bald Eagle Falls, and the quaint names that she and her friends had for the facilities. "I need to use the loo!"

Open-mouthed, Sarah watched her walk away.

★ Chapter Thirteen ★

REG WASHED HER FACE and held a cold cloth over her eyes. She was incredibly tired, even though it was still only late afternoon. It seemed like every contact she had with Warren left her more and more tired. For some reason, he was draining her of all of her energy.

No. She was tired because of a virus. Or because of her travel. Or something in the air or the food. It wasn't because Warren was draining her of energy, because she wasn't actually channeling his spirit. If she were to believe the fiction that she had invented, then he wasn't even dead, but in a hospital somewhere while his ghost walked around looking for trouble.

She touched up her makeup and took her time returning to the two witches and their bizarre ideas. She sat back down with them and looked back and forth at them to see what they had decided.

"There aren't really that many hospitals around here," Letticia told Reg. "We should be able to get to all of them in a few hours. All you have to do is be open to the presence of the spirits and figure out which hospital Warren is in. Then we can go inside and find him, assuming he's not in some restricted area. Once we find him, then we can turn it over to Ling and over to the police to put together the rest of the pieces of the puzzle and figure out who he is under threat from."

"How do we know he's in a nearby hospital?"

"It would need to be somewhere close by for him to be communicating with you. That takes a huge amount of energy."

"Besides," Sarah pointed out, "his plane was in the area when it went down. He would have had to come in somewhere fairly close by."

"Then wouldn't the police have found him? Wouldn't they have tied together the man who went missing from a plane crash site and the one who washed up on the beach?"

The two witches looked at each other. Something passed between them, but Reg couldn't make out what it was. They knew more than they were telling her.

"He's close by," Sarah said. "I'm absolutely sure of that."

Reg took out her phone and looked at it. A moment later, the screen lit up and it started to ring. Letticia looked at her sourly.

"That's a neat trick."

Reg remembered that Letticia didn't like technology, particularly cellphones. But that wasn't Reg's fault, and they were in Reg's house. She wasn't going to live like a homeless person just because Letticia couldn't abide a ringing phone.

The caller ID told her it was Corvin. Reg turned the screen away from Sarah so she wouldn't see who it was. She needed to take the call. Twice she had met with Corvin and their plans had been foiled by Starlight, and she didn't want him getting the wrong impression. Playing hard-to-get might work with some guys, but she had a feeling that Corvin wasn't one of them. His ego was too big to be chasing her around making a fool of himself. If she didn't make some sign to him, he would move on to the next woman on his list.

"Sorry, I need to take this," Reg said, and swiped the screen to answer the call. She said "Hello," but didn't pursue the conversation until she was in her bedroom and the door was shut. "Sorry about that," she whispered to Corvin. "I have visitors and I needed to find somewhere private to talk."

"Good," Corvin purred into the phone. "I'm glad that we're alone. Who is visiting? Anyone I know? A client or something else?"

"Sarah and a friend of hers."

Corvin waited, not saying anything else. Reg wondered whether she should tell him any more details.

"Letticia," she offered finally. Maybe Corvin would know her. Maybe he wouldn't. Reg didn't have to be guilty of leaking any details to him. Just because she had mentioned Letticia's name.

"Letticia?"

"I don't know her last name, I don't think Sarah said. An older woman."

"She's the leader of Sarah's coven."

"Oh. Well, sure. I guess that's why Sarah went to her for advice."

"What advice did Sarah need?"

Reg was uncomfortable. "Why do you need to know? I thought you were calling to talk to me, but if you want Sarah I can put her on the phone. It's my understanding that Letticia doesn't like phones, so if you want to talk to her, you'll have to come here."

"Is that an invitation?"

Reg paused. "No. I was being facetious."

"I could come there and be facetious too."

"No. Please don't. It's crowded enough here already."

"Crowded? Who else is there?"

"Sarah and Letticia. And Starlight. And me. That's more than enough for this little place." She almost added "and Warren," but managed to bite her tongue.

"So what did Sarah need the old crone for?"

"Isn't that sort of rude? Whether you like the woman or not, it's really poor taste to be calling her names…"

"What?" Corvin laughed. "I'm not being insulting, Reg. A crone is a term of respect for an older witch. Sort of like an empty-nester, only wiser."

"Oh." Reg added that one to her mental file. She needed to do more extensive research if she didn't want to get caught up on things like that. She didn't claim to be an expert, but people were going to expect her to have at least some understanding of the culture in Black Sands. "I didn't know that."

"I wouldn't expect you to, since you've just recently started to pursue your calling."

"I'd like to get together again," Reg said, before he could ask her anything else. "I assume that's why you called?"

There was a scratching on the bedroom door. Reg ignored it. Starlight didn't need to follow her everywhere she went. If she opened the door for him, he'd only turn around and decide he wanted to leave again two minutes later, when he discovered that she didn't have any food or entertainment for him.

"I would like to get together again," Corvin agreed. "Are you feeling better?"

"Better?"

"You thought you might be coming down with something. You were tired, not sleeping well."

"Oh, that. Well... still not any better, but I'm trying to just push through and pretend I'm not. Sarah and her friend have some ideas."

She made it sound like they were coming up with an herbal cure for her, rather than that they were determined to find a dead man who wasn't necessarily dead.

"That's good. I hope you're feeling more like yourself soon. So, are you free to go out for dinner tonight? Maybe a movie, if you don't think you'd fall asleep in the middle of it."

"Um... I don't think tonight is going to work, actually. But I didn't want you to think I was putting you off. I do want to do something, I just have other plans for the rest of today."

"Things don't really get popping in this town until after midnight. We could still do something later on."

His voice was soothing. He didn't have quite the same presence over the phone when she couldn't see and smell him, but she still ached to see him again and to continue where they had left off.

"I don't think I'll be able to stay up that late. I really am sorry."

"Don't worry your head about it. We'll work things out. Where are Sarah and Letticia taking you tonight?"

Reg opened her mouth to answer, then realized that he was fishing again. Why was it so important for him to know all of the details of her life? She didn't insist on knowing how he spent every minute of his day. She wasn't even sure there was such a thing as a full-time warlock. Did he just do magical work, or did he have to have a day job to pay the bills? She pictured him in jeans and a tight shirt, ready to do some manual labor to make ends meet, and gave herself goosebumps.

"Call me tomorrow," she told Corvin. "Actually, don't bother calling me, just come on over tomorrow, and we'll work something out. Okay?"

"Alright," he sounded pleased with that, even if he hadn't managed to worm any further information out of her. She would need to be more careful about what she said about him. She didn't know if he liked to know things just for himself, or to spread gossip, or because he was a reporter for some community newspaper that needed a big scoop. "I'll see you tomorrow, Regina Rawlins."

She blushed at the way he said her name in a low, seductive tone, and then he was gone. Reg patted her face. She was going to need to splash cold water on herself again, but not to wake herself up, this time.

She went over to the door and opened it, finding Starlight sitting on the other side, his ears back so he looked like an owl, apparently not impressed with being shut out of the room.

"Oh, don't look at me like that. You don't even want to be in here," Reg motioned to the room. "You just want to be in here because it's where I am."

He yowled at her in a particularly vexed way and entered the room but, as she expected, he didn't jump up on the bed to go to sleep, but immediately circled back around to Reg and brushed past her legs, his fur tickling her skin. She watched him closely, not about to be lulled into a false sense of security and get bitten on the leg again.

"You don't fool me, puss. You probably know I was on the phone with Corvin, and you don't want me to get together with him again."

Starlight looked up at her, clearly communicating his disdain.

"Corvin is the reason you got that piece of hamburger today. However much of it you got away from me. And if we go out again tomorrow night, maybe I'll bring you something home again. You'd like that, wouldn't you?"

He sat down and regarded her.

"No cat is going to tell me what I can and can't do," Reg told him. "No more biting, or there will be no table scraps for you. It's no wonder you got sent to the pound."

After she said the words, she remembered why he had been at the shelter, and regretted them. He hadn't been given up by an owner who couldn't stand his hijinks anymore. His owner had died, and there had been no one else to take him. As a foster child, Reg could relate to that feeling of being unwanted and abandoned. Just discarded, of so little value that no one would take her for more than a short period of time.

"Oh, I'm sorry, Starlight," she told him, bending down to scratch his ears and his chin. "I didn't mean that. I'm glad you're here and I'm not sending you back to the shelter. I know it wasn't your fault that you were there, and it's not your fault that we haven't been getting along with each other either. We just both have different expectations. It can't be easy for you, all of the strange comings and goings around here. You just want to sit down and relax, and there are all of these weird people coming and going."

He purred his forgiveness, rubbing against her hand and sucking up the attention. The poor beast was just starved for affection. If she gave him lots of attention and watched for those times when he was feeling overwhelmed by company, maybe everything would be just fine. She'd figure out what things triggered his bad behavior and change them.

Reg laughed at herself. All through her childhood, she'd been the subject of those evaluations. The ABCs of behavior modification. What is the antecedent? What behavior does it trigger? What are the consequences of the behavior? Change the environment, and you could fix the child's behavior. Only, it was never quite that cut-and-dried. People were messy and behaved in unexpected ways. Reg liked to know what reactions she was going to get from her behavior, and she didn't want some do-gooder mixing it all up. Changing Reg's environment and people's reactions to her behavior drove her out of her mind. She needed things to be predictable and within her control.

"Cats can't understand people and cats aren't psychic," she told Starlight. "So why am I still talking to you?"

But she knew exactly why. Because once Reg was finished with talking on the phone and expounding her philosophies to Starlight, she was going to have to go back out to talk to the two witches, and things were going to spin out of Reg's control once again.

★ Chapter Fourteen ★

"OKAY," REG FACED THE two crones. "So what do I do?"

"You don't need to do anything yet," Sarah said. "You can just enjoy a nice, relaxing ride, and Letticia and I will take you to the hospitals. We'll make sure he's safe and that his loved ones know he is alive."

It sounded simple. But Reg had a feeling that it wasn't going to be anything of the sort. Her life had not been simple since arriving in Black Sands.

"You don't want me to drive?" Reg checked. If Letticia didn't like technology, she probably didn't want to drive, and Reg had no idea whether Sarah drove. Maybe she just used a broomstick.

"I'm quite capable of driving," Sarah assured her.

They traipsed out to the garage and Reg saw the big, black jeep. Somehow, it wasn't what she had pictured Sarah driving. An old station wagon, maybe. Something understated. Letticia hopped into the front passenger seat, leaving Reg to select a seat in the second row. There were no seatbelts, but she was sure she would be just fine with Sarah driving.

Until Sarah actually started driving.

Reversing out of the garage, the tires squealed, and Reg was thrown forward against Letticia's seat, bruising her mouth and nose.

"Oh, I'm sorry, dear," Sarah apologized blithely. "Hang on to something."

Reg did. She hung on for dear life all the way to the first hospital. It wasn't exactly the nice, relaxing ride that Sarah had suggested it would be. She was relieved when they reached the hospital and immediately jumped out, needing solid ground under her feet. Her face was throbbing and she was feeling dangerously carsick.

Letticia stayed in the jeep. Sarah flicked on her flashers and climbed out.

"Do you feel something, Reg? I had hoped that we would just be able to stay in the car unless you felt like Warren was here."

Reg leaned against a pillar. "I needed to get out for a minute."

"Of course," Sarah agreed, frowning.

A white compact car pulled up behind the jeep. Reg heard it thunk into park and heard the door slam after the driver unfolded himself from the seat. She concentrated on breathing long, slow breaths.

"You are a menace on the streets, woman," a familiar voice criticized. "They should take away your license!"

"I don't have one." Sarah smiled at him.

It was Corvin. Reg stared at him. Was he part of a hallucination? Was she really that sick? Maybe the whole thing was just a fevered nightmare. When she woke up from it, everything would be back to normal.

"What are you doing here?" she demanded, in spite of herself.

"He followed us," Sarah said. "You really shouldn't have taken his call."

"How did you know...? And I didn't tell him where we were going!"

"You didn't need to."

Did Corvin have some mystical extrasensory powers as well as his natural attraction? Had he read her mind?

"Everyone in the neighborhood can hear when Sarah's out in that deathtrap," Corvin pointed out. "She's not exactly difficult to track."

Sarah sighed. "What are you doing here, Corvin Hunter? You don't have any business with us."

"For one thing, I want to make sure that you don't kill my date before I get a chance to see her again."

Sarah eyed Reg, obviously disappointed with her. She had, after all, warned Reg that Corvin was dangerous and that she shouldn't be seeing him. So far, Reg had done nothing but flout her advice in that department. But Sarah didn't repeat her warnings in front of Corvin.

"So, what's going on?" Corvin asked casually, looking at the hospital. "Are you here to visit someone?"

Reg wasn't sure what to say about it. She took a couple more deep breaths. The nausea was starting to fade. Corvin looked from Reg to Sarah, waiting for an answer. At first, Sarah seemed to have no intention of giving Corvin any information. But as he stared at her, Reg saw her face begin to flush. He remembered how Sarah said that even as an old woman, she still felt Corvin's pull.

"We're just looking for someone," she told Corvin, patting at her hair. "Not that it's any of your business."

"Looking for who?" Corvin prodded.

Reg turned away from them, hoping it would help her to resist Corvin. She could still feel his eyes on her and could still smell his rose scent.

"He's not here," she told Sarah. "We should go. And you…" Reg looked back toward Corvin, but stared way past him, off into the distance, to avoid his pull. "You can stop following us, or we'll call the police."

"Oh…" He chuckled. "You'll call the police, will you? And just what do you think they're going to do?"

"They can tell you to back off and help me to get a restraining order," Reg growled. "You can't stalk three defenseless women all over Florida."

"All over Florida? A restraining order wouldn't be valid outside this jurisdiction. And if you think that the police would be able to do anything to stop me…" He laughed again. "That's not the way it works around here, Regina."

Reg looked at Sarah, not understanding. Sarah sighed and shook her head. "I'll explain it to you in the car."

Without looking at Corvin again, trying hard to avoid breathing in his scent, Reg got back into the jeep. Sarah went around to her side and climbed up into the driver's seat. Reg watched her close her door and put her seatbelt on. They pulled out of the loading zone, and Corvin's car fell in behind them.

"So explain," Reg ordered. "Why is it he doesn't have to listen to the police? Is he some big crime boss around here?"

"You've felt his influence," Letticia said. "Do you think the police would not? Do you think they would be able to resist him? It takes strength to be able to walk away from him." She looked over her shoulder back at Reg, as if evaluating her. "Few women would have what it takes to push back against him."

"What about men?"

"His natural influence there is less, but still substantial. And combine his charm with a small spell or two…"

"So you're telling me he can control the police? He doesn't have to listen to anybody?"

"It would take a lot to convince the police of anything. Him standing with a smoking gun over a dead body, maybe. As far as getting them to stop him from following you, no. There are rules in our community, though, and he could be taken before his coven if he broke them."

"But him stalking and harassing us isn't against the rules?"

"No. You can put up wards against him. Learn to use your powers to protect yourself against his glamour. But you can't restrict his freedom of movement if he hasn't done any harm."

Reg's head spun. She rested it against the inside of the jeep, then decided that was a really bad idea when Sarah bumped over a curb going around the corner. She leaned back against the headrest and held both hands to her temples.

Magic wasn't real. Spirits weren't real. She didn't have any powers and neither did Corvin or anyone else. Yes, he was handsome and had natural charm and powers of persuasion, but that was all it was. There was nothing unnatural or paranormal about it. Despite what the self-proclaimed witches said, Reg could go to the police at any time to deal with Corvin. She just didn't want anything to do with the police. She didn't like that she was already on their radar when she had only been in town for a few days. She didn't want to attract further attention.

"I can help you with some charms and wards," Sarah offered. "That is one of my areas of expertise."

"Do they work?" Reg asked.

"She sells them on Amazon," Letticia advised, her tone dripping with contempt, "so they must work."

"I do not!" Sarah snapped back. She glanced in the rear view mirror at Reg. "I sell them on Etsy."

Reg choked on her own laugh of disbelief. She'd heard Etsy was a good place to sell crafts. She'd just never imagined anyone selling witchcraft there.

"If he's bothering you, I can help you out." Sarah repeated the offer. "But you have to resist him with your will too. Wards won't be much help if you are going to date the man."

Reg shook her head. "I'll think about it. Thanks for the offer."

The next hospital wasn't very far away. Apparently, there were a lot of hospitals in Florida. Probably something to do with the number of retirees and the resultant aging population. Reg wondered how many they were going to have to go to before they found Warren. If they really could find Warren. She wasn't quite sure how she was expected to know from sitting or standing outside the hospital whether Warren was inside. That went far beyond her intuition abilities. Figuring out what a client needed to hear by listening to them and watching their body language was a far cry from standing outside a hospital trying to feel some ghostly vibrations.

"Do you have any maps?" Reg asked, looking out her window toward the ocean.

"Of course. In the door pocket," Sarah told Letticia.

Letticia dug a handful of jumbled maps out of the pocket of the door and handed them back to Reg. She sorted through them, trying to put them into some kind of order. She unfolded a large one that showed the ocean and beaches and other natural areas around Black Sands. She looked at the wide expanse of ocean. Where had Warren been headed? Where had he gone down? Ling had not said why he had been flying in the first place. He obviously hadn't had any passengers, but was it a pleasure trip or was he transporting a cargo? If he was acting as a courier, then to whom? And was it legal or illegal?

"You're awfully quiet back there," Sarah observed. She looked into the mirror as she drove up over the curb into the parking lot of another hospital, making Reg bite her tongue.

"Just looking at these maps, trying to figure out where—"

"We're here."

"Where?"

"At the General. Do you need to get out? Can you feel him here?"

Reg barely even glanced out the window. She couldn't feel anything and randomly driving from one hospital to another without even talking to the admissions desk seemed the height of stupidity.

"No, not here," she snapped.

Letticia looked around her seat at Reg and shook her head. "She doesn't have a clue what she's doing."

Reg didn't, but she pushed back immediately. "I do too! I don't see you coming up with any answers. Why don't *you* tell me where he is?"

"Talking to spirits is not one of my gifts," Letticia said simply. She raised her eyebrows. "I'm not sure it's one of yours, either!"

"I've been talking to them since I was a little girl," Reg insisted, remembering what Corvin had said about her imaginary friends. "I'm not a fraud."

"Then why don't you tell us where he is? If your connection with him is so strong…"

Reg stared at the map, feeling her face flush red. "There," she said, stabbing a finger at a random beach. "That's where he came ashore. And the nearest hospital is…"

"He wouldn't necessarily be taken to the nearest one," Sarah said, "it depends on their specialities."

"This one." Reg pointed to a large building with a blue letter H superimposed over it.

"McNara?" Letticia asked. She shook her head. "That's more of a long-term care facility. Not somewhere they would take the victim of a plane crash."

"We've already looked where they would take the victim of a plane crash," Reg snapped back. "And the police have presumably looked all of the places where they would take the victim of a plane crash. So let's look there."

Letticia shook her head. She faced front again and shrugged at Sarah. "Go, if you want. I don't see how it makes any difference."

Sarah made a quick course correction that threw Letticia and Reg against the inside of the vehicle with a crash. Reg righted herself and looked back over her shoulder to see if Corvin had managed to make the turn in time. He apparently had not. There was something to be said for erratic driving when they didn't particularly want to be followed.

Reg was more careful to hold on for the remainder of the drive, and at some length, they pulled into the parking lot of the long, low building. It didn't look like a hospital, at least not the ones that Reg was accustomed to. But it had an H on it on the map, and Reg was sticking to her guns. If Sarah and Letticia could make uninformed decisions and hop from hospital to hospital on a whim, then Reg could pick the one that attracted her.

"Oh, this is nice," Sarah remarked.

Reg closed her eyes, feeling a wave of warmth wash over her, followed by a chill that she was becoming increasingly familiar with. "No," she objected, "not again!"

Sarah's head turned in slow motion, and she opened her mouth to ask something. Letticia's head turned a few seconds later, also in slow motion. She reached around the seat she was sitting in and caught Reg's arm with her long, bony fingers. Reg fought against the waves of memory that were not hers.

A pain in her forearm grew, forcing its way into her consciousness. The jeep again resolved around Reg. She jerked her arm, trying to get out of Letticia's grip.

"Let go, let go! You're hurting!"

Letticia released her. Reg looked down at where Letticia's fingers had been digging into the meat of her arm. There were clear impressions from all of her fingers, with crescent-shaped cuts at the ends of the fingers where her nails had drawn blood.

"Ouch! What did you do that for?"

"I'm sorry," Letticia said, not sounding one bit sorry, "it was the quickest way to bring you back. You said you didn't want to channel him, and Sarah already said how far he's been dragging you under."

Sarah looked apologetic, even though she wasn't the one who had hurt Reg. "Sometimes when a medium goes too far... well, bad things can happen. We want to be sure we're going to get you back again."

Reg took a couple of deep breaths. "Well. I guess he's here."

"Apparently so," Letticia said dryly. "Shall we go find him?"

Reg nodded. All three of them got out of the car. Reg looked around. Would the three of them look suspicious if they all walked in together, looking for a man who was supposed to be dead? Or was there safety in numbers?

Not that there was anything to be afraid of. They were in a hospital. Warren, if he were there, had just been in an airplane accident. Not something that was contagious and was going to infect them.

Sarah barged past Reg to the reception desk inside the cool, atrium-like lobby. She gave the woman there one of her patented grandmotherly smiles, raining beneficence upon her.

"Here I am to see my grandson," she announced.

The woman at the desk smiled in response.

"And who would that be?"

"Warren Blake."

The woman paused for a moment, frowning. She shook her head before tapping the name into the computer. "No... I don't see a Warren Blake on our records."

"But he's here," Sarah insisted. "A young man. Just last week. He was in a plane crash and just about drowned."

The receptionist shook her head slowly.

"I'm sorry, that doesn't sound like anyone we have here. Are you sure you have the right place?"

"Why don't you look at his picture," Sarah suggested, pulling out her wallet.

The receptionist showed great restraint in not rolling her eyes. She looked at Sarah with apparent interest, leaning toward her to see the snapshots the confused grandma had.

"Hold these," Sarah ordered, putting a few dimes into the receptionist's hand as she went through her wallet and her purse. She placed what appeared to be a blank white card on the counter. "You see, there's Warren. You remember him coming in. It might have been a bit confusing for you, but this should clear it up." She held out a roll of candies. "Life Saver?"

The receptionist's expression was clouded. She took one of the candies and put it in her mouth. Holding the coins in her hand, she looked down at the blank card.

"Yes... of course. I remember him. David Forrester, right?"

"Yes, that's right," Sarah agreed. "David Forrester. That poor young man."

"He's very handsome," the woman said, looking at the card.

Sarah picked it up and tucked it back away in her wallet. As she busied herself with putting her possessions back away, the receptionist handed back the loose change.

"What room did you say he was in?" Sarah asked.

"One-eighty."

"Thank you very much! You have a nice day, now, dear."

The receptionist nodded her head. Looking at the various signs, Letticia pointed to the right. "This wing over here."

Reg managed to keep her mouth shut until they got out of sight and earshot of the receptionist. "How did you do that?" she asked. "What exactly was it you just did?"

"Oh, just a couple of little charms to help clear up the confusion," Sarah said with a satisfied smile.

"Why would Warren have been admitted as David Forrester?"

"I can't tell you that right now. But I can tell you... there is magic at work here."

"No..."

"Come on, let's go have a look at your young man and see if we can't sort it out."

★ Chapter Fifteen ★

THE THREE OF THEM walked purposefully through the hallways as if they knew exactly where they were going, hoping to avoid anyone asking any questions. The signage was clear, and in a few minutes, they found themselves in the little unit cluster that held Warren's room.

There was a nurse on duty at the desk in the center of the unit, and she attempted to stop them from going any farther without explaining what business they had there. It was Letticia who jumped into action this time, approaching the woman with a series of odd questions that distracted and confused her.

Sarah pulled on Reg's arm, and they found Warren's room.

Reg recognized the man as the one in the photo Ling had shown her. He had lost weight, his face looking quite gaunt. He didn't look sick or injured, but instead looked like he was peacefully asleep and would wake up the moment they talked to him or touched him. He was hooked up to a number of machines that beeped and whooshed. There was an IV draining into his arm and a bag filling with yellow fluid hung below the level of the blanket on the bed.

"It's him," Reg confirmed, in case Sarah had any doubt. She put her hand tentatively on Warren's arm. "Warren? Are you okay? Warren?"

There was no answering muscle movement. His arm remained slack and still under her touch.

Reg raised her voice. "Warren. Can you talk to me, Warren?"

Sarah made a warning noise, and Reg realized too late what she had done. The combination of her proximity to Warren, actually touching him, and the instruction to talk to her reopened the channel they had previously used, the one that Warren had been trying to get back through ever since then. Sarah reached out to stop Reg too late.

"You came!" Warren's voice came from inside Reg. "You found me. But where is Ling?"

"Ling isn't here," Sarah said. "We had to find you first, make sure you were here. We didn't want to put Ling through that disappointment if we didn't find you."

"You need to bring her. She could be in danger. They could come after her."

"Who could come after her? Who did this to you, Warren?"

"Did what to me?"

"Can you see your body? Look at yourself right here."

Reg found herself staring at Warren's form in the bed, her eyes wide with astonishment. She looked all around the room, taking everything in.

"What happened? Why am I here? Am I sick?"

"They told us you were in a plane accident. Do you remember being in a plane accident?"

Reg watched the disjointed images flash through her brain. Warren's plane, his pride and joy. The thing that he would use to build his business and become independent. He'd be able to give Ling everything she wanted and deserved. All he needed was that plane and a good plan and hard work, and he'd be able to make a good living for them.

The images wavered in front of her, the plane getting smaller and melting out of sight. Had they wrecked his beautiful plane? They wouldn't have dared, would they? It was his baby.

"My plane," Warren's voice groaned. "How could they do that? Not my plane!"

"It wasn't just your plane," Letticia said, coming into the room. "Look at what they've done to you! You were supposed to die in that wreck."

"I'm not dead. You said I was dead, but I'm not. I'm still alive!"

Letticia moved to the bedside. She looked Warren over. She stood by him and held her hands out, just over him, moving them around as if feeling for some force that surrounded his body. Back and forth, up and down, like some human form of MRI looking for anything unusual in his energy field. Sarah was quiet and so was Warren, watching it all through Reg's eyes.

"What's wrong with me?" Warren finally asked. "Did I hit my head?"

"Do you remember anything about how it happened?"

Reg remembered people, but their faces were blurred and indistinct. What had they done to him? Had they drugged him? Hit him over the head? Had they put him in the plane and crashed it, or had they dumped him somewhere else, intending that his body would never be found? Who had brought him to the hospital?

"I don't know. There was a man in a dark coat. Who wears a long, dark coat in Florida? And a man with dreadlocks. There were... I don't know how many of them there were. I told them I wouldn't do anything illegal, and they laughed. I don't know why they were laughing."

A man in a dark coat. Reg had seen one man in a long, dark coat recently.

"They put a spell on you," Letticia informed Warren. "A binding spell. It is holding you here, keeping you from waking up."

"A spell?" Warren's voice was incredulous. "You mean like a magic spell?"

"Yes."

"There's no such thing as magic!"

"Then wake up."

Warren was silent, considering this. Maybe he was trying to move, feeling out his body, trying to wake himself up. But whatever he tried, it wasn't working.

"Something is wrong. Maybe they drugged me or hit me over the head. You have to help me."

"We're trying to help you," Letticia said calmly. "But we need more information about who it was that did this to you. We need to know the person who cast the spell if we're going to break it."

"I don't know who it was!" Warren's voice held an edge of panic. "The names they gave me were false. I checked them out and they weren't who they said they were."

"A man with a black coat," Letticia said slowly. "There are a number of warlocks around here who wear black coats or cloaks at least part of the time. Dreadlocks are not uncommon either. What was it they wanted you to do? You said that you wouldn't do anything illegal, and that you checked them out, so you must have known that what they wanted was against the law."

"It wasn't what they said it was. I knew it wasn't. They were offering too much money, and there was too much…" Warren's voice hesitated, trying to find the right words. "Too much whispering and the way they looked at me when I came into the room. You can tell, if someone only talks when you're out of the room, and when you get back, the whole room goes quiet…"

"What did they say it was?" Sarah asked.

Reg tried to see it in her mind. She could feel Warren's energy flagging and knew he wasn't going to be able to keep using her for much longer. She tried to get him to fill her mind with the pictures, so she would understand what he had seen and heard, even without the names of the men who had crashed his plane. She closed her eyes, trying to take it all in. He filled her up with a flood of pictures and then he was gone.

Reg nearly toppled over, but Letticia caught her on one side and supported her until Sarah could take Reg's other arm and they held her up between them.

"Are you okay?" Sarah demanded. "Reg? Can you hear me?"

Reg nodded her woozy head. She tried to get control of the spinning and to cobble together an answer.

"He's gone. Is he… is he still okay? He's not dead, is he?"

Sarah watched the machines as they continued to cycle through their usual sounds. Letticia stared into the space above Warren's body.

"He's still there," Letticia said. "He's just weak. Manifesting like this takes lots of energy. A strong mind and lots of willpower. It will leave him in a weakened state, and he's already vulnerable. He's already been damaged."

"By the crash?" Reg whispered.

The two witches walked Reg backward until they reached a visitor chair, and then they lowered her into it. Reg tried not to let her eyes close, knowing that if she let herself go to sleep, it might be hours before she was able to wake up again. The way she was feeling, it might be days before she woke up again. They'd have to hook her up to tubes like Warren to keep her alive.

"No, he wasn't damaged by the crash," Letticia said. "He probably wasn't even in the crash. Or if he was, he was rescued right away. It's not physical damage that worries me, it's the psychic damage."

"You really think this is some kind of spell?" Reg shook her head. She'd heard of a vegetative state before. She'd heard of locked-in syndrome. A person could appear to be just fine in his body, but an injury in his brain kept him from ever waking up again, keeping him in a twilight prison for years or even decades.

"Don't discount it just because you don't understand it," Letticia said. "There are many kinds of poisons and drugs that can keep you in a state of suspension. And there are incantations and forces of will that can do it just as well, without ever leaving a mark on the body."

Medical science could explain a lot of things, but it couldn't explain everything. There were still things that modern science could not explain away. Reg had watched documentaries about psychics and the scientific tests that had been attempted to prove or disprove psychic ability. She'd studied them extensively to be able to play her part. And even though she didn't believe in her heart of hearts that real psychic ability existed, she couldn't discount that there was something. Even her own abilities, which she attributed to intuition and imagination, were scarily accurate at times.

"So how do we break it, then?"

"Like I told Warren," Letticia said, "we have to find out who did this first. It isn't until we know who did it that we can attempt to reverse it. The maker has a lot of psychic energy tied up in keeping Warren bound, and until he releases that bond, Warren will sleep. Or he'll get lost in the twilight."

"But how can we make him release it?"

Letticia and Sarah exchanged looks. Letticia shook her head grimly. "We'll cross that bridge when we come to it. First, we have to find him."

★ Chapter Sixteen ★

R EG WAS EXHAUSTED. EVEN after resting in
Warren's room for some time, she still needed help
from Sarah and Letticia to get back out of the building
and to the jeep, which was still parked outside the main doors
of the building.

"You're lucky no one towed it!" Reg said when she saw
the black jeep sitting there. "This is a ten-minute loading
zone, and we were in there for a couple of hours."

Sarah laughed. "No one is going to tow my car," she said
without concern.

"Why? Do you have a spell cast on it?"

Sarah and Letticia helped push Reg up into the vehicle
and got her settled. She got the front seat this time, and as
Letticia pulled the seatbelt across her and clicked it into place,
Reg had a suspicion it was so that she wouldn't be thrown
around the interior of the jeep in her weakened state. Letticia
then got into the back.

"I have a number of charms and wards in place," Sarah
confirmed. "Anyone who wants to interfere with it in some
way is just going to get distracted and decide to do something
else instead."

"What do you mean?" Reg waited until Sarah had gone
around the jeep and gotten back into the driver's seat. "You
mean they walk up to give you a parking ticket or tow you
away, and then they decide that they need to chase butterflies
instead?"

Letticia snorted loudly in a surprised laugh. Sarah eyed
Reg and chuckled more sedately. "That would be a good
one," she agreed. "Usually it's not butterflies. Maybe their

radio starts acting up. Or the phone rings. Or their boss has an important project they need to work on right away. Just something that distracts them from what they were going to do."

"So you can just park wherever you please and drive however you want," Reg said in disbelief. "Actually—that explains a lot."

All three of them laughed. Reg closed her eyes as Sarah started the engine.

"Please… just drive slowly home. We found Warren. We don't need to rush."

She could feel a look pass between Sarah and Letticia without even seeing it.

"We found him," Letticia said, "but that doesn't put him out of danger. In fact, if anyone knows we found him, he may be in even more danger. Whoever put him there may decide that the binding spell on the boy and confusion over the caregivers aren't enough and turn to something more drastic. Something that doesn't require him to spend his energy maintaining a hold."

"You mean they would kill him? They couldn't!"

"There is evil in this world, Regina."

"We have to find out who did this to him."

"Yes. But I agree with Reg on one thing" Letticia directed her words at Sarah. "We could take the trip home a little more slowly while we consider our course of action."

Sarah grudgingly kept the jeep to the speed of the traffic around them and slowed for intersections and corners. Reg let sleep steal over her. She was so exhausted by her ordeal. Her mind kept flipping between disbelief and understanding. She pondered all that Warren's spirit had had to say, trying to sort out what had happened to him, and then her logical mind took over, objecting, insisting that there was no scientific proof of the psychic experience she had invented at the hospital.

It was only her wild imagination, just like when she was a child. She was making up stories to fit the circumstances, not uncovering the truth. She could invent and adapt, but it was just a combination of intuition, the research she had done for her part, and her out-of-control imagination. It didn't help that the two women who should have had the sense to bring her down to earth were instead feeding her more nonsense.

The feeling of swinging back and forth between the two schools of thought drifted into the physical sensation of swinging on a swing. She was in a park, a playground with old, rusted swings and climbers. Reg swung back and forth, back and forth for hours, the swinging satisfying part of her brain that was always anxious and restless. As she swung, sitting by herself, she watched the other children and adults in the playground as they came and went.

And then Mrs. Gordon came. She was a fat woman who didn't like to leave the house, so Reg knew the moment she saw the woman headed toward her that she was in trouble. She jumped off the swing, but her legs and her body were so accustomed to the swinging movement that her knees buckled and she fell down, dizzy with her contact with the earth.

"What have I told you a million times?" Mrs. Gordon demanded. "You're supposed to come home when there's no one else at the park. It's not safe for a girl your age to be hanging out here all by yourself, and we'll have the neighbors making calls to Social Services, saying that I'm not taking care of you properly." She got within reach of Reg, and cuffed her across the head. "You are supposed to be home in bed."

Reg raised her hand to block any further blows, looking around in confusion. "I was going to come when everybody else went home…"

"Then why didn't you?" the red-faced woman challenged. Mrs. Gordon grabbed Reg's arm and pulled her to her feet, holding her there like a dog on a shortened leash.

Reg motioned to the playground. "I'm not the last one. Polly is still here…"

Mrs. Gordon's eyes followed Reg's finger to the empty climbers. "Don't you get started with your imaginary friends again. We are not dealing with this nonsense!"

Reg's shoulders slumped as she looked at Polly. The younger girl gave her a happy smile, not seeming to understand the trouble she had gotten Reg in. Reg put both hands over her face.

"You were supposed to tell me when it was time to go home," Reg murmured into her hands.

"What's that?"

"I was talking to Polly..."

Mrs. Gordon shook her. "You're way too old to be using imaginary friends as an excuse. You're a big girl and you know better. You know as well as I do that there's nobody here." She shook Reg harder. "Say it! You know that there's no one here."

"There's no one here," Reg repeated, a stray tear leaking from the corner of her eye and tracing a path down her cheek. "I'm sorry."

Mrs. Gordon started to haul her in the direction of home. "You're going straight to bed. No supper. If you have to go hungry, maybe you'll learn something from this."

In opposition to Mrs. Gordon's pull, Reg could feel Polly's pull on her insides.

"No, don't go," Polly pleaded, "Don't leave me alone here!"

But Reg couldn't answer Polly, or her punishment would be that much worse. The tears ran down her cheeks faster. She looked back despite herself. Mrs. Gordon jerked her arm, wrenching her shoulder.

Reg knew from the look on Mrs. Gordon's face that she wanted to punish Reg by telling her she couldn't go to the park anymore. She was right on the edge of it, looking for something that would hurt Reg more than the slap across the head or withholding of supper. But forbidding the park would mean that Reg was underfoot right from the time school let out, and that would punish Mrs. Gordon as much as Reg.

"I'm sorry," Reg told her again. "I'm sorry, I'm sorry."

Ling was clearly uncertain about why Reg had called her back to the cottage. She was looking Reg over every time Reg glanced at her.

"I was thinking about coming back," Ling confessed. "It was so good to hear Warren's voice again. But I also thought... it might not be healthy for me to keep coming back, right? I mean, I don't want to avoid the grieving process. I want to be able to heal and get past this." Her eyes teared up. "However much I don't feel like I can get over Warren. Other people do. They go on with their lives."

"Ling..." Reg didn't want to draw it out and make Ling suffer any longer than she had to. She put the tea tray down on the coffee table and sat down. "I didn't ask you here because I wanted to do another reading for Warren. He's been on my mind plenty, but that's not why I called you."

"Oh." Ling was still. Her eyes wandered around the room as if she might be able to pick up on what it was. "Okay..."

"You remember how Warren kept saying that he wasn't dead?"

Ling nodded. "Of course."

"He was right, Ling. Warren isn't dead!"

Ling's expression immediately became guarded. She wasn't about to let Reg hurt her and scam her and lead her along. She thought she knew Reg's game, but she was wrong. Reg leaned in closer.

"Warren is at McNara. He was checked in under the name of David Forrester. It's hard to explain, but... he's in a coma there. My friends and I are trying to figure out what we can do to help him, if there's anything we can do."

Ling's eyes were wide with shock. "But... how could that be? That doesn't make any sense."

"I know it doesn't, and I wish I could explain it all to you in a way that made sense, but I can't. He is alive, and he's worried about you. He's worried that the men who crashed his plane might come after you."

She blinked and shook her head. "The men who crashed his plane? But it was an accident. That's what the police and the crash investigators said. Something... a malfunction."

"They were wrong. If they could be wrong about the fact that Warren was dead, they could be wrong about the crash, couldn't they? It wasn't an accident. It wasn't a malfunction. They sabotaged it or they steered it into the water."

"Why?"

"We're trying to figure that out. I am, and a couple of friends are helping me. We don't have all of the answers yet, but I wanted to tell you, so you weren't mourning Warren when he's still alive."

Reg was glad that Ling was already sitting down. She looked completely devastated. Reg didn't quite understand; she had expected Ling to be elated. But human emotions weren't always logical. It would take Ling time to get from the place where she had been mourning for her dead husband to celebrating his life. If they could keep him alive and find a way to free him from the coma. It was too early to be celebrating yet.

"Ling, I know it's a lot to take in, but I need your help. How much do you know about Warren's business? Do you know who he was supposed to be doing a courier job for? Did he tell you any of his suspicions about it?"

"It wasn't really a business... just a job now and then. He wanted to get his own business set up, not to have to work for someone else... but that was still in the future. He needed time to get established..."

"But he did jobs now and then. Who was he doing a courier job for when he crashed?"

Ling thought about it. She shook her head. "I don't know. He said they were strange. Like, they were into role play or reenactment. I pictured... drama geeks... not anyone that would be dangerous."

"Did he tell you that he checked them out and they weren't who they said they were? And they weren't transporting what they said they were?"

Ling shook her head again. "No," her voice quivered. "He didn't tell me that."

"Did he have any records? A day planner, computer, flight plans?"

"He had a computer... but it was with him. It went down with the plane."

"Dang it... did he have a backup? Did he sync to the cloud so he could have it on his phone?"

"To be honest..." Ling rubbed at a spot on her saucer, "he wasn't very good at writing things down or keeping records. You'd think that being a pilot, he'd be really good at academic stuff, but he wasn't. He had learning disabilities, and he wasn't very good at writing things down. He kept it all in his head."

And now a jumble of what he had kept in his head was residing in Reg's, but she couldn't find a way to sort it out and file it properly. She felt a sudden kinship with Warren. Not just because she was carrying his memories around in her head, but because she knew what it was like to grow up with learning disabilities. To try to live in a world where so much depended on reading and writing when reading and writing came so hard.

"I'm sorry. I really want to help you," Ling said.

"Well... you have my number, so let me know if you think of anything. But Warren was worried they might come after you, so you might want to... find somewhere else to stay for a while. Call in sick at work and fly under the radar until we figure this all out."

"Do you really think there's any danger? They don't know me and Warren didn't tell me things about work. It isn't like he left a lot of papers around the house. I don't see why they would have any concerns about me."

"I don't know. Do you trust Warren?"

"Yes, of course I trust him."

"Then you should listen to his warning, don't you think? If he'd called you up on the phone and told you to stay away and go into hiding, you'd do it?"

"Yes. But that's not what happened. I don't…" Ling hesitated. "I don't have any proof. That doesn't mean I don't believe you, but… you could be making it all up. It doesn't sound like Warren. It doesn't make any sense to me."

"Maybe… maybe you should go see him," Reg suggested. "Maybe then you'll feel what it is he's trying to tell you. And you want to be sure that he's really alive, and I'm not just playing with you, trying to get money out of you somehow, right? I'm not making you pay me to tell you where he is or to make you buy more sessions to talk to him. I already told you where he is and the name he's there under. You can check it out for yourself."

"And if he's there, will you talk to him for me?"

Reg's stomach knotted. Her brain was so exhausted from channeling Warren already. Every time she talked for him, it took more out of her and made it harder to come back. From what Sarah said, the same thing was happening to him. The more he tried to communicate with them, the weaker he got, the more tenuous his hold on life.

"I don't think I can," she told Ling as gently as she could. "And I don't know if Warren can."

Ling put her hands over her face, quelling any tears. "This is crazy, you know that? I just came here one time to try to get some peace. To say goodbye to Warren for the last time. And you're dumping all of this stuff on me. None of it makes any sense."

"I'm sorry."

"I'll go to this place, and I'll see if he's there… but if he isn't, I don't know. I'm not just going to take being strung along." She made a determined face.

Reg nodded. "Okay. But don't ask for him at the front desk or at the nursing station. He's in room 180. If you ask someone where he is, they'll just tell you he isn't there. Go look for yourself. Just walk in and act like you're supposed to be there and know where you're going."

"Why are they hiding him there?"

"The staff… they don't really know, I don't think." Giving more details would just be more mumbo-jumbo to

Ling. She wasn't going to understand that it was all some sort of magical plot. So why did Reg believe any of it? "They're just... confused. They've been told a different story, told he is someone different."

"So I'll set them straight, if it really is Warren. And he'll get better. And everything will go back to normal again."

Starlight jumped up onto Reg's lap. She pulled him against herself, feeling his warm, compact body. What about her? Was everything ever going to be normal again? If she left Black Sands, would she be able to go back to normal and pretend that nothing had ever happened? Would it just be some wild story about her misspent youth that she'd look back on with fondness when she was old?

Or would the disquiet cling to her like a spiderweb for the rest of her days? And how long would that be?

★ Chapter Seventeen ★

WHEN LING WAS GONE, Reg felt like she had done all that she could. She needed to have a bite to eat and then she could lie down and go to sleep and replenish her energy. When Ling came back in a day or two, having decided to accept the story Reg told her, then they could take the next step. Reg would describe what she could remember from Warren's memories, Ling would identify the men, and the witches would help to break the spell, releasing Warren from his magical coma. They would all live happily ever after.

In an ideal world, which, so far, Black Sands had not turned out to be.

Reg ate peanut butter straight out of the jar, topped up Starlight's water dish, and headed to the bed. Starlight, disgruntled by this treatment, followed her, yowling and complaining. Reg kept an eye on him to make sure he wasn't going to attack her legs, and climbed into bed. She wrapped herself up in the blanket and closed her eyes, sinking into the pillow.

In a few minutes, Starlight had jumped up onto the bed, but Reg was too close to sleep to be bothered to push him back off. As long as he didn't bite her ankles, she didn't care, and her ankles were well-wrapped in the blanket. Starlight snuggled against her, making a warm little pocket against her, and he started to purr. Reg drifted off. Feeling glad for once that she had adopted a cat and had someone warm and comforting to keep her warm. Better than the boyfriends she'd had over the years.

She couldn't have been asleep for more than a few minutes when Starlight got up abruptly. He meowed as if answering some call, walked over top of her, and jumped to the windowsill. Reg tried to just go back to sleep, but his behavior was disquieting, and she found that she couldn't close her eyes and return to her state of unconsciousness again.

"Starlight? What's the matter? What do you see out there?" she asked him.

Maybe there was a bird or a squirrel or some other type of wildlife in the yard. They were close enough to wild country that there might even be a deer. Or a gator.

Reg definitely couldn't go back to sleep thinking that there might be a gator in the yard. Even if she wasn't outside and knew that Starlight wasn't outside, it still scared her.

"What is it, kitty? Can't you just come back to the bed?"

He didn't even turn and look at her, but put his paws up on the glass as if trying to get out. He was definitely watching something out there.

With the blanket wrapped around her, Reg slid her feet off the bed and shuffled over to the window. It was dark outside. Not full dark, but pretty close. If there was a gator outside, she wasn't going to be able to see it.

But she did see something. Not a shape down low to the ground, but something upright, moving against the trees.

She told herself it was a deer. Or maybe just the shadow of the house or another tree. But she knew by the way it moved that it was not a deer. It wasn't anything wild. Not a wild animal, anyway.

Her window was open a crack to let the light breeze in, along with the smells and sounds of the outside. She could hear the figure moving across the yard, getting closer and closer to her window. She hadn't left the lights on, so he probably had no idea she was standing there by the window waiting for him.

The dark shape drew closer. A man in a cloak or a long coat?

"Who's out there?" Reg demanded, her voice quiet in the stillness of the night.

The man froze. She couldn't see his features, but she could tell he was looking toward her, trying to analyze her and decide on his next move.

"Little pig, little pig, let me come in."

Reg shivered at the creepy whisper. She forced toughness into her voice. "The big, bad wolf? Really? That's inventive."

He didn't respond right away. "You're supposed to say, 'not by the hair of my chinny chin chin.'"

"Seriously?"

"I didn't have an answer prepared. I didn't expect you to see me."

Starlight moved on the windowsill and meowed.

"Oh," Corvin said. "I see. It was your familiar who saw me."

"He says the way you're crashing around out there, it's a wonder you haven't woken the whole neighborhood."

There was another pause. "Did he really say that?" Corvin asked finally.

Reg pressed her lips together. Did he think she could talk to animals? As ridiculous as it sounded, it wasn't really any more far-fetched than being able to talk to someone who was dead or in a coma. Maybe there were mediums who could talk to animals. There were plenty of pet owners who would pay to know what their furry babies had to say.

"Are you going to come in, or continue to crash around my yard?"

"It's Sarah's yard."

"Should I call her to see if she wants you back there?"

She heard a twig snap as he shifted his stance. "Uh... no. I don't see any need for that."

"Come to the door, then."

Inviting him into her home might seem like a stupid thing to do, but Reg knew he was going to end up there sooner or later. She might as well be able to keep an eye on him and not waste her energy trying to prevent what was going to happen inevitably anyway.

Corvin obediently went to the cottage door and Reg let him in. He hesitated in the doorway, looking in. Looking for Starlight, maybe?

"Are you going to come in?"

"Is that an invitation?"

Reg rolled her eyes. "Yes," she said in exasperation. "Come in."

He nodded and entered. He shut the door behind him and slid the deadbolt into place. Reg hadn't used the deadbolt since her arrival. She frowned. No one would be able to come in if she needed help. Except Sarah must have a key for the deadbolt. It was her cottage. But Reg suspected she'd have to turn around and go back into the house to find it, and she wasn't particularly fast. A lot could happen in a short period of time.

Corvin's eye darted around the cottage again. Starlight had been lurking in the spare room, and entered the living room area. He yowled when he saw Corvin and headed straight toward him.

"Mind your own business, cat," Corvin told him. "I was invited."

Starlight looked at Reg. He sat down and started to wash, flicking his ears at her every few licks. Reg understood clearly that he was not happy with her. If he was psychic, like Sarah suggested, maybe he had some knowledge about Corvin that Reg did not. Though Reg had already been told that he was dangerous.

"So what were you doing lurking around my yard?" she demanded. "Our date isn't until tomorrow. Couldn't you wait?"

"I wanted to check on you and make sure everything was alright."

She glared at him. "Really? You expect me to believe that?"

"Why wouldn't you?"

She held the stare for a few seconds longer. She could feel his pull. She tried to resist it, breathing shallowly and looking past him.

"Maybe because a warlock of your description put a binding spell on Warren Blake."

His brows drew down. He sat on the couch, frowning at Reg. "You found Warren Blake?"

"Yes. You didn't expect that, did you? Thought you had him hidden away where no one would ever be able to find him. But you didn't count on me being able to—" Reg cut herself off, not sure how to describe what it was that she had done. She hadn't followed his trail. She hadn't been told where he was. Even if she had channeled Warren for real, he hadn't been able to tell her where he was. She had just looked at the map, pointed to the place, and walked in and found him. That kind of psychic phenomenon was just the sort of thing she didn't believe in.

"I said from the start you were powerful," Corvin said, his eyes glittering as he studied her. "I wouldn't put anything past you, once you had the faith in yourself to follow your own instinct."

Was that what it had been? Instinct? She had looked at a map and, knowing nothing about where he had gone down or what the water currents were like, had pointed to where he had been hospitalized. No amount of calling around to hospitals would have found him, because he wasn't even there under his own name. They had tried their best to hide him.

Who had? Corvin?

He didn't seem upset by her discovery. But why would he? The binding spell held. She couldn't do anything to prove that he was the warlock who had put the spell on Warren, couldn't do anything to make him release the young man. Reg was no closer to being able to save Warren than she had ever been. He was still just as dead to Ling as he ever had been.

"No drinks today?" Corvin asked.

"You got me out of bed. I don't need a drink, and if you do, you can go to the bar and get one yourself."

He chuckled. "Feisty, aren't you? Got out on the wrong side of the bed?"

"I shouldn't be out of bed at all. I'm exhausted. You have no idea how tiring it is to maintain a connection with Warren."

Or did he?

"I won't keep you, then," Corvin said. "But I would like to hear about what you found. Where was he? Could he tell you what had happened to him? I take it this information about the binding spell comes from the two witches?"

"Yes. I wouldn't know a binding spell if it hit me in the face. Well, maybe now I would, but I wouldn't have before today."

His eyes were narrow. "You still haven't told me where he was."

"And I don't think I will."

"I'll bet I could convince you." He was leaning forward in his seat. His voice was soft and seductive. Reg caught her breath. She looked around for Starlight. At her look, he marched across the room toward them.

"What do you think he is going to do?" Corvin challenged.

"I don't know. But I'll bet you do. You know more about this stuff than I do."

"I won't do anything," Corvin said, shifting so that he was leaning against the couch, leaning away from her. "I'm just sitting here having a civilized chat."

Starlight jumped up onto Reg's lap. She petted him and he stared at Corvin.

"I'll bet you always had cats while you were growing up," Corvin suggested. "I can just see you curled up on a hammock with a book and a cat, whiling away the summer."

Reg snorted. "You couldn't be further from the truth."

"No? Really?"

"If you're supposed to have psychic powers, I'm sorely disappointed. No cat, no hammock, and no whiling away my summers."

"Did I at least get the book right?"

She shook her head. "I don't read for pleasure."

"Hm." He rubbed his short beard, looking thoughtful. Reg saw it for what it was, an act. An attempt to make her think that he was relaxed and unfazed by recent events, when really he was concerned. "You're an enigma, Reg Rawlins."

Reg covered a yawn, unable to restrain it. "A tired enigma. I think you'd better go. I'll see you tomorrow evening."

"Yes. You will." He didn't seem inclined to leave.

"Do I need to call the old crone to get rid of you? Or just sic the cat on you?" Reg slid her hands under Starlight, as if getting ready to launch him at Corvin.

"No need," Corvin held his hands up in surrender.

Starlight twisted suddenly to nip at Reg, making her jerk back and let him go.

"Testy, testy," Corvin teased Starlight, earning himself a dark-eyed glare.

But Corvin got up and headed toward the door without pushing Reg any further. "You're coming to my place tomorrow, right?"

So there would be no cats to protect her? Was that what he was thinking? Reg was pretty sure that she had told Corvin to meet her at the cottage.

"I'm thinking maybe we should meet on neutral ground," she countered. She gathered from his behavior that she had to invite him in for him to enter without consequences. Maybe because Sarah had put up some ward. And if she had, maybe Reg should let the ward do what it was intended to and not override it.

She was definitely not going to his place.

He couldn't do anything to her if they were out in public, like when they had met at The Crystal Bowl.

Corvin seemed disappointed, but not particularly surprised. "The more you retreat, the more I pursue," he said softly, leaning toward her again.

Starlight growled and hissed, unsheathing his sharp claws into Reg's legs. Reg winced and tried to focus on her cat instead of the warlock.

"Yes, you're right," she told Starlight. "We're both tired and it's time for bed."

Corvin eyed her. Reg got up, still holding the cat, and started walking toward the door. "Time for you to go."

He got up, face a tight mask, and swept after her. He drew the coat close, as if he were cold, and looked her up and down one last time before leaving.

"You are a fascinating woman, Regina."

With that, he slipped through the door and disappeared quickly into the darkness.

★ Chapter Eighteen ★

R EG HAD HOPED THAT she would be able to come to some kind of conclusion while she slept. It had often been the case that she would go to sleep with a problem on her mind, and when she woke up in the morning, she would have a solution, or at least the beginning of one. Since her first session with Ling, she had been thinking and dreaming of Warren, and she had hoped that when she fell into sleep, she would have a dream that would reveal the path that she should go. The memories that he had provided her with would all be miraculously sorted and put in order, so that she could pick out all of the important clues.

But that didn't happen. She awoke in the morning feeling groggy and unrested, with the pictures in her head just as murky and confused as ever. She showered and dressed and put on the coffee machine, hoping to bring some clarity, but none of it helped.

"Maybe I should go for a walk," she said to Starlight. "Sometimes that helps."

He nudged her and rubbed against her, begging for food. With a sigh, Reg opened a can of tuna. She had sworn she wouldn't spoil him, but he had to have something to eat. The smell of the tuna had Starlight just about climbing straight up the cupboard. Reg thought about Erin and her cat, Orange Blossom. And about years ago when Reg and Erin had been teenagers, and opening a can of tuna in the house was practically a guarantee that Erin would be racing for the bathroom and puking, her sensitive nose a curse to everyone in the family.

Sometimes, Reg thought she would have preferred an overdeveloped sense of smell to psychic sensitivity or a wild imagination, whichever it was she had been blessed with. She sniffed the tuna, which didn't bother her a bit, even first thing in the morning, and put a bowl down for Starlight. He immediately thrust his nose into it as if he'd been starved for days, purring loudly.

The doorbell rang. Reg looked at her phone. A little early for callers, unless it was Sarah. And Sarah didn't ring the bell, she just knocked and entered. The doorbell was immediately followed by loud, purposeful knocking.

Reg looked at Starlight, who looked up with his ears back at the violence of the rapping.

"I know *that* sound," Reg told Starlight, her heart sinking.

The first volley of knocks was immediately followed by a second, and a shout through the door. "Open up, Miss Rawlins!"

Reg went reluctantly to the door, unlocked it, and swung it open.

Detective Jessup stood there, hand on hip, looking as intimidating as possible for her small frame. She had a male partner who hadn't been with her on her previous visit, a few inches taller and twice as broad, his face red and sweat on his forehead even in the cool of the morning.

"Regina Rawlins," Jessup pronounced Regina like the Canadian city, "You're to come with us, please."

Reg didn't move. She looked them over, trying to read their faces. "What's this about?"

"We'll discuss it at the station."

"No, I don't think so," Reg said slowly. She tightened her fingers on the door like she was going to close it. Jessup put her heavy shoe in the door.

"Ma'am, I think you'd better cooperate."

"I haven't heard you say I'm under arrest."

"No," Jessup said grudgingly, "but you are wanted for questioning."

"In what?"

Jessup just stared at her.

"Come in to the police station, and we'll get it all straightened out," her partner advised. Reg and Jessup both glared at him, and he got still redder.

"I don't think so," Reg countered. "I know my rights, and I don't have to go anywhere. If you want me to cooperate, then you're going to have to act like a human being and try communication."

"You're wanted for questioning in connection with the disappearance of Ling Lau."

Reg felt lightheaded. "What?"

She lost her grip on the door. Jessup grabbed her by the arm, but she wasn't dragging Reg off to the police station, she was helping to hold Reg up and get her inside. Jessup's partner took the other arm and together they walked her into her living room and gently deposited her on the couch.

"Are you okay?" Jessup asked. "Take deep breaths. Do you want a glass of water?"

Reg shook her head. "I don't know. What happened? Ling is missing?"

"She was reported missing by her family this morning. The last place they knew she was going was to see you, and we already know what kind of an operation you're running out of here."

"She was here," Reg agreed. She was gasping, unable to draw a deep breath like Jessup had instructed. "I talked to her. Then she left. She was going to see…" Reg trailed off as she thought about it. Ling had gone to see Warren, who was supposed to be dead and was being held in a binding spell by someone with magical powers, and then she had disappeared? It didn't take a rocket scientist to figure out what had happened. Reg swore softly.

"What is it?" Jessup demanded. "What do you know?"

"Oh, no… they got her too."

"Who got her?"

"I don't know…"

Reg blinked, trying to see through the fog, and saw Jessup roll her eyes at her partner. Had he even introduced himself? Reg was too wrecked to even squint at his name bar. He was too far away and it looked like a lot of letters.

"So you think she's been kidnapped by some unknown party," Jessup summarized. "I'm so glad you were able to clear that up for us."

Reg moaned. She covered her eyes, resting her elbows on her knees. "You're not going to believe any of this."

"Thanks for the warning. Now get talking."

"I don't know what to say... why did I let her go by herself? I should have sent her with... the others."

"Start at the beginning. Ling was coming here to talk to you. Why? To do another of your seances?"

"I asked her to come." Reg uncovered her eyes, but kept them closed. She rubbed both temples, head pounding. It was hard to believe it was first thing in the morning. She felt like she'd been through the wringer. She could hear one of them moving around, and discerned that Jessup's partner was in the kitchen, putting on the kettle. She couldn't even bring herself to care.

"Why did you ask her to come?"

"Because... I found her husband. Warren Blake. And he's not dead."

This announcement was greeted with silence. Reg opened her eyelids a fraction of an inch to look at Jessup. Jessup had her notepad out, but she wasn't writing anything down. She was just looking at Reg, her expression inscrutable.

"You called her here to tell her that her husband wasn't dead."

"Yes."

"And how exactly does that fit into channeling spirits? What did you expect to get from her when she got here?"

"Nothing. I just... she needed to know. He's her husband and she has the right to know that her husband wasn't killed in that plane crash. He's still alive and well. Or... still alive."

"And where is he?"

"He's in McNara, a hospital. But he's not under his own name, so you can't call and ask for him. He's under David Forrester."

"You found out that Warren is checked in there under a false name."

"Yes."

"And how did you figure that out?"

"It's a long story…" Jessup didn't believe that Warren was even there, there was no way she was going to believe Reg's long story about the witches and about finding Warren there in a magical coma.

"We've got all day," Jessup replied. "We're talking about two missing persons here. Allegations of fraud. Who knows what else."

"If you go and see… you'll see for yourself." As long as they hadn't already spooked the culprits. With Ling showing up there, had they taken her out of the picture? Would they decide that holding Warren in a coma was no longer going to be enough? So far they had avoided actually killing anyone outright, but would that hold when the police started poking their noses into the operation?

"If he's still there," Jessup said, correctly interpreting Reg's hesitance. "But maybe he won't be. Maybe there will be no sign that he was ever there."

"I don't know. I'm not a part of this. I didn't do anything to Warren."

"Why is he in the hospital? He was injured in the plane crash?"

"I didn't actually talk to a doctor… so I don't know how extensive his injuries are. We just found him, and talked to him, and we're trying to figure out what it all means—"

"You talked to him."

"Yes—"

"And what did he have to say?"

"He wasn't conscious. He was… in a coma, I guess? So he couldn't talk… in a normal way."

"But you're good at channeling spirits, so maybe you put on another show."

The kettle was whistling. Reg looked over at the man to give him directions, but he seemed perfectly at home in the kitchen, finding everything he needed.

"I... channeled him," Reg admitted. She didn't know what else to say. There was no other way to explain what had happened. She couldn't explain it in a logical, scientific way. If she were going to convince them of her innocence, she was going to have to put on the best act of her life. She had to convince them that she really was psychic and that was how she had found Warren. "There was no other way for me to communicate with him."

"So you must know all of the details of the plane crash and what happened to him."

Jessup's partner put the tea service down on the table, and even though Reg didn't want it, she prepared herself a cup, hoping it would calm her brain and help her to get her thoughts organized. Her fingers shook as she poured the water and picked up her cup.

"No. He was confused. He couldn't remember a lot of the details."

"Of course not. That would be too easy, wouldn't it?"

"I'm not trying to pull one over on you, Detective Jessup. I'm trying to explain what happened. They... drugged him or did something to him so he couldn't remember exactly what had happened. I don't even know if he went down with the plane, or if they dumped him somewhere.... or just checked him into this hospital..."

"I thought psychics were supposed to be able to figure things like that out."

"Well, I'm trying. But it's not instant... I called Ling to see if she knew anything about these guys that Warren had been dealing with, or if he had any papers, journals, flight plans, something that might help us to piece together what had happened."

"And you don't think we would already have requested all of that in connection with the plane crash?"

"You could have missed something... there might have been something that you didn't know was important. You thought that crash was an accident."

"But you don't."

"No. It was the men he was supposed to be doing a job for. They did something to him, and they crashed his plane."

"How would crashing his plane get them what they wanted?"

Reg sipped her tea and concentrated on the question. What had the men wanted? If they wanted Warren to transport their illegal goods, then how would hurting him and crashing his plane help?

"They must have... they must have used it first. Then they crashed it to get rid of the evidence."

"They could fly without Warren?"

"I don't know... maybe they could. Or maybe they forced him to fly, and he just doesn't remember that part. There are a lot of holes." Reg tried to pull the memories together into something cogent. She had it all, or most of it, if she could just sort it out. "There was a man in a long, dark cloak, he said. Or an overcoat. And a man with dreadlocks. I don't know how many others." She searched the memories for pictures of them. "The man with dreadlocks is black. Very dark and thin. There are others..." The center of Reg's forehead was pulsing. She pressed into it with her thumbs.

Starlight rubbed against Reg's ankles. She bent over and picked him up. He purred and bumped his head against her. She rubbed the white spot on his forehead and the pain in her own head seemed to ease a little. She rubbed his chin and stared into his mismatched eyes.

"There are others... but those two are the leaders, the ones making the decisions."

"Warren told you that?"

"He... sort of. I can see... some of what he remembered. He couldn't hold the connection, so he tried to give me everything he could, all at once... but it's all jumbled and disjointed."

"So you have pictures of them in your head. Can you draw me pictures?"

"The one in the overcoat... his face is always obscured..." She didn't want to say that they had used magic spells to keep her from seeing their faces clearly. There were lots of legitimate ways people could hide their faces. Hats pulled low, collars pulled up. Masks. Makeup. Beards.

She thought about Corvin's beard. It was real, not something pasted on like a stage prop. But it was short and neat. Some men could grow a beard like that in a couple of days. Was he hiding what he really looked like so that Warren could never describe him?

"What about the others?"

She tried to picture the man with dreadlocks. Had the dreads been real? Not just a wig or fake hair attached to a hat? Was it also a disguise? A misdirection?

"The man with the dreadlocks is very black and skinny—"

"But his face? Can you draw his face?"

Reg rubbed Starlight's spot. "I don't know... I could try, but I'm not very good at that kind of thing, and the pictures are... they're blurry and fleeting. He tried to give me so much at once... it's like drinking from a firehose."

Jessup scribbled in her notepad, but it didn't look like she was writing words. "Unknown men, with no motives, intentionally crash a plane and put Warren Blake in hospital under another name... could you be any more obscure?"

"I'm trying."

"So you had Ling here, dumped all of this on her, asked her questions about Warren's operations and friends, and then she went away. Was she going back home?"

"No, she was going to go to McNara. To see Warren."

"And then was she supposed to get ahold of you? What was the next step?"

"She didn't really believe any of it. She wasn't working with me. I just told her about this... and she went to see." Reg ground her knuckles into her forehead. She didn't need to be channeling Warren to see how stupid she had been. "I shouldn't have let her go alone. I knew these men didn't want Warren to be found, so why would I let Ling go over there all by herself to find out she'd been lied to and that he was still alive? Whatever they did to him, they could do to her... or worse..."

"You should have come to the police," Jessup's partner spoke up. "Civilians shouldn't be trying to handle this kind of thing on their own. You knew there was an investigation into the plane crash. As soon as you found out Warren was alive, you should have contacted us."

"I just thought... there'd be a bunch of questions I didn't know the answers to. If I could just sort out everything he said and gave to me, then I could have something coherent to tell you..."

"You've withheld evidence."

"I don't have any evidence."

"Warren Blake himself. You should have called us from the hospital. He's key to our investigation," Jessup pointed out.

"I... yes, I suppose I should have. I was so tired after channeling him, I couldn't think straight. I just wanted to get home and sleep."

"You put an innocent woman at risk."

Reg tried to focus on Ling. What if they had killed her? What if they had put her in a magical coma as well? She closed her eyes and reached out for the woman.

"Oh, now we get a show," Jessup's partner said sarcastically.

"Shut up," Reg told him, trying to focus her concentration outside the cottage. Ling was out there somewhere. Reg had to make contact with her.

Jessup whispered something to her partner, but Reg didn't hear what it was and didn't try to work it out. Let them talk. She had a job to do. Reg had put a client in danger, and she had to reach her again.

She didn't have a picture or personal item to help focus her search. But she had Warren's memories, intimate portraits of their life together. She had met Ling before, which made it easier to search for her, like searching for a friend's face in a crowd.

Reg thought she could feel Ling's energy. She rubbed her fingers into Starlight's fur, trying to gather his psychic force to strengthen her own. She didn't call aloud to Ling; this reading wasn't for show. But she called out mentally, repeating Ling's name, trying to establish a link between them. She kept running up against barriers. She couldn't connect with Ling's consciousness.

Finally, she let out her breath, relaxed and smoothed Starlight's ruffled fur, and opened her eyes. Jessup and her partner were both staring at her.

★ Chapter Nineteen ★

ELL?" JESSUP PROMPTED. "I'M waiting for the crazy talk."

Reg shook her head. "I think… she's okay. She's not dead or unconscious like Warren. Sarah said…" She trailed off. She'd been trying not to mention Sarah or Letticia. They wouldn't want to be involved with the police, and the police would just get annoyed at them. The two crones lived in a whole different world from Jessup.

"Sarah who?" Jessup asked. When Reg didn't answer, she pressed again. "Sarah Bishop?"

Reg blinked. "How do you know Sarah Bishop?"

"She's your landlady, isn't she? We've done our background. We wouldn't just come in here blindly not knowing the situation."

"It's nothing. I was just talking to her about Warren."

"And what did she have to say? What does it have to do with Ling's situation?"

Reg rubbed her forehead again, wishing she could just go to bed. The police had no idea how much mental effort it took to communicate over a distance. And they weren't going to like anything Sarah had to say about what they had decided about Warren.

"It's just nonsense," she said. "An old woman's ramblings."

"Are you going to tell me, or do I have to get her in here?"

Reg preferred to manage the information. Sarah would just blab everything unfiltered and her talk of magic spells would get her slapped into the loony bin.

"It's nothing… just… Sarah said that it would take a lot of effort to keep Warren unconscious. So I don't think… maybe they don't have the resources to do the same thing with Ling."

"Okay…" Jessup's eyes were narrow, waiting for more details.

"I was worried that if they couldn't do the same thing with Ling, they might just… eliminate her."

"Which is why you should have told us about Warren last night instead of Ling."

"I guess." Reg stared into Starlight's eyes, not wanting to have to look into Jessup's.

"But you don't think they've killed her," Jessup's partner said.

"No, I can feel her out there, but she's not responding to me, which I think means she's still conscious and alert. People put up mental barriers when they're conscious. You can't communicate with them on the same level as you could if they were unconscious."

"Or dead."

"Right."

The seconds ticked by while Jessup and her partner watched Reg, evaluating her.

"I'm not crazy," Reg said. "I know this all sounds crazy, but it's just… it's just a phenomenon that we don't understand yet. One day, science will be able to explain it."

"Psychic phenomenon," Jessup's partner said.

"Yeah."

"In the meantime, we're expected to take this on faith."

"You can go to McNara and see that Warren's not dead."

"If he's even there. And if he is, that doesn't mean that the rest of this nonsense about cloaked wizards and dreadlocks dude is true."

"No… but it is. I'm not just making it up."

"That's what you do for a living," Jessup snapped. "You make things up. You fool people into paying you for made-up nonsense."

Reg bit her lip to keep from fighting back. She stared at the little card on the table in front of her. *Readings and other services are for entertainment only.* If she didn't want to be charged with fraud, that was the line she had to stick to, whether she was imagining or actually making some kind of real connection.

"I entertain people," she said stoically. "Just like any Vegas magic act."

How many times when she was little had she cried and insisted to an angry foster mother that she was telling the truth, not making up stories about her imagined friends? It felt like a betrayal of herself to tell Jessup it was just illusion and imagination. She'd been whipped and locked up and mistreated for telling the things that she saw and heard. She'd been called a liar and worse. All because she saw things other people didn't.

Jessup and her partner exchanged looks. Finally, Jessup pushed herself to her feet. "We'll go check out McNara," she said. "You'd better stay here."

"*Here?* Are you putting me under house arrest or telling me not to leave town?"

Jessup considered. "Don't leave town."

Reg walked the two officers to the door, glad that the dizziness had passed and she was able to walk unassisted. She looked at Jessup's partner's name bar, squinting to make the letters stay still. *Hawthorne-Rose.*

"We'll be in touch," Jessup said.

"Will you call me after you see that it's Warren?"

"I'm not making any promises. If it is Warren, we're going to need to talk to a lot of people. One of which will be you, to get a proper account of how you found him there."

Reg swallowed. She was grateful for the warning that she was going to have to figure out something to say. Maybe with some time, she could put together a story that made some sense and didn't involve pure luck or psychic inspiration.

Reg waited the rest of the day for a call from the police officers, but it never came. Had they identified Warren and become embroiled in the investigation, too busy to call her? Had they been bamboozled by the magical wards, deciding he wasn't there after all or going off on some other wild goose chase? Had Warren been gone, spirited away by the men who had crashed his airplane?

However much she wanted to know, she wasn't about to call them and find out. That would just be asking for trouble. A suspect who showed too much interest in an investigation was just that much more suspicious. Like the firebug who returned to watch the firefighters putting out the blaze he had started.

During the afternoon, the doorbell rang, waking Reg from a nap, and when she tottered to the door, still half-asleep, she found a young boy there. He was perhaps ten years old, blond, with wide blue eyes and childish round cheeks.

"Yes?"

She expected him to say that he'd hit a ball into the yard or that he was raising money for his scout troop. Instead, he held a folded piece of paper out to her.

"I'm to give this to you."

"Oh. What is this?"

He turned and ran away without answering. Reg looked down at it. It was a thick, substantial paper with a rough texture. Reg closed the door and unfolded the sheet, her heart racing in anticipation. A ransom note? An order to appear before Sarah's coven for some innocent infraction?

The thick calligraphic script was made by a practiced hand, not a computer. The ink was a deep indigo, with variation in shade from the thin strokes to the thick.

Miss Rawlins

I request the pleasure of your company at the Eagle Arms tonight at seven o'clock. (Neutral enough for you?)

Ever yours,

Corvin Hunter, III

It was certainly nicer than an email. Reg felt herself blushing at the amount of effort Corvin had obviously put into it. She would need to put some time into getting herself dolled up for the evening in return. It was obviously more than just a casual dinner. Reg hesitated, then walked over to the main house and knocked on Sarah's back door. It was a few minutes before Sarah answered it, looking flushed and out of breath.

"Come in, dear, come in. What can I help you with?"

"I was just wondering… what kind of place the Eagle Arms is."

"The Eagle Arms?" Sarah looked Reg over carefully. "Who is taking you to the Eagle Arms?"

Reg cleared her throat and looked down.

"Corvin?" Sarah demanded. "I've told you to stay away from him. No good can come of a relationship with him."

"We're not in a relationship… it's just one date."

"That's the beginning of a relationship."

"It's not serious," Reg said. "And besides you haven't explained to me why I shouldn't see him. He is a very charming man, and he's interested in me… what's going to happen?"

"Any number of things," Sarah said darkly.

"Like…?"

"He could turn you into a toad."

"Somehow, I don't see that happening!" Reg laughed.

"They never do."

"Sarah. Is it a fancy place? The Eagle Arms? It sounds… dark and British. Do I need a floor length dress? A jacket? Jewelry? Do I need to put my hair up?"

Sarah sighed. "I said to come in. It looks like we have some work to do."

Which confirmed Reg's suspicion that she was going to need to go full-formal. Sarah turned out to have the equivalent of a dress shop tucked away in the closets of the main house. Reg had hoped to borrow some accents from her, but hadn't expected her to have a dress that would be Reg's size or style.

"I haven't been fat all my life," Sarah said, as she measured a dress against Reg. "It's just one of those things that happens as your body slows down and you settle into eating at restaurants instead of doing for yourself. And hemlines are easy to adjust."

"Ooh, that's pretty," Reg reached out and touched a blue silk gown with crystal beads sewn into it.

Sarah pulled it out of the closet and examined it closely. "Everything seems to have held," she observed. "Nice lines. You've got the figure for it. Give it a try."

Reg took the hanger and draped the dress over her arm. The shade of blue worked nicely with her complexion.

"I'll try it," she agreed.

"I have some earrings that will look stunning with it. And maybe... a small locket to set off the neckline."

"This is so generous of you, thank you!"

"What are friends for?" Sarah put a few of the dresses she had pulled out back away again. "Did I see the police over at the cottage today?"

"I guess you did. I didn't see you around."

"I still see most of what goes on around here."

"Well, they came by... we had a little discussion about Warren and Ling, and they headed over to McNara to see if they could pick up Ling's trail."

At Sarah's puzzled look, Reg filled in further details.

"Ling went over there last night to see Warren... and never got home. Her family called the police and reported her missing."

"You sent her over to see Warren? I'm not sure that was such a good idea."

"I guess I get that now. I just thought... she needed to know that Warren was alive. And I wanted to know if she knew anything about the men that... did that to him."

"But she didn't know anything about it," Sarah guessed.

"No. Nothing."

"And that ignorance would have kept her safe, had you not involved her."

Reg sighed heavily. "Things are a lot more complicated than I ever would have imagined. This whole... paranormal world... is very disconcerting."

"I'm sure it's very different than what you are used to. Which is why you should ask for help and advice instead of just running headlong into things."

Reg nodded. "Uh-huh."

Sarah led her into yet another of the bedrooms and started to go through all of the little compartments of a complicated jewelry wardrobe. She eventually found the crystal earrings she was looking for, and a little heart locket.

"You go shower and get dressed," she advised. "I'll be over when you're done with some appropriate shoes and I'll put your hair up."

"You don't need to do that…"

"Go on. I'll be over shortly."

Reg decided to do what she was told. She took her treasures back to the cottage. Starlight jumped off of the couch and looked at her, putting his ears back and opening his mouth like there was a bad smell. Reg raised the dress to her nose and sniffed it, but couldn't detect any mold or mothballs smell that might be offensive.

"What?" she asked him.

He just continued to look at them with that disapproving, wrinkled-up-nose expression.

"I know you don't like Corvin either. But I seriously don't know what your problem is. I don't know what everyone thinks Corvin is going to do to me. He might be a warlock—maybe—but he's a man, and I know how to handle men. He's not going to do anything to me that I don't want done."

Starlight sneezed and stalked away. He stationed himself by his food dish and stared at her.

"I'll feed you before I leave. You don't need anything right now. If I feed you tuna three times a day, you're going to be as wide as the couch."

With that, she left him alone with his untouched dish of dry kibble and had her shower.

Sarah was obviously on the same wavelength as Reg, as she showed up at the cottage just as she finished doing her face and putting her earrings in.

"Let me help you with the necklace," Sarah offered. "The catch sometimes gets stuck."

Reg held up her hair while Sarah reached around her to settle the necklace into place and do up the catch securely. She gave it a little pat. "That should do it. Now let's do something with your hair."

She had Reg sit down at the kitchen table that so far Reg had not used, and worked her magic. In a few minutes, Reg was looking in a hand mirror at the large knot of braids wrapped with a jeweled net.

"That's pretty," Reg admired.

"It's very elegant," Sarah agreed, sounding pleased.

Reg angled the mirror to look at her face. "I guess I'm ready to go."

"Stand up and let me look at the dress. Does the hemline need to be adjusted?"

Reg stood up and showed off the gown that skimmed over her figure like it was made for her. The sweetheart neckline was chic without showing too much cleavage. When Reg checked the length, it was just a smidge too long.

"Maybe just a bit."

Sarah shook her head. "Actually, I think it will be just right with the shoes."

"Oh, the shoes!"

"You're not going out in sneakers or flats," Sarah informed her. She opened up a shoebox, and Reg almost expected a pair of ruby red shoes. Instead, they were strappy, silver spike heels embellished with sparkling zircons.

"Oh, those are beautiful!" Reg took them from Sarah, sure that they wouldn't fit. But everything else Sarah had given her had fit perfectly, so why did she doubt it? It was almost like magic.

Reg slipped the shoes on and did them up, and of course they fit like a glove. They raised Reg's height just enough that, as Sarah had said, the hemline on the dress did not need to be adjusted, just skimming the floor.

"I feel just like Cinderella," Reg laughed. "All ready for the ball."

"Just be sure not to get turned into a pumpkin," Sarah warned, not smiling at her own words. She might be helping Reg with her outfit, but she still did not approve of Reg having dinner with the dangerous warlock.

★ Chapter Twenty ★

REG WOULDN'T LET SARAH drive her to the restaurant, but instead hiked up her dress and drove herself. Who knew what she would look like when she got there if she let herself get thrown around in Sarah's jeep. She didn't need to be showing up for dinner with a bloody nose.

A valet took the car when she got to the Eagle Arms. Reg had never had her car valet parked before, and wasn't sure about letting someone else have the keys, but peer pressure forced her to accept the service, and she let the young man take her key and drive her car away.

She arrived just before seven and glanced around to see if Corvin were already there. A beautiful hostess stepped up to her. "You're Mr. Hunter's party?"

"Yes. How did you know?"

"This way, please."

Reg followed the woman through the main dining room to a private room in the back with rich wall tapestries and flickering candlelight. Corvin stood up to greet her.

"Is this little Regina Rawlins?" he murmured. "My dear, you have outdone yourself." He took her hand gently and kissed the fingertips, making Reg feel immediately awkward. Who did that? And what was she supposed to do in response? Curtsy?

"Uh… and you look very nice too," she offered, giving a little bob. He was in a black tux with tails, white shirt, vest, and bow tie.

"Come have a seat," he pulled a chair out for her, and Reg sat down carefully as he pushed it in.

Reg was feeling warm, though she was sure the climate in the dining room was perfectly regulated. If she was warm within two minutes of walking into the room, how was she going to get through the night?

"You obviously got my note," Corvin said, seating himself.

"Yes, of course." A thought occurred to Reg. Should she have sent a note back to him acknowledging it? Was there a proper protocol to receiving a formal invitation? There was bound to be. The gamin who had delivered the note had not stayed, and she had no idea where Corvin lived. But Sarah undoubtedly did. "Sorry... maybe I should have sent something back?"

"Not necessary. Unlike with email communication, I was sure that the invitation was in your hand."

"Right, that makes sense."

Corvin motioned to Reg's glass. "Wine?"

"Uh..." Reg looked at it, remembering her reaction to the alcohol at her last dinner with Corvin. If she didn't want to be vulnerable to him, she needed to make sure he didn't get a chance to tamper with her drink, and that she didn't let herself become impaired by alcohol. "No, thank you."

He raised his brows. "It's already been decanted," he pointed out, an offended edge to his voice. "And it's not cheap. I know you drink."

"Not tonight," Reg said firmly. When he opened his mouth to argue further, she cut him off. "I don't owe you anything."

Corvin closed his mouth. He readjusted his position in his seat, stretched out his arms, and adjusted the sleeve cuffs protruding from his jacket sleeves to some exacting measurement. Reg could smell the rose scent, heady and warm. A more eloquent argument than anything he could have said. She almost gave in and agreed to have the wine, but biting the inside of her lip, managed to hold firm.

Corvin poured wine into his own glass; dark red, almost black in the dim lighting of the room. He gave it a swirl and a sniff. "I've ordered hors d'oeuvres, but perhaps I should have checked that with you first as well."

Reg smoothed her dress. "No, it's fine. I'm sure they will be lovely."

He studied her, frowning. "You are a puzzling woman."

"Got to keep up my mystique."

He leaned back. The relaxation of his body language calmed Reg. She didn't want the entire date to be a sparring match.

"So, tell me… I am interested in hearing the story of how you discovered Warren, and what you found out about him."

Reg tried to read him. Was he one of the men who had crashed Warren's plane and put him in hospital? Or was it just idle curiosity? She still hadn't decided. Sarah said that there were various warlocks who answered the description Warren had given. But she had also said that Corvin was dangerous. She hadn't jumped to the conclusion that Corvin had been one of the men who had attacked Warren, so Reg shouldn't either. Sarah knew the players better than Reg could. She had continually warned Reg against Corvin, but she hadn't prevented Reg from seeing him, and she hadn't said that he was the one who had plotted against Warren.

Sarah had also said that it would take a lot of energy to keep Warren bound. Would Corvin be able to expend that amount of effort and still sit across from her looking casual and amused? No sweat on his brow or other signs of exertion?

"Not really much to say," she said. "He was being held at an obscure hospital under another name, to try to keep anyone from finding him. Confusion charms and a binding spell and all of that."

"But you still managed to find him."

"Luck," Reg said lightly.

"I don't think luck had anything to do with it. You shook me off your trail and managed to get past all of the wards to make contact with him. And found out… what…?"

Reg considered. "I think you already know what I found."

He betrayed surprise. "How would I know?"

"He described a warlock who bore a startling resemblance to you."

"He showed *me* to you?" Corvin challenged.

Reg reviewed the images Warren had given her the best she could. But as before, she could only find shadowy figures with blurred faces. They had either hidden their faces from Warren, or whatever spells they had put on him had muddied his recollection. The warlock with the long coat could have been Corvin. But he could have been a lot of other men too. There were no identifying features that could exclude Corvin or provide proof that it was him.

"I can't tell whether it is you or not."

Did she detect a slight shift in his shoulders? An infinitesimal relaxation? "I didn't have anything to do with Warren Blake," Corvin advised. "I rarely have any interactions with non-magical folk. I find it taxing to have to worry about the masks and pretenses required to deal with them without revealing myself. I would rather expend my energy on other tasks."

"So you don't know anything about what happened to him or who did it."

Warren picked up his glass and sipped his wine. "What did he tell you? If he was placed there under such suspicious circumstances, I can only assume that what happened to him was not the simple plane crash caused by mechanical issues that the police thought it was."

"No." Reg shifted toward Corvin, aching to give him all of the details. "There were several men. Some kind of illegal enterprise. He refused the job, and they… I guess they decided he was taking it anyway, like it or not. He couldn't remember what they did to him, whether they coerced him into flying or did that themselves, but they did whatever it was, and crashed his plane afterward. And hid him away where nobody could find him."

"Almost nobody."

Reg's cheeks warmed. "Almost nobody," she agreed. "Certainly not the police."

"What kind of job was it?"

"Courier. Moving some kind of product. But he decided it wasn't what they said it was. Thought it might be drugs or some other illicit trade. And he didn't want to be a part of it."

Corvin nodded thoughtfully. "But it obviously wasn't simply drugs. A drug dealer would have slit his throat and put him in the ocean with his plane."

"Then who do you think it was? What would they want transported illegally?"

A waiter came in with the hors d'oeuvres Corvin had ordered ahead, a variety of canapés that were not immediately recognizable. Reg would have to be adventurous. She transferred a couple of the small treats onto her plate.

"There are many different things that might be trafficked in the community that are illegal in the non-magical world or regulated or prohibited by our traditions."

"Such as…?"

"Ingredients for potions or charms. Relics. What you might call human trafficking."

"Sex trade?" Reg demanded. "Slave labor?"

Corvin made a humming noise. "Closer to slave labor," he said, "but the subjects are not always… entirely human."

"What does that mean?"

He shifted uncomfortably. "Perhaps we should just leave it at that."

"You're going to drop a bomb like that and then expect me to just ignore it? Non-human slave labor?"

"I think it would take much longer to give you a clear picture than you could get in the time we have to discuss it."

"I don't need a clear picture. Just an idea. What kind of non-humans are you talking about?"

He shrugged and took another drink of his wine, staring at her without answering.

"Is that what you think Warren was involved in? Is that why they're trying to keep him quiet?"

"No, I doubt it. It isn't just unusual to involve a non-practitioner in such a venture. It would be… unheard of. Simply not tolerated."

"It would be worse to involve an ordinary person than to actually traffic in… non-humans?" Reg couldn't believe she was even having such a conversation. Before coming to Black Sands, she would have assumed that anyone discussing magic and non-humans was completely off his rocker. Instead, she was discussing it with a self-proclaimed warlock as naturally as if they were talking about cheating on the SAT.

"Definitely," Corvin agreed. "The trade is… highly discouraged. But involving non-believers would be subject to the highest levels of discipline."

"What kind of discipline is there for…" Reg wasn't sure what terminology was appropriate. "People like you?"

"There is a wide variety of disciplinary measures. Everything from shunning or removing someone from their coven or community to… entrancement."

"Entrancement?"

Corvin popped one of the canapés into his mouth. He chewed it slowly, but Reg wondered whether he was really enjoying it or just using it as an excuse to delay his answer. She looked down at the canapés on her own plate, working up her courage to try one.

"Entrancement is similar to the state you say Warren is in. But the binding of a practitioner is… a very grievous step."

"Worse than binding Warren."

He nodded. "Of course."

"Why isn't binding Warren a serious infraction?"

"It could be done to protect the community. Or as a way to stay Warren without harming him. Binding someone who doesn't have powers is usually a temporary measure and it requires the ongoing energy of the binder to maintain it."

"And that's different than entrancement…?"

"Entrancement removes that person's powers from the community and also requires a price to be paid to keep him…

imprisoned for the duration of the sentence. So it is a double-blow to the community."

Reg tried to wrap her mind around it. She shook her head. "I still don't understand how it's okay for someone like Warren but not for someone who supposedly has powers."

"Binding is seen as a viable solution to keep a non-believer out of harm's way. Killing him would be…" Corvin hesitated, staring off and searching for the right turn of phrase, "…I guess the concept that comes closest is bad karma. By doing harm to someone else, you do harm to yourself and your future prospects. It's much better to bind a man than to kill him. But to bind a *practitioner*… it is a penalty worse than death."

"Because…?"

"Because those powers are an asset of the community. It's like cutting off your own arm or leg."

"Oh." Reg picked up one of the canapés and popped it into her mouth. The burst of flavor shocked her and for a moment she just stared at Corvin, completely losing track of their conversation. She closed her mouth and just chewed the savory bite for a moment, trying to analyze the complex flavors. "What are these?"

"Just a hint of things to come."

She didn't know whether he meant the main course, or some other path he intended to take her down. For the next few minutes, she was completely focused on trying each different type of canapé on the plate. She felt strangely light-headed, even though she had avoided the wine.

Corvin leaned forward in his seat. "There are many other pleasures I could introduce you to, Regina."

Reg swallowed the last bite. "I'm sure there are."

"Then why do you continue to resist me?"

"I want to stay in control… and I've been warned against you."

He smirked. "Some old crone who is jealous of the attention you're attracting."

"I thought you said crone was a term of respect."

He shrugged. "It can go either way."

"Starlight doesn't like you either."

"You can't trust a cat. All they care about is where their next meal is coming from. He doesn't want you to be distracted and to forget to feed him."

"I think he has more loyalty than that."

"A cat? Cats have no loyalty."

"They said at the shelter that he'd recently lost his owner, and was grieving for him. That doesn't sound like an animal without any loyalty."

"People put human emotions onto animals. That's a mistake, animals don't have the same emotions as humans do."

"How do you know that?"

"Years of observation."

"But you can't talk to animals, can you?" She remembered their conversation of the night before. "So you don't really know, you're just guessing."

"I'm observing." He gave a little shrug. "Maybe some cats are loyal to their owners," he conceded, "but most of them couldn't care less, as long as they get fed."

"You don't like them, do you?"

Corvin didn't answer immediately. He had another sip of wine. "No," he admitted finally, "I don't."

"Maybe that's why they don't like you."

He shook his head and opened his mouth to object, then shrugged again and left it at that.

"Who do you think hired Warren?" Reg asked. "There can't be that many people in such a small community who would do this kind of thing. Crash his plane and put a spell on him. You must have some idea of who it is."

Corvin rubbed his beard. "People come and go. There is a core population that has been here for a long time, but there are others who are—if you'll excuse the expression—fly by night. They come, check things out, see whether they can get something established, and then move on in a short period of time."

Reg shifted uncomfortably, recognizing herself in his comment. She was one of those people, coming into town and seeing whether she could make a living there. There were a lot of towns she had blown into, tried out a new scheme for a while, and then left before trouble could catch up with her. If she decided Black Sands wasn't the place for her, she'd pack her bags and be gone again before anyone could look for her. With Jessup looking at her, she was already considering pulling up stakes before they could stick anything on her.

"So is there any new group like that?" she asked Corvin. "According to Warren, it wasn't just one guy. There was a man with a long black coat, and another who was skinny and had dreadlocks, and some others. Does that sound like anyone you know?"

Corvin's eyes glittered, greedy for the information. "Not off the top of my head. But they could be flying under the radar—literally and figuratively—to avoid being identified by the police or the covens."

Reg nodded. The waiter returned to clear the appetizers, smiling and nodding at them both. Reg expected him to offer her a menu, but he did not, assuring them that their dinners would be ready shortly. She raised her brows at Corvin.

"You ordered my main course too?"

"I did."

"You know you're a chauvinist?"

He blinked at her. "I'm a what?"

"Did it ever occur to you that I might not want you to order for me? That it would be a good idea to ask me what I like instead of just assuming you know what I like or don't like?"

"I know the menu and what's good here."

"That's not what I said."

"You liked the hors d'oeuvres, didn't you? Don't you trust me to make a good choice?"

Reg shook her head. "I like to make my own choices, not to have them imposed on me by some paternalistic—"

"Regina."

Reg stopped her rant.

He spread his hands in a query. "Why don't you wait and see if you like it?"

"And what if I don't?"

"Then you can order something else."

She glared at him. "There's a difference between charming, old world manners and being a presumptuous—"

It wasn't his words that stopped her mid-sentence, but his expression and his hand over hers on the table.

"Stop fighting me," he urged, voice a low croon. He stroked his thumb across the back of her hand, sending a shiver up her spine and goosebumps popping out all over her arms. "You're here to enjoy yourself, so stop trying to be in control of everything and let it happen."

★ Chapter Twenty-One ★

REG'S NATURE WARRED AGAINST her undeniable attraction to Corvin. When he laid on the charm, the pull was so strong it left her breathless.

"I'm just…"

"We're in the best restaurant for a hundred miles. I have arranged for the best refreshment and repast available. You are to be waited on hand and foot. Why would you want anything else?"

"I don't like you assuming that you know what I like."

"But I do."

His tone was so certain, Reg was left with her mouth open, unable to find an argument. Was it possible that he did know her tastes without ever even asking? Had he been able to discern them from some sort of spell or telepathy? Or was he just full of ego and hot air?

"Give me a chance," Corvin urged. "The wine, the meal, just enjoy it like you were meant to."

Reg pushed air out, trying to start breathing again. "Fine," her voice was almost a whisper, "I will try it."

"The wine too?"

He had poured his out of the same bottle. He hadn't poisoned or tampered with it. If Reg limited herself to one glass, there was no danger of intoxication. So what was the harm in trying it?

"Yes. One glass."

He smiled, pleased. Without further urging, he poured her a glass. Reg smelled it and swirled it around. She wasn't exactly a connoisseur, but she knew the basics. She tasted the wine, holding it in her mouth for a minute before swallowing.

"It's very nice," she told Corvin. And it was. It had depth and a pleasant finish. She put it down, not taking a second sip. She would stretch it out to last the full evening. That way she could be certain of staying in control.

"So, tell me about your life," Corvin suggested. "This profession is new to you. What were you doing before you came to Florida?"

Reg blew out her breath slowly. "Ooh... well, that's the million dollar question, isn't it..."

He smiled expectantly. "Well...?"

"I've done a lot of different things. I have... a wanderlust. I like to move around, try out different things. So I've never really settled into one career. I just sort of... taste test."

"Jack of all trades, master of none?" Corvin suggested.

"Yes. Very true."

"So, tell me about some of them."

Reg thought about what to share with him. "I have... sold real estate..."

Corvin raised his eyebrows. "Really. And that wasn't something that you have to stay in long term to make a living at? I thought that you had to do quite a bit of training."

"If you do it the right way," Reg agreed. Of course, to do it the right way, one had to actually own the property or have a contract with the property owner. What Reg had done had been more along the lines of selling properties she had access to, but didn't actually have any legal title to. A few computer-generated reports that looked legitimate, and most people could be convinced to pick up real estate on the cheap without involving a lawyer.

Corvin chuckled. Reg wasn't sure how much of the truth he was able to read in her face and voice. She was usually pretty good at masking her thoughts.

"I've sold all kinds of things," she continued. "Property, jewelry, cars... umm... antiques."

"Actual legitimate antiques?"

"Maybe not exactly legitimate."

"Am I sensing a pattern here?"

"You may be."

"When you say you've moved around a lot, would I be right in guessing that moving on wasn't always solely your decision?"

"Oh, no," Reg protested. "It was always my decision. I didn't wait around for anyone to tell me to go."

Though Reg *had* overstayed her welcome at Erin's. She should have been more careful not to take advantage of her sister's hospitality. But at least she had gotten out of Bald Eagle Falls before the police department had caught wind of any suspicious goings-on.

"And what about Black Sands? Are you going to stay here long-term? Or is this just another pin in your map?"

"I don't know. It's a nice place, but I've already had the police knocking on my door twice, and that's pretty quick… I'm not going to wait until they fabricate charges."

"Twice?" Corvin repeated.

He didn't seem surprised that she'd been visited by the police, but her mention of two visits had caught his attention.

Reg nodded. "I guess you're not completely up-to-date yet. See… after I found Warren… I talked to Ling, and she went to see him."

Corvin nodded seriously, watching her with sharp eyes. "What happened?"

"Unfortunately… I don't know. She disappeared."

"From where? Before or after she got to the hospital?"

"I don't know. The police were going to go to the hospital to inquire, but I didn't hear anything back from them either."

"They came to you to see if you had something to do with her disappearance?"

"She'd told her parents that she was coming to see me, and that was the last anyone heard of her, so naturally, they came to talk to me."

"Naturally," Corvin agreed.

"But they were pretty hard-nosed about it," Reg said. "They started out with… misconceptions… and were pretty insistent that I had to go to the police station to be questioned."

"You don't have to go with them if they don't put you under arrest."

Reg took another sip of her wine. Dinner had been delectable stone crabs. She was full and satisfied, but not stuffed. With something in her stomach, the wine shouldn't go to her head.

"I don't like having the police poke their noses into my business," she told Corvin. "And it's not good business if people seeing the police coming in and out of my place all the time. They start to think that there's something shady going on."

Corvin's smile was ironic. She'd just been confiding in him the different rackets she'd been in, so he wasn't buying the plea of innocence.

"Well, if they didn't come back, that's a good sign, isn't it? They must have found a lead in another direction, or evidence that what you told them was true. If they got to the hospital and everyone disclaimed knowledge of Ling going there, they would have been back to question you further."

Reg nodded. She had been holding out hope for that reason. On one hand, she was grateful that Jessup and her partner had stayed away and not thrown any further accusations around, but on the other hand… she wanted to know what they found. She wanted to know they had found out about Ling and that Warren was still at the hospital where she had left him. Maybe even that they had found Ling at Warren's bedside, where she had fallen asleep holding his hand, and that was the only reason she hadn't been home to her parents.

"Yeah. It's good… but I want to know what's going on."

"Not really any of your business," Corvin said. "You didn't have anything to do with what happened to Warren, so why should you be concerned?"

Reg took another drink, but was really just trying to cover up the fact that she was studying him, reading his body language, trying to decide whether he was telling her to stay out of it because it was his own caper and he didn't want her screwing it up.

"Like you said about karma," she said slowly, after putting her glass down again. "You do harm to someone, and it comes back to bite you. You do something nice for someone when you don't have to, and maybe the universe throws some of that good stuff back your way."

"Uh-huh." His tone was unconvinced.

"I don't like thinking that Ling could be in trouble because of something I did. She was safe thinking that Warren was dead. When I opened my mouth... she disappeared."

Corvin nodded. "You should have just stayed out of it."

"And why were you following me yesterday? *You* weren't exactly minding your own business."

His lip curled up at the corner. "I was just keeping an eye on you. Making sure you didn't get yourself into any trouble."

"Again, why? I'm not a little girl. I'm a full-grown woman and I've had plenty of experience taking care of myself. I don't need a man to protect me."

"You may have experience in the outside world, but you don't have experience here. You don't know the first thing about protecting yourself against spells and enchantments."

"I was with two witches. Or so you all led me to think. They seem to be pretty competent."

"There's competent... and there's skilled."

"Letticia is the leader of the coven, doesn't that mean she's skilled?"

Corvin rolled his shoulders in a dispassionate shrug. "I don't see why you would object to being protected by me, but accept them. My skills are... not insignificant."

"Sarah said—"

He slid his hand over hers again. "Why let these women's petty jealousies control your appraisal of me? You can make decisions based on your own experience and intellect instead of listening to someone who has an ax to grind."

"Yes..." He had a point there. She was a grown woman. She might not have a lot of experience in paranormal circles, but she had life experience. What Corvin said made sense. All of her senses drew her to him. People talked about chemistry, about falling in love, meeting Mr. Right, and she had never understood it. Her relationships with men had always been careful decisions, weighed on a balance.

But her body was telling her that Corvin was the one for her. Her soulmate. Sarah had refused to give Reg any real answer about why she shouldn't have a relationship with Corvin. She just kept repeating general warnings without any kind of backup. She had admitted that, even as an older woman, she was attracted to Corvin. Maybe that was the key to why she kept trying to push Reg off. Jealousy, just as Corvin had suggested.

Corvin wrapped his fingers around Reg's, forming a comforting shield around them. She leaned closer to him, wanting that feeling to envelope her entire body. The smell of roses filled her nose and she wondered whether it was a cologne or whether it was actually his natural scent, some kind of pheromone. It did seem to increase in more intimate circumstances. Corvin lifted his other hand and traced Reg's breastbone with the lightest possible touch. It raised delicious shivers all up and down Reg's spine and arms. She closed her eyes, savoring it.

Corvin's fingertips touched the chain of the locket, and he suddenly jerked back as if burned. Reg's eyes flew open and she looked at him, concerned.

"What happened?" He was holding one hand in the other, his face contorted. "Did you cut yourself?" Reg ran her finger down the chain where he'd touched it, searching for a burr in the metal links.

Corvin rubbed his fingertips, then shook them as if trying to flick something off. "Where did you get that?" he demanded, glaring at the locket. "Where did that vile thing come from?"

Reg looked down at the locket, shocked at his reaction. She closed her hand around it, holding it protectively, in case he tried to grab it away from her.

"I borrowed it from Sarah. What's wrong?"

"That witch! It's a ward," he snarled, "and don't tell me you didn't know that! You've been teasing me all evening, pretending to be interested and then withdrawing. All the time, you knew you were wearing a ward against me."

"I—I didn't! Sarah just said it would go well with the dress. Everything is from Sarah, right down to the shoes. I didn't have anything suitable for a place like this, so she helped me out."

"Is that so. You think she just accidentally gave you a ward against me? She's been trying to turn you from me from the moment we met."

"I know. I know she has. But I didn't realize... she didn't tell me that there was anything... unusual about it. I thought it was just a pretty, old necklace."

"She's put something in it." He eyed Reg's hand, still closed around the heart-shaped locket. "The whole thing is buzzing with magic. It is no accident that you're wearing it tonight."

Reg opened her hand and looked at it. She couldn't see or hear anything unusual. She slid her nail into the crack between the two halves of the locket to open it up. It didn't click open. She tried harder to force it, but couldn't pry it open. She felt for a catch to release it. It was probably spring-loaded somehow.

But no matter how she tried, she couldn't find a way to open it.

"If there's something in it, I don't know how to get it out," she told Corvin.

"Take it off."

Reg hesitated. Sarah had felt it necessary to protect her, and it had obviously worked. But why? Why was she so concerned about Reg getting closer to the warlock?

"If you didn't know about it and didn't ask her for it, then take it off," Corvin challenged.

In the back of her mind, Reg remembered that she had talked with Sarah about getting a ward to discourage Corvin's advances. Not when she had been getting dressed for the date, but the day before, in the car with Letticia. She hadn't actually asked Sarah for it, and Sarah had said nothing about it when helping Reg to dress for the date.

Under Corvin's angry glare, Reg reached behind her neck for the clasp. She would show him that she could be trusted and that she hadn't intended to harm him or to keep him away from her with the ward. Then he would calm down and wouldn't be angry toward her. She could feel that warm, enveloping feeling again.

She fumbled with the catch, feeling its shape and trying to figure out how to release it. It didn't feel like any of the clasps that were standard on the jewelry she wore. It must be older, a different kind of clasp that she wasn't familiar with.

"Can *you* do it?" she asked Corvin, swiveling her body to put it within his reach.

He moved back, his breath hissing out. "No. I can't touch it."

"Can you see how to open it? I can't work it out."

He remained apart from her, shaking his head and not attempting to touch it or to describe it to her. Reg slid the chain around her neck until the catch was at the front near the locket so she could see how to open it. She thumbed the spring-loaded catch, but it wouldn't move. She wiggled it and worked her nail under it and tried to find a way to release it.

"How did you get it on?" Corvin demanded, watching her attempts. "Just reverse the process."

"I didn't put it on."

Reg remembered Sarah's comment that it had a sticky catch, and that she was the one who had draped it around Reg's neck, done it up, and then patted it when she had it in place. "That should do it."

"Sarah did," Corvin deduced.

Reg nodded, letting go of the necklace.

"Take it off over your head."

Reg attempted to do so, but in spite of the fact that she was sure it was large enough to be taken off without undoing it first, she wasn't able to get it off. She looked at Corvin helplessly.

"I'm sorry. Really, I didn't plan this."

Corvin sat back in his chair, pouting, his arms folded over his chest.

"Blast that woman."

"I'm sorry... but we can still have a nice evening together, can't we? I've really enjoyed myself so far. Don't let this ruin our night."

He studied her, still looking petulant.

"Come on," Reg urged. "Please."

He sighed, then made what appeared to be a huge effort of will and sat up, uncrossing his arms. He didn't take her hand again.

By the time dessert came by, Corvin seemed to have gotten over his temper tantrum, and was once again the attentive host. The dessert could have been billed as a brownie, but that didn't begin to describe the rich chocolate, whipped cream, and drizzles of chocolate syrup. Reg had never had anything that compared. She could no more call it a brownie than she could call the sun a lightbulb.

"That's unbelievable," Reg told Corvin. "How could something like this even exist? This restaurant should be bursting at the seams and booked five years in advance."

He gave her a slow, catlike smile. "I know how to take care of a date."

"Wow. I thought the canapés were amazing. But this was just... wow."

He traced a finger down her arm, drawing out more anticipatory shivers. Reg grabbed his fingers with her other hand, unable to stand it.

"Come home with me," Corvin whispered.

Even after the pleasures of that evening, Reg was wary of the invitation. She shook her head. "No."

"Regina."

"Come to mine," Reg countered. At least she knew her own cottage. There were no weapons, bonds, or dungeons there. She didn't know what kind of medieval torture to expect after the warnings from Sarah, but at her own place, at least she was close to Sarah's protection and knew her surroundings.

Corvin hesitated.

"It's a compromise," Reg said. "Come on."

He stared deep into her eyes. Reg felt like her skin was on fire. Finally, Corvin nodded.

★ Chapter Twenty-Two ★

CORVIN MOTIONED TO A big, sleek black car waiting at the curb. "Our carriage awaits."

It was not the white compact he had been driving the day they had been out looking for Warren. It was a luxury vehicle, lots of leg room and all of the latest features. But Reg shook her head.

"We'll take mine." She held her valet tag out to the boy waiting to assist her.

"Yours. Why can't you trust me, Regina?"

"I want to take mine. I'll drive and we'll go in my car," she said firmly. She wasn't going to be distracted by nice wheels.

Corvin nodded to the valet, who hurried off to get Reg's car. Corvin leaned close to Reg, his warm breath on her ear and neck. "Do you really think you're still in control?"

Reg shivered and couldn't repress a smile. She couldn't deny she was being driven by her desires, barely keeping her head. But she could at least act like she was making safe, logical decisions.

Corvin gave a knowing grin. When the valet drove the car around, Corvin held the door for Reg and shut it once she had managed to hike up her dress and slither into the seat. He folded his body into the passenger seat beside her. Reg rolled down the windows, wanting as much fresh air as possible. She wasn't drunk, but she certainly felt intoxicated.

Corvin gazed out the window. "Do you ever wish you didn't have any powers?"

Reg pursed her lips, thinking about it. "I don't know. I never even thought of them as powers... just as my imagination... part of my brain that didn't work right..."

"And do you want to be like everyone else? Just normal?"

"Well... sure." Reg could remember screwing her eyes shut and covering her ears, trying to banish the ghosts and the voices. After so many punishments, psychologist visits, and med changes, she had ended up having a breakdown. She hadn't slashed her wrists, but she had certainly considered it.

After that, things had been different. She had succeeded in blocking out the worst of the visions. It wasn't until she had started the gig as a fortune-teller that they had started to return. "All I ever wanted was to be like everyone else." She shrugged and sighed. "But they say normal is overrated."

"Is it?"

Reg had no idea what normality would be like. Did her imagination and intuition really amount to a psychic gift? Was it supposed to be something good? Were the diagnoses she'd received over the years all just a misunderstanding of a paranormal phenomenon or was she truly damaged?

"I don't know. I guess I'd have to experience being normal to tell."

"And would you? If you had the option, would you take it?"

"Yes. Maybe. I don't know. It's not like that's ever going to happen."

She got to the house and parked in the back. Hopefully, Sarah would not see her car and figure out that she was home. She wouldn't show up, asking how Reg's date had gone.

She opened the gate and Corvin followed close behind her, his feet whispering over the cobbled path. Reg turned her key in the lock and swung the door open. She looked at Corvin, standing behind her, unmoving. She raised her brows and reached back for him.

"Invite me in," Corvin said.

Reg smiled. "Come in."

His lips spread in a smile that showed his teeth and he went with her over the threshold into the cottage. He bolted the door behind him as he had the last time, but Reg didn't mind. She didn't want to chance Sarah barging in on them.

She heard Starlight jump down from the bed and his soft footfalls as he approached the living room. When he saw Corvin, his lips parted in a snarl.

"I'll take care of him," Reg told Corvin. She grabbed Starlight and took him to the spare room, where she shut him in. He yowled in protest and clawed to be let back out.

Reg bit her lip. She hadn't expected him to be so loud or so upset.

"He'll be fine," Corvin assured her. "He'll settle down in a few minutes."

They had another drink from Reg's stores. Her nerves were all afire. She couldn't calm down and relax with him as she had at the restaurant. They sat together on the couch. Corvin held her lightly by the shoulders as he leaned in and kissed her. Reg's heart was beating so hard it hurt. She wanted nothing more than to be with him, to be completely his.

Corvin released her from the kiss and looked down at the locket.

"I can change everything for you."

Reg was sure he could. Every touch rocked her world. He had access to tastes and pleasures she had never even dreamed existed. Corvin knew her, understood about her childhood and the pain her gifts had brought her like no one else ever could.

"You can remove the ward if you want to," Corvin whispered. "It will only work for as long as you desire a protection against me."

Reg grasped the locket in her hand, prepared to yank it and break the chain. The catch opened and the two ends of the released chain slithered down either side of her neck and it lay free in her hand. Reg put it on the coffee table.

He reached for her again, hands stroking her collarbone and throat and dropping down farther. When he kissed her again, it was like an explosion. Reg's senses reeled. She was drowning. She pushed back against him, wanting to stop and yet to go both at the same time.

Corvin broke the kiss, but he didn't let go or back away, his face filling her vision, his eyes wide, dark, hungry pits she couldn't see the bottom of.

"Yield to me," he murmured.

Reg took a deep breath.

"Yes."

★ Chapter Twenty-Three ★

S HE AWOKE SLOWLY, DISORIENTED, feeling as though she had never slept so deeply in her life. She opened her eyes and looked around the tidy cottage bedroom with its pristine white sheets and coverlet, the smell of the sea breeze blowing in the window. It was bright, the full light of morning. Her body was relaxed and sated and all of the fog and fatigue gone from her mind. It was as if everything were suddenly crystal clear.

Reg reached across the bed for Corvin, but he wasn't there. Reg sat up and looked around, holding the blanket to her chest to keep herself covered. Had he gone? Left her there alone?

There was something wrong.

She was only vaguely aware of it at first, but it slowly spread through her.

She thought at first that she had lost her hearing. Everything was so quiet, like stepping into an empty theater.

But she could hear the pulsing of her heart. The shifting of the sheets as she moved. The waves lapping at the shore, where she still hadn't gone to gather seashells. She could hear birds outside and the buzzing of bugs.

But something was missing.

Reg slid out of bed and pulled on her housecoat. She belted it around her waist and left the bedroom.

Corvin was sitting on one of the chairs in the living room, sipping a cup of tea and looking down at the locket in his hand. Reg remembered how he hadn't been able to touch it the night before, and her stomach tied itself in a knot.

What had she done?

Corvin turned and looked at Reg, though she was sure she hadn't made any sound or movement to attract his attention.

"There's my sleeping beauty," he said. "How are you feeling this morning?"

His voice echoed in her head. It was too loud. She wanted to cover her ears.

"I... I don't know..."

Her own voice too was too loud. It was as if the room were in a great, yawning silence, only she could hear everything. Reg's nerves jangled at every sound. She jumped at every movement. The room seemed to echo with its emptiness.

"Would you like some tea? Some breakfast?" Corvin inquired.

"No. I don't think so."

He stared down at the tea in his cup. His eyes were big and bright. He almost purred with contentment.

Something had definitely changed. She had changed something.

Corvin cocked his head as if listening to something. "They're very loud," he said. "I don't know how you could shut them out."

And then in a rush, Reg realized what was wrong. They were all gone. The voices. The memories from Warren. The presences from the other side. It wasn't the room that was empty, it was her head.

She stared at Warren, wide-eyed.

"What have you done?"

He smiled like the cat who had swallowed a canary. Reg looked around the room, feeling rudderless. It was like she was alone in her own head for the first time in her life.

Starlight yowled to be let out.

Like a zombie, Reg walked to the spare room door and opened it. Starlight pushed his way out. He rubbed against her leg, looking up at her. Then he sat back and washed his whiskers. He advanced into the kitchen and looked over at

Corvin. He looked back at Reg. His glare was like an accusation.

"And now the fun begins," Corvin intoned.

Reg looked at him, no idea what he meant. There was a brisk knock at the door, and the handle turned, but it was bolted from the night before, so there was a soft thud on the door when Sarah had expected it to open and instead ran into it. Reg looked at Corvin and didn't move.

"She's not going to go away," he told her.

It took a long time for Reg to get her feet moving. She shuffled over to the door and slid the bolt. She opened the door.

Sarah took one look at Reg and color rushed to her cheeks. Her eyes snapped. She entered the room and looked around for Corvin.

"You beast! How could you do such a thing? I'll have you before your coven!"

Corvin smirked. "I had her consent. I haven't broken any rules."

Sarah turned her head to look at Reg. "You gave him your powers willingly?"

"I..." Reg tried to make sense of their conversations and what had happened the previous night. "I don't know. I guess... I did. I don't really remember..."

"He glamoured you."

Sarah looked at Corvin, who was casually swinging the locket by its chain. Scowling even more deeply, she strode over to him and snatched it from his hand.

"That is not yours."

"I didn't break the ward."

"No," Sarah agreed, shooting a look at Reg. "I did everything I could to protect you. I told you that you were playing with fire. Why would you break the protections I put in place? You brought him into your house. You removed the ward. Why?"

Reg hugged herself. There was a yawning emptiness in her, like she was hungry, but it wasn't hunger. She felt naked and vulnerable in front of Corvin and Sarah, and it wasn't because all she had on was the housecoat. "I didn't know!"

"You had to know. You had to give him leave!" Sarah sent another accusing glare in Corvin's direction.

"She expressed a wish to give up her powers," Corvin said smoothly. "She invited me in, broke the ward, and yielded them up. What more do you want from me?"

"I didn't understand," Reg protested. She closed her eyes and covered her ears, trying to reset the silence in her head. It was like the feeling of her ears being blocked after swimming or flying, waiting for them to pop and restore her hearing. She knew it wasn't physical, but she didn't know what to do. "He tricked me!"

"Well, what did you expect from a warlock?" Sarah said scathingly. "I told you he was dangerous. You thought he would be honest with you about his intentions?"

"I didn't... I never even knew it was possible..."

"All the more reason to be careful and listen to your elders! You played the part of a willful child and look what happened!"

Reg just wanted to fold up into herself and disappear. "I'm sorry. What am I supposed to do? How do I...?"

Sarah looked at Corvin. He shook his head.

"No. She's not getting them back. I gave her what she wanted, she gave me what I wanted. It was a fair exchange."

"It's never a fair exchange with one like you." Sarah turned back to Reg. "He would have to restore them willingly, of his own free choice. No one can force him or take them from him. And these soul-suckers never give them back by choice."

Reg rubbed her eyes. What had she done? How could she have been so naive and stupid? She had thought that he liked her, that he felt as passionately toward her as she did toward him, but his attraction was just like the sweet scent of a predatory plant, luring insects into its depths to be consumed.

She didn't know how she was going to manage with everything in her head suddenly so quiet. It was like waking up and finding her legs had been amputated. How did people manage day-to-day decisions and life without guiding whispers in their heads?

Corvin drank the last sip of his tea and studied the leaves in the bottom.

"I need to talk to Reg privately," he told Sarah.

"So you can take advantage of her more?" Sarah accused.

"What else is there to take from her?" Corvin countered unsympathetically, raising his brows.

Sarah looked at Reg, waiting for her to object. But Reg had nothing else to say to her. It was hopeless. What Corvin had taken from her would never be restored.

Sarah shook her head, shot one more dark look at Corvin, and turned toward the door.

"Don't run away," she told Reg. "Stay here until you get your bearings again. Don't leave without talking to me first, understand? I don't want you disappearing. I have some things to do, but I'll be back."

Reg sat down on the couch, clutching her head. How did Sarah know that was exactly what Reg wanted to do? She wanted to get in her car and drive away and leave Black Sands and Corvin Hunter far behind her.

Then Sarah was gone. Reg was once again alone with Corvin, but this time she felt no attraction to him. She felt violated and bereft.

Corvin closed his eyes for a moment, then opened them and looked at her. "All of these images... these memories... they're from Warren?"

Reg nodded slowly. "When he was getting too tired... I tried to get all he could give me before the connection broke... I thought it would make more sense than trying to explain it all with words."

"It's all a jumble. I can't figure out what is what."

"Yeah." Reg breathed shallowly. "I was trying to get it into some kind of order... but it's like a jigsaw puzzle... I wasn't having much success." She raised her eyes to him. "But you know Black Sands better than I do. Do you know the places in his memories…? They must have some meaning to you."

"It's a lot more to manage than I expected," Corvin said. "It's going to take me some time to integrate everything properly…" He smiled. "You didn't think you were very gifted. You thought it was just a little intuition, a little imagination…"

"Uh-huh."

"You sold yourself short. You had very powerful psychic gifts. So much more than I was expecting."

Tears started to leak out of Reg's eyes. She was powerless to stop them. She'd had something. She'd had a gift, and she'd thrown it carelessly away. She hadn't had any idea what it was like to live like a normal person. How incredibly lonely and isolating it was.

"Tell me your ritual for contacting the dead," Corvin instructed.

Reg shook her head and sighed. "Nothing special… just have a cup of tea with the client… ask a few questions about the person who died to get a good feeling for them. And then… reach out with my mind and… feel for them…"

"Is there anyone *you* would like to talk to?"

"No." Reg's head had been full of dead people. They had talked to her all the time. She'd never had the need to seek one of them out for her own purposes. They were always there.

"Tell me about… Polly."

"Just a little girl I used to play with. I didn't ever know her when she was alive. She just… lived near me when I was little. Or… died near me."

"Who is Norma Jean?"

"Who?"

"She has a very strong attachment to you," Corvin said. "She watches over you. Did you want to talk to her?"

"No."

Corvin's eyes rolled up so that only the whites were visible. "Well, look at you," he said in a breathy voice. "Is this little Regina? All grown up?"

There was a lump in Reg's throat. The cadence and accent were so familiar. They had lived in the corner of her mind for almost as long as she could remember, but it had been many years since she had heard it in life.

"Norma Jean…?" she said tentatively.

"You can call me momma," the voice said, "my dear, sweet girl."

"No, stop!" Reg told Corvin urgently. She grabbed his arm and shook him to bring him out of it. "I don't want to talk to her!"

Corvin went rigid. It was a moment before he opened his eyes and looked at her.

"Your mother?" he asked.

"I never knew my mother," Reg said. "She died when I was just a little girl. I don't want to talk to her or anyone else."

He chuckled. "A little disconcerting to be on the other side of the reading?"

"Just leave me alone. I don't want to talk to anyone."

"I'm just trying to figure it out. How you used these gifts… what I can do now."

"Why don't you just go away? Go back to your house and leave me alone."

"I couldn't do that. Then I would miss your visitor."

"What visitor?" Reg demanded, worried about Corvin channeling someone else she knew.

"The one who's going to be here in a few minutes."

★ Chapter Twenty-Four ★

R E G   H A D   L O N G   B E E N   able to predict the unpredictable. She just knew when things were going to happen. She knew when the phone was going to ring before it did. She knew when she was going to get moved to another family, though probably anyone with a little experience could have worked that out. Other things, like what cards she was likely to pick up in a poker game or what song was going to play on the radio next. She just took it for granted, assuming everyone had similar experiences. Like deja vu.

It wasn't until Corvin said she had a visitor coming that she realized she would have known that, if she'd still had her powers. Instead of a sense of knowing what was coming, there was a blank. Just nothing but the emptiness of eternity.

They both sat there for a few minutes in silence, Corvin listening to the voices now in his head, and Reg listening to the expanding silence. She would sooner die than listen to that silence for the rest of her life.

There were footsteps on the cobbles outside the door, amplified by the quiet of the room. Reg got up to get the door, not sure what else to do.

"Be careful," Corvin warned suddenly. "Do not tell him anything."

"Who…?"

"Keep it under wraps," Corvin insisted. "Don't tell him what you—we—know."

There was a hard knock on the door. Reg knew what that knock meant without any gift of prescience. Cops.

She opened the door, expecting Jessup and her partner, but she only saw Jessup's partner. The man whose name she could not remember. She studied his name bar. The letters still swam. Apparently, her learning disabilities were not tied to her gifts. It was something she had wondered.

Hawthorne-Rose. Officer Hawthorne-Rose.

"Uh… yes? Can I help you?" She didn't invite him in.

"I'd like to talk to you, Miss Rawlins."

"Go ahead."

"I'd like to come in."

Invite me in.

She really didn't want men intruding on her space. She should have told Corvin to take a hike the night before. She should have gone home, left him at the restaurant or in the yard outside with no way to get in, and gone to bed.

"It's not a good time."

Why didn't Corvin want her to tell Hawthorne-Rose anything? Was he involved in Warren's accident after all? Had Reg's first instinct about the cloaked man been right? Had it been another manifestation of her gift, not just a random connection?

"I'm afraid I'm going to have to insist," Hawthorne-Rose said. He put his foot in the door and put his shoulder to it, pushing it open the rest of the way. He didn't need to be invited in. Had Sarah's spell only been to keep Corvin out? Or had Reg broken it when she had let Corvin in?

Hawthorne-Rose looked around suspiciously. He saw Corvin sitting there and his eyes narrowed.

"What business do you have here?" he demanded.

"I could ask you the same," Corvin said mildly.

Hawthorne-Rose took a walk around the living room and kitchen, peering back into the bedrooms to make sure that it was just the three of them.

"Where's Detective Jessup?" Reg asked, uncomfortable with the two men in the cottage. She would feel a lot better if there were another feminine presence to balance them out. Corvin and Hawthorne-Rose both felt predatory, with Reg playing the part of the prey trying to stay away from their claws.

"Detective Jessup is… tied up. She asked me to come over to get some more information from you."

"I don't know any more than I did the last time you came over," Reg insisted, wrapping her arms around herself. Why hadn't she dressed as soon as she got out of bed? She felt exposed.

"You're the psychic," Hawthorne-Rose said, stepping closer to Reg. She fell back, trying to put more space between them. He pursued.

"No," Reg insisted. And it was true, she no longer was a psychic. All the psychic power she had possessed was gone. "I play people. Cold read them. Tell them what they want to hear. I don't have any real powers."

Hawthorne-Rose sneered. He grabbed Reg's arm and jerked her up close to himself. "Don't mess with me, girl."

Reg gasped and tried to jerk out of his grip. She hadn't been expecting any physical intimidation. Corvin jumped to his feet. He knocked over a sheaf of Reg's flyers and sent them skating across the floor. But they didn't stop like they should. They took flight and swirled around Hawthorne-Rose and Reg in a mini-tornado. Reg covered her face. Hawthorne-Rose batted at them, catching some and knocking others to the ground, until the flyer tornado was gone. Reg frowned at Corvin. That wasn't one of her powers. She couldn't move things with her mind.

Something niggled in the back of her brain. She remembered that day with Erin, stealing the cans and bottles from neighbors' back yards. Reg had grabbed a couple of garbage bags and had left Erin to pick up the plastic bin. But Erin, gawky and awkward, had tripped and fallen with the bin, sending cans and bottles flying, bound to alert the entire neighborhood to what was going on when they crashed everywhere. Reg had seen what was happening, had reached for Erin and the box, and had prevented the cans and bottles from flying, settling them back into place in the bin without being able to reach them. An impossibility. There had been other times. Times when she thought it would be funny if a paper skittered away or a bully tripped over his own untied shoelaces, and somehow, what she had imagined had happened.

But she couldn't control things with her mind. That wasn't possible. If she had once been able to, she had now given those powers to Corvin, and his little flurry of papers was not enough to deter Hawthorne-Rose from his purposes.

The policeman glared at Reg as if the papers had been her fault. He crumpled and threw away the ones he had caught out of the air, and again grabbed her, even more roughly.

"Enough of that!" he growled. "Do you think this is a game? I want answers out of you. Real answers!"

"I told you what I knew already," Reg protested, trying to pull out of his grip.

"You're going to tell me more."

Reg shook her head.

"What did Warren tell you?"

Reg swallowed. "Warren was unconscious the whole time I was there. He couldn't say anything."

"Do you think I don't know that?"

Reg shook her head, confused.

"I know he was unconscious," Hawthorne-Rose said sharply. "You told me that. But he still communicated with you." He grabbed her chin, staring into her eyes and not allowing her to look away from him. "Tell me what he told you."

Reg swallowed. She thought of Corvin's words before Hawthorne-Rose came in. *Do not tell him anything.*

"Nothing." She tried to shake her head, even though he still held her in his grip. "How could he?"

"I know what you are and I have heard what you do. I know you communicated with him, and I want to know everything he told you."

"Where's Detective Jessup?"

"Detective Jessup isn't coming. She can't help you this time."

This time? How had Jessup helped her before? She hadn't done anything for Reg. She had asked questions, and Reg had done her best to answer them, but there had been no real trouble. Hawthorne-Rose had stayed in the background while Jessup had talked to Reg.

Hawthorne-Rose pushed Reg back until her back was against the wall. His hand slipped down, and rather than holding her chin, his hand was clamped under her jaw against her throat, threatening to choke her.

"What did he tell you?"

"She doesn't know anything," Corvin said. "Leave her alone."

Hawthorne-Rose turned his head. "Shut up, witch."

Hawthorne-Rose had shifted his position enough for Reg to see Corvin over his shoulder. Corvin's face flushed red. Reg didn't know if he was angry or embarrassed at being called a witch. Was it a slur?

Did Hawthorne-Rose know that Corvin was a warlock? And believe it? When they had visited before, Reg had thought both officers were unbelievers. Reg had done her best to convince them that what she was telling them was legitimate, but neither had acted like they believed anything she said.

Had Hawthorne-Rose been acting the whole time? Had he believed what Reg had been trying to tell them? Had he ditched his unbelieving partner and come back for more details?

"You said he gave you pictures," Hawthorne-Rose reminded Reg. "I want them."

"Not... physical pictures. Not like photographs. Pictures in my mind."

Corvin had said not to tell Hawthorne-Rose anything, but this was something Hawthorne-Rose already knew.

"I know that," Hawthorne-Rose growled. He pressed his hand into Reg's throat. "Give them to me."

"I... I can't!" Reg's voice squeaked higher. Even before Corvin had taken them away, she wouldn't have known how to share them with Hawthorne-Rose. She had been good at channeling the dead, and apparently even those who were unconscious, but telepathy with the living was much harder. It wasn't like a Vulcan mind-meld on Star Trek. There were natural barriers. It would have been difficult to simply share the mental pictures with Hawthorne-Rose.

He squeezed her throat, cutting off her air. Reg reached up and grabbed his hand, desperate to pull it away and to breathe. But he was too strong for her.

"Let her go!" Corvin ordered. But he didn't offer to Hawthorne-Rose that he was now the possessor of the memories. *Don't tell him what we know.*

Corvin moved forward like he would attack Hawthorne-Rose, but stalled in his tracks. Hawthorne-Rose barely gave him a glance. He was completely focused on Reg.

"Give them to me."

Reg struggled for breath. The room started to go black. Hawthorne-Rose released his hold, letting her breathe. Reg sucked in oxygen, trying to kickstart her brain and understand what was going on. This wasn't a police interrogation. She'd dealt with her share of angry police officers in the past, but Hawthorne-Rose's actions didn't fit any of the established patterns. This was something else altogether.

It was then she felt Hawthorne-Rose pushing against her thoughts. He was inside her brain, banging clumsily up against her mental barriers, searching for the information. Even worse than what Corvin had done, tricking her out of her powers, he intended to take Warren's memories from her by force.

He wasn't just a believer, he was a practitioner.

Reg tried to push back against the intrusion, but without her powers she felt as weak as a newborn mouse. Corvin held all of her strength to resist such an assault.

She looked past Hawthorne-Rose at Corvin. He was obviously struggling, trying to get past some barrier or spell Hawthorne-Rose had put up. But he had no experience with psychic powers and how to wield what he had stolen from

Reg. She tried to communicate her thoughts to him, forgetting once again that she no longer had that ability.

She struggled even to read his expression. For so many years, she believed that her ability to cold-read someone was a skill that she had developed and honed, something anyone could do with some effort. In all that time, it had never occurred to her that her ability to read someone had really been a psychic gift.

One that could be taken away from her.

"Get out!" Reg told Hawthorne-Rose through gritted teeth. She tried to push back against him physically, unable to do it mentally. "Get out of my head!"

He swore under his breath. "Where is it?" he demanded, pressing against her throat again. Reg struggled, unable to push him off of her.

Hawthorne-Rose released his grip on her for a moment, but it wasn't to give her a chance to reconsider and answer him. He bent down and scratched at his ankle, which Reg through was a bizarre thing for him to take a break for, until she saw him straighten back up with a knife in his hand.

"You need a bigger incentive?" he demanded.

Reg panicked and tried to break away from him. He pressed her against the wall with his body and stretched her right arm out beside her. He pressed the knife tip against her palm, holding it against the wall. She felt like a butterfly being pinned to a display board.

"Let's read your lifeline, shall we?" Hawthorne-Rose sneered, pressing the knife harder. "I'm thinking I might shorten it a little." Reg felt him start to cut into the flesh of her hand and thrashed, trying to break free.

But he was strong and had a good hold on her. He wasn't going to let her go until he had what he wanted.

"Stop," Corvin begged in a strained voice. "Please don't hurt her. I can get her to talk."

Hawthorne-Rose didn't stop immediately. He rocked the knife, drilling it in deeper. Reg cried out. Her body convulsed. The room grayed at the edges.

"What makes you think you can get further with her than I can?" Hawthorne-Rose demanded. "I'm pretty persuasive."

"I can do it," Corvin insisted. "I know how to convince her."

Reg blinked, trying to bring the world back into focus. She tried to read his face, but felt like she was suddenly blind. What would have been so easy before he took her powers seemed an insurmountable task. She had no idea what his plan was. It had to be a trick; after all, Corvin could have just given Hawthorne-Rose the information he was looking for.

Hawthorne-Rose considered. After a long pause, he pulled the knife back and motioned Corvin closer with the bloody blade. "You've got two minutes to convince this little gypsy to give it up before I start cutting her again. You'd better be good."

He stepped back, releasing Reg's body. She just about fell to her knees, she was so weak and frightened. Hawthorne-Rose appeared to have released Corvin as well, and Corvin stepped quickly forward, slotting himself between Reg and Hawthorne-Rose, catching her drooping body and holding her up. Reg held on to him, desperate, but with no idea how he was going to save her from the dirty cop.

Their faces were only inches apart.

"Trust me," Corvin mouthed, making no sound.

Reg just stared at him, frozen. Corvin leaned in, exuding the scent of roses, and kissed her.

At first she struggled, repulsed, wanting nothing to do with him again. He had stolen her powers. He had violated her. Despite his glamour, she didn't want the intimacy with him that she had craved just hours before.

But as her brain flooded with images, she realized what he was doing. He was willingly returning her gifts.

Reg clutched herself to him, ignoring the pain in her hand. She drank back the psychic powers she had spent her life fighting against.

For a few moments, there was equilibrium between them, when they both had a portion of the powers, and could communicate with each other clearly without any need for words. Corvin was clumsy with the unfamiliar gifts, his thoughts painfully loud in Reg's head. She struggled to temper them and to understand what he knew. His own magical gifts and powers were just as unfamiliar to her as her gifts were to him, but during that brief contact, she learned all she could of them and how they could work in concert.

★ Chapter Twenty-Five ★

ORVIN BROKE THE KISS, and for a few seconds, they just stared into each other's eyes as they each adjusted to being separate again.

"You can do it, Regina," Corvin whispered.

Reg took a few deep breaths, trying to calm and focus her whirling brain. If they were going to get themselves out of there, she needed to be on top of her game.

"Alright," Hawthorne-Rose snapped, stepping in and shoving Corvin away from Reg, "That's enough." He stared at Reg, his dark eyes full of malice. "Are you ready to give them to me now?"

Reg swallowed. "I need my cat."

"What?"

"My familiar."

Hawthorne-Rose looked around and saw Starlight sitting on his haunches, watching everything. He jerked his head for Reg to go get her pet.

Reg stepped unsteadily away from the wall and went to Starlight. Her legs felt like jelly. She scooped Starlight up into her arms and buried her face in his fur. Newly sensitized, she could feel the warm, familiar, psychic energy he exuded.

She sat down with him on one of the wicker chairs.

"I need your help," she whispered to him.

He purred and licked her hand, his long tongue rasping over the place where Hawthorne-Rose had cut her. The pulsing pain eased. Reg petted Starlight and scratched his ears and chin, staring into his mismatched eyes while at the same time focusing on the white spot in the middle of his forehead. Together, they almost buzzed with energy. Reg pushed the memories from Warren into a quiet corner of her brain and turned her thoughts to Hawthorne-Rose.

He stiffened, his attention riveting on Reg.

His mind was immediately probing inside her own, eager for the information Warren had given her. As she had just done with Corvin, Reg shared the connection he had opened up and used it to delve into Hawthorne-Rose's own consciousness. She was careful not to push too hard, hoping not to tip him off as to what she was doing. She saw again the men Warren had remembered, but their faces were clear instead of being obscured. Reg saw that the man in the long black coat was not Corvin, but another face that was vaguely familiar. She thought for an instant that it was Hawthorne-Rose himself, but it wasn't.

She had seen him somewhere. At the restaurant Corvin had taken her to? They hadn't seen anyone but waiters and other staff at the Eagle Arms. The man in the coat was not a waiter or valet, and he hadn't been dressed white tie like Corvin had been.

She replayed it in her head. The man tossing back a drink. Taking her hand.

Reg dug her fingers into Starlight's fur, trying to unlock the identity of the man. She felt Starlight's consciousness with hers inside Hawthorne-Rose's head, and then a flash of knowledge. Uriel.

Not from the Eagle Arms, but from The Crystal Bowl, the first day she had arrived. He had talked about setting his own rules. Not being constrained by others. Just the type of person she would expect to be working around the law and the accepted rules of the community.

She felt the first stirrings of resistance. Hawthorne-Rose realizing that she was snooping around in his brain while he was searching hers. His body jolted and he said "no" out loud.

Reg didn't know how long it would take Corvin to weave his spell. She dug in, not letting Hawthorne-Rose push her out. He had withdrawn from her mind and was trying to close the connection. She had no experience in keeping open a connection the subject wanted closed, but she fought him the best she could, like two people on opposite sides of a door, one trying to pull it closed while the other pulled to keep it open. Starlight prowled around her consciousness, helping to strengthen the connection. She'd had no idea that the little cat had such a strong psychic gift.

"No," Hawthorne-Rose said again, fighting to shake her off. She tried to see Corvin out of her peripheral vision, wondering how he was doing, but she couldn't see or feel him.

"Okay, Reg," Corvin said. "I've got him."

Reg let the connection slide away from her. Hawthorne-Rose was breathing heavily, glaring at her.

"What just happened?" he demanded.

Reg raised an eyebrow innocently. "What?" She straightened her housecoat, once more feeling confident in her own skin. She was whole again, the theft of her powers a fading memory.

Starlight kneaded Reg's leg, his claws pricking her and then withdrawing several times. He purred and blinked one eye at her.

Reg was expecting to be tired, but maybe using Starlight to boost her signal or sleeping soundly while Corvin held her powers had renewed her strength.

Hawthorne-Rose took a step toward Reg, looking threatening. He gripped the knife tightly in his hand, his eyes were fixed on her. Then he looked down at his foot, as if he had stepped in something. He wiggled it experimentally. He jerked toward her and then stopped. His gaze turned instead to Corvin.

"You."

Corvin blinked. "Yes?"

"Release me."

"Uh… no. I don't think I will. Regina has the right to protect herself in her own home."

"This is not her."

"She asked for my aid to set the ward."

"I was already in the house. You cannot set a ward against someone who is already in it!"

"Hmm…" Corvin pondered this. "No… it seems to me there were some exceptions to that rule. Something like… if you raised your hand in violence against the homeowner…"

Hawthorne-Rose's face turned a deep shade of purple, but despite his best efforts, he seemed unable to move from the spot. Reg let out a sigh of relief.

"What did you find?" Corvin asked Reg. "Anything?"

She nodded. "There was a man at The Crystal Bowl. His name was Uriel…?"

Corvin nodded. "Uriel Hawthorne," he agreed.

"Hawthorne?"

"It's not an uncommon name in our community. There were Hawthornes in Salem. But it's possible that…"

They both looked at Hawthorne-Rose. He turned his face away from Reg.

"Is he related?" Reg asked. "It felt like… you were quite close."

"You didn't have any right to—"

"Well, I don't know all of the rules," Reg said sweetly. "You'll have to explain them to me. But you did threaten me and force your connection on me, didn't you? I just… used it for myself."

He closed his eyes and Reg could feel the energy rolling off of him, like heat waves from an open oven. She looked at Corvin, worried.

"What's he doing?" Corvin asked.

"It's… I think… he's warning Uriel." Reg looked around, panicking. "Uriel is close by!"

Corvin swore. He darted out the door of the cottage. Reg looked at Hawthorne-Rose to make sure that he wasn't freed by Corvin leaving, but he still seemed to be firmly rooted in place. Reg looked out the windows, but couldn't get a clear view of Corvin or Uriel. She could hear yelling and crashing around, but she couldn't very well go out and try to help to subdue Uriel with nothing but a bathrobe on. She hurried into her bedroom and started to pull on clothes as quickly as she could. By the time she had shirt and pants on and went back out to the living room, wrapping a bandage around her throbbing hand, Corvin was coming in the door, wrestling Uriel in with him.

Uriel was taller, but Corvin had more weight and bulk, and managed to wrestle Uriel into a chokehold, the taller man forced down to his knees.

"Now then," Corvin growled, "who wants to explain what's going on here?"

Uriel and Hawthorne-Rose glared at each other, both defensive and self-righteous.

"You said you could handle her," Uriel shouted at Hawthorne-Rose. "Just a girl with a little clairvoyance. No trouble at all."

'He wasn't supposed to be here. How could I have predicted that? And the cat."

"So, what, it was three against one? What good is it to have someone in the police department if he's completely inept? A girl with hardly any powers. And a cat."

"And a warlock! In case you didn't notice, he's a bit of a problem!" Hawthorne-Rose shot back.

Corvin pulled Uriel's head back in order to smirk down at him.

"I held him to start with, but then she…" Hawthorne-Rose looked at Reg, shaking his head. "She's no novice, Uriel. She's much stronger and more skilled than you led me to believe."

Corvin looked back and forth between the two intruders. "And which one of you is binding Warren? Or is it someone else?"

Neither of them answered. They kept their faces masked, careful not to give it away. Reg picked Starlight up again and thought about Warren. She felt for his consciousness, and then felt for a connection back to one of the men, for the binding spell that one of them held over him even now.

"It's Uriel."

He looked at her, furious.

"Can you break it?" Corvin asked.

"I... I don't know how." Reg swallowed. Sarah had said that there was more than one way to break the binding spell, so she was pretty sure that she didn't have to kill him to do it. She looked back toward the main house. Was Sarah even home? She had said she was going out and Reg didn't know how much time had passed since then.

Corvin closed his eyes. Reg didn't know if it was in frustration, or if he was trying to think of a course of action. She waited. Uriel tried to twist away from Corvin to free himself, but Corvin tightened his grip.

"If we can get into Uriel's lair, I might be able to figure out how he cast the spell in order to counter it."

Uriel showed no concern over this suggestion. Reg guessed that no one knew where his lair was or that it was protected by enough wards he had no fear of anyone breaking into it.

"Do you want me... to find out where it is?" Reg suggested. She loathed the idea of trying to get information from Uriel against his will, just as Hawthorne-Rose had just tried to do to her, but she couldn't think of any other way to break the spell.

Corvin nodded. "If you can... that would probably be the most humane way. Otherwise... we're going to have to get our hands dirty."

Reg looked down at her bandaged hand. She didn't want to be driven to torture. And Corvin had talked to her about karma, how committing violence against someone else would return to her.

"Okay. I'll try."

"You can't do that!" Hawthorne-Rose shouted at her. "There are rules about using telepathy without a person's permission!"

Reg stared at him in disbelief. "And what was it when you did it to me?"

"That was a police investigation. That's different."

"I don't think so!" Reg opened her mouth to marshal her arguments, then realized that she was letting him distract her.

Maybe with extra time, they could get someone else's help or Uriel could create some kind of barrier. Or maybe Uriel could use the connection he had with Warren to kill him before they could get there to help him. Could he do that? Reg had seen things like that on TV. If someone dreamed they died, they would die in real life, wouldn't they?

She turned deliberately away from Hawthorne-Rose and looked at Uriel. He again tried to break away from Corvin's grasp and get up, but Corvin wasn't letting him go. Reg didn't know if he was able to bind Uriel as he had bound Hawthorne-Rose, but he didn't seem to need to. For the present, both men were under Corvin's control.

Reg sat down with Starlight. She entered Uriel's consciousness, pushing through his defenses, and tried to find an image of his lair. What would it be like? A mad scientist's laboratory? A basement dungeon? A bright and cheery kitchen? It had to be somewhere important to him, somewhere that he spent a lot of time. If he was a powerful warlock, he had to spend time on his craft.

She saw crates of supplies, and stopped for a look. Magical ingredients and artifacts to create potions or cast certain types of spells? As soon as she started to explore the crates in his mind, she felt resistance. Uriel did not like that. He did not want her there. She smoothed the short fur over Starlight's white spot, pushing harder mentally. She could feel Starlight's consciousness there with her, curious about what she had found. The crates contained animals and animal parts. They seemed to be cloaked in darkness, and filled Reg with sadness when she saw them.

But she was supposed to be looking for his lair. They needed a way to break the binding spell. When she thought of Warren and the binding spell, she felt Starlight's attention slide in another direction. She tried to reconnect with him, to stay with him, redirecting him back to the crates and where Uriel's lair might be.

Starlight pulled away again, so Reg followed. The cat had been a good partner; maybe he had an instinct about Uriel that Reg didn't.

She again felt the connection between Warren and Uriel. The binding spell. It felt thick and strong. She explored it for a few minutes, trying to find weak points. Did magic have to be broken with magic, or could her psychic gifts break a magic spell? She tested her strength against the binding spell, and it gave more than she expected. She gathered Starlight's consciousness and tried to direct it toward the binding spell along with her own.

Uriel began to buck and fight against Corvin. Corvin nearly lost his grip. Reg tried to ignore their physical struggle and continued to push against the binding spell. She imagined Starlight's teeth and claws shredding at the thick cord, fraying it and cutting their way through it. Starlight made a deep rumbling; Reg wasn't sure whether it was a purr or a snarl. She held him firmly and applied her own mind against the spell, bringing out a mental arsenal of scissors, knives, and anything else she could think of that would be used to cut a strong cord.

Uriel was howling. Corvin still fought to keep him under control. Reg worried that if Corvin put too much effort into fighting Uriel that his binding spell on Hawthorne-Rose would be broken, but it continued to hold.

Uriel's spell on Warren was getting thinner and more strained. Reg pictured it as a thread of dental floss; thin and very strong. But a thread like that was not strong enough over such a long distance, and she could just put it between her teeth and break it off. She braced herself and gave it a single, violent pull.

Uriel cried out again and slumped over. Reg opened her eyes and stared at him. Corvin was trying to hold on to him and to see his face at the same time to see if he was playing a trick. Reg shook her head.

"He's out."

Corvin laid Uriel out on the floor. Hawthorne-Rose was no longer complaining. His face was as white as chalk. Reg let Starlight go, and went over to Uriel, worried.

"Is he okay? I didn't... I didn't go too far, did I? I didn't want to harm him."

Corvin put his fingers over Uriel's pulse and shrugged. "Good, strong heartbeat. I'm not one of those for seeing or feeling auras…" he made sweeping motions over Uriel's body to demonstrate. "But physically, he seems fine."

Reg tested her connection with Uriel. It was still there, but he was no longer fighting and resisting her. She didn't sense any pain. She explored, feeling for the binding spell, but couldn't find it.

"Hold on…" she told Corvin, though what he was supposed to do or stop doing, she wasn't sure. She felt for Warren's consciousness, but couldn't find it. Did that mean he was dead? Had severing the binding spell meant severing Warren's tenuous hold on life as well? But if he were dead, she was sure she would have been able to contact his spirit. She'd made contact with him several times, and it had gotten easier every time.

Warren.

She called out to him, but wasn't getting any response. Reg looked at Starlight. He washed his whiskers, unconcerned.

She closed her eyes and concentrated. Finally, Reg bumped up against Warren's consciousness. She let out her breath in a sigh of relief, and tried to channel him. But the doors were closed. There was too much resistance.

Reg opened her eyes. "He's awake!"

Corvin looked over at Uriel, who was still unconscious.

"No—Warren. Warren is awake."

★ Chapter Twenty-Six ★

T HEY LEFT HAWTHORNE-ROSE bound by
Corvin's spell and Uriel bound with twine they had
found in one of the kitchen drawers, and headed over
to McNara. Corvin's big car was still at the Eagle Arms, so
they climbed into Reg's. Corvin couldn't very well complain
that it was too small for him, as Reg had already seen his little
compact the day she and the witches had gone looking for
Warren. And he couldn't complain that she was a bad driver,
not considering how Sarah drove. But he still didn't look
comfortable sitting in the passenger's seat. Reg guessed that
he liked to be the one in control.

She understood the sentiment.

She didn't get there as quickly as Sarah would have, but
they still made pretty good time. They ignored the reception
desk and the confused receptionist calling after them to stop
and check in properly. Reg wondered if all of Uriel's spells
were breaking with the severing of the binding spell. Would
all of the nursing staff at McNara be wondering who the
young man in room 180 was and what he was doing there?

They burst into Warren's room, worried and out of
breath. Warren appeared to be sleeping, but he stirred and
opened his eyes at their noisy entrance.

"Oh. Hello."

While Reg was happy to see that he was still there, and
that he was well, she had been hoping to find Ling there with
him. And maybe Jessup too, busy taking their statements. But
other than Warren and the machines, the room was empty.

"Do you remember me?" Reg asked.

He gazed at her, brows down. "I don't know… you seem sort of familiar…"

"My friends and I talked to you before. When you were… unconscious." Reg didn't want to say that he had been dead or in a coma. Unconscious seemed more tactful.

"Oh… I'm sorry, I don't… I don't remember why I'm here."

"You were in an accident. Your airplane. But you're okay now."

"Right." He nodded along, as if that made perfect sense.

"Do you know where Ling went?" Reg asked.

Warren blinked a few times, thinking about it. He looked around the room as if looking for clues.

"Ling… she was here."

"Today? When you woke up?"

"No. When I woke up… I was alone."

"The men who you were dealing with, that transportation job, do you know where their warehouse is? Or where they live? Anything?"

"The warehouse…" Warren sounded like he was coming out of a dream.

"With all of the crates," Reg suggested. "Do you remember the crates he wanted you to transport?"

She had seen the crates in Warren's memories. She had seen them in Uriel's. They were important. She needed to find out where they were. If Uriel and his band of thieves had kidnapped Ling and Jessup, that seemed the most likely place to hide them.

"Yes," Warren sat up. He rubbed his eyes. "Yes, I picked things up from the warehouse that needed transportation. But why would Ling be there?"

Reg looked around the room. "Do you have something to wear? We need to go check it out right now."

She and Corvin went through the drawers and little cupboard locker in the hospital room, but didn't find any street clothes for Warren. Reg bit her lip and offered him a second hospital johnny. "Here, just put this one on back to front, and then you'll be covered up. We don't have time to find anything else."

Warren frowned, but seemed to be picking up on her sense of urgency, and after carefully removing the various tubes and machines, pulled the second robe on.

"What happened? Can you tell me?"

"You told those guys that you weren't going to smuggle whatever it was they were trying to transport. They crashed your plane and... knocked you unconscious. You've been here since then. Ling came to see you, and she disappeared. I think... I think they got her too. That's why we need to go back there to see."

Warren nodded, eyes wide. "I knew there was something off about those guys. There were just too many unanswered questions. And the way they would huddle together to discuss things, and then the conversations would stop dead when I walked into the room. It was obvious they had something to hide."

They hustled Warren past the nursing station desk and past the reception area without stopping to explain where they were going and how their coma patient was suddenly up and walking around. Before the hospital had a chance to get security to try to stop them, they were out to the parking lot and piling into the car.

"I really should have signed their papers..." Warren said, looking back.

"You can go back and sign them later."

"Yeah..."

Reg was feeling more and more anxious. The longer it was, the better the chances were that Uriel and Hawthorne-Rose would be able to get out of their bonds or summon their troops for rescue, and then they would all be riding toward the same destination, ready for a fight. Corvin and Reg were just two people. They hadn't been able to deal with Hawthorne-Rose or Uriel on their own, needing the cat's help. Like most cats, Starlight didn't like car travel and they hadn't bothered to bring him with them. Now they had another person they needed to defend, someone without any paranormal powers.

"Down Main," Warren directed. "To the waterfront."

Reg pressed the gas pedal down farther. She weaved in and out of traffic, keeping an eye out for any police cars. Maybe it would be good if they attracted the attention of the police. They could take them to the warehouse and show them what was going on. They could get help.

She heard a voice in her head. *You should have come to the police. Civilians shouldn't be trying to handle this kind of thing on their own. You knew there was an investigation into the plane crash. As soon as you found out Warren was alive, you should have contacted us.*

Now, she was going to do it again. Fly right into a potentially deadly situation without any police support, expecting everything to come out right in the end. Maybe they should call the police and get them to raid the warehouse instead of running blindly into it themselves.

But she didn't want more police officers missing or hurt. She didn't want to have to explain how they knew what they did. She didn't want to have to talk about psychic phenomena to nonbelievers. She still didn't believe half of it herself, in spite of all she'd had to do to free Warren from the clutches of evil warlocks. It was too much to expect anyone to believe. She wasn't going to believe it herself after she'd had a chance to think about it.

"It's the third one down…" Warren gestured. "The one with the yellow doors."

"Stop back here," Corvin instructed. "We don't want to give ourselves away."

Reg pulled in behind a big white van, out of sight of the warehouse.

"What are we going to do?" she asked. "Just go in there?"

Corvin looked at her. He glanced over at Warren.

"Can you tell who's in there?" he asked Reg.

Time for more performing in front of a nonbeliever. It had never bothered Reg when it was just an act. But that had all changed. Reg closed her eyes and concentrated on the warehouse, trying to give nothing away by her expression.

She didn't need to channel anyone or faint or do anything big. Just take a remote look to see who was in there.

She stretched her consciousness out toward the warehouse. She saw the crates again, the ones she had seen in Uriel's mind. She again felt the clouds of sadness surrounding them. She could feel other consciousnesses in the building and struggled to identify them. She had met both Ling and Jessup face to face, and was pretty sure they were there. But was there anyone else? They didn't want to walk in on Dreadlocks or any of the others in the enterprise. Reg explored the building, wishing that they had brought Starlight with them after all. He would have helped her to focus and be more sure of herself. She was tiring after all she had already been required to do.

Corvin reached over and took her hand. Reg jolted and opened her eyes, glaring at him for startling her.

"Sorry," he apologized. "I just thought... I might be able to help."

Reg stared at him, not pulling away. He was, she had learned, not to be trusted. But he had returned her gifts to her and had helped to bind Uriel and Hawthorne-Rose. Was there any possibility that he was part of their venture? Or maybe he hoped to take it over, whatever it was, now that Uriel and Hawthorne-Rose were out of the way?

Corvin's mind was open to her. Maybe because he had held her powers not so long ago, or maybe because he had some psychic skills of his own and was able to consciously lower his defenses. She felt for his intentions. Nearest the surface was his desire to help her and to rescue Ling and Jessup. That, at least, was genuine, and maybe that was all she needed to know in order to use him.

There was, though, much that was buried deeper, too deep for her to explore before making her decision. Among other intentions and desires was a hunger, a deep, gnawing hunger that he had locked away as deeply as he could, but she could still sense it. He resisted when, curious, she tried to pursue it.

"I can help," Corvin repeated.

Reg withdrew. She nodded. Still holding his hand, she tried to use him like she had Starlight, drawing on his power to boost her own flagging abilities. She didn't want his thoughts, only his strength. She could immediately feel the difference. She confirmed to herself that both Ling and Jessup were in the warehouse, but she couldn't make contact with them, so they were probably awake, not unconscious. That was good news. She couldn't sense anyone else in the warehouse or guarding it from outside.

"It's just them," she told Corvin. "Just Ling and Jessup."

"Let's go in, then."

The three of them got out of the car. Warren was looking at Reg with a puzzled expression, but said nothing. They circled the building, checking the doors, which of course were all locked. Warren grimaced. "If I had my clothes… I did have a key…"

"Fortunately, I have a few skills other than witchcraft," Corvin said. He examined the locks on the back entrance. Reg waited for him to pull out a set of lock picks and open it like a burglar on TV, but instead he picked up a cinderblock from the rubbish in the alley, and smashed the doorknob off with it. He reached into the hole it left, cleared the debris, and swung the door open.

Reg stared at it, openmouthed. Corvin chuckled.

"Lives are at stake," he pointed out. "I don't think now is the time for delicacy."

They all entered the building.

Even though Reg already knew there was no one in the building other than Ling and Jessup, she still tiptoed and listened for any hint of someone else guarding the building. She didn't know if it were possible for someone to be there, hiding himself behind a spell. But she wasn't going to walk right in as if she owned the place.

She led the others, feeling Ling and Jessup's location. It was like intuition, but it wasn't. She would have said that she was just guessing where they were, but she knew it wasn't true. It was a difficult thing to put into words.

Reg opened the door to a small administrative office and saw both women lying bound on the floor. She let out a long sigh of relief. Warren hurried to Ling and Corvin to Jessup, pulling away their gags.

Jessup swore. Her voice was hoarse and weak.

"Hunter. Tell me you disarmed the snares before you busted in here."

★ Chapter Twenty-Seven ★

REG LOOKED AT CORVIN. She hadn't seen him do anything special as they approached the building or the room, but that didn't mean that he hadn't quietly removed any spells before walking through them. But by his pallor, she gathered that he hadn't.

He cleared his throat. "What snares?"

"You think they would leave us here with no guard and no magical protection?" Jessup demanded.

"Uh…"

Reg resisted the urge to run back out the way they had come before something bad could happen. But if Jessup was right, it was already too late, and she didn't know what she would be running into.

She looked at Corvin. He got up and walked back to the office door they had come in. It had whooshed shut behind them on a pneumatic closer and clicked into place. Reg had thought nothing of it. Corvin wiggled the handle, but it was locked. He looked around. Reg knew he was looking for something heavy to break it off as he had with the outside door. The room was bare. Corvin shouldered the door experimentally.

Reg shook her head. "It opens inward."

Corvin studied the door. "Yeah, you're right."

Considering the hinges, Reg looked around for a screwdriver or other tool she could use to pry the pins out of them. But just like when Corvin had looked for something to break the handle, she came up empty. Even MacGyver couldn't have found a tool to get them out of the room. But he probably would have at least had a Swiss Army knife in his pocket. Reg patted her pockets, but she knew she wasn't carrying anything. She had just pulled on the first pants she had found. She hadn't even grabbed her phone or purse. If she hadn't needed the keys to start her car, she wouldn't even have brought them. Reg eyed the hinges, wondering whether her keys could be used to pry the pins out.

She sighed. Not likely. Besides, they were probably magically protected against tampering.

"Do you have your phone?" she asked Corvin.

He patted his pockets as if he weren't sure, and pulled out an ancient-looking Blackberry. He pressed a button and looked at the screen. "Battery has been drained," he said. "No big surprise."

Warren had managed to pick out the knots binding Ling's wrists to free her hands. Ling looked drawn and pale, but unharmed. He looked around.

"If the door is locked, try the window," he suggested.

Reg crossed the room and checked the window. It was not a sealed unit, but had a bottom portion designed to slide on a track, with a screen to let in fresh air. She flipped the lever to unlock the window and slid it open.

They all just looked at it. A three-year-old might have been able to wriggle through the opening if the screen were punched out. But none of them were going to be able to push their heads or shoulders through.

Corvin knelt back down to untie Jessup. She was in her police uniform, but her utility belt and all of its accouterments had been removed. No gun. No tools.

She moved stiffly, rubbing her wrists and shoulders and flexing her legs. "Hawthorne-Rose?"

"He's at Reg's place," Corvin nodded to Reg. "A little... stuck at the moment."

Jessup rubbed her temples. "Everything just fell apart. As soon as he saw Ling at the hospital... I knew he was dirty."

Corvin nodded sympathetically.

Jessup gazed at Reg. "Heaven help us from interfering civilians! Why couldn't you have just called the police when you found Warren? Or better yet, when you thought he was alive? You sent his wife right into the teeth of things."

"I'm sorry. I... didn't think anyone would believe me. I mean, I know some police departments use psychics occasionally... but I didn't think they were ever really taken seriously."

"No. And you can see why, given how flaky and unreliable they are!"

Reg looked away, her face flaming. Ling and Warren murmured together quietly, obviously happy to be back together again, but not facing the issue of their all being locked in a tiny room together as the day started to heat up. Reg could see from Jessup's and Ling's condition that they had already suffered from one day's captivity. Another without water might just finish Ling off. Jessup looked stronger, but that didn't mean she'd last much longer than Ling. They needed to find a way out.

"Reg has been a big help," Corvin said. "Don't blame her for all of this. She broke the binding spell."

Jessup's eyes widened. *"She* broke it?"

Corvin nodded. "Not bad for a raw beginner!"

"I just assumed..." Jessup trailed off.

Reg leaned against the wall, trying to sort everything out. "You... know about magic?" she asked Jessup.

"Yes. But don't go spreading that around. It needs to stay under wraps." Jessup leaned back, pushing sweaty hair out of her face. "Not that you're going to have a chance to say anything to anyone. The outlook at this point is... pretty bleak."

"Don't say that. We'll figure it out."

"Unless you have experience breaking out of enchanted prisons, I highly doubt it."

Reg set her jaw stubbornly. She had never been one to take no for an answer. A lot of people had told her she couldn't do things... but she'd usually done them anyway.

Corvin grinned at her as if he knew exactly what she was thinking. "Well? What's the plan, Reg?"

"I don't know yet." Reg looked around the bare room. "How does it work, this trap? Is it just the locked door? Or if we get out of here, will here be something else in its place?"

"Probably every hallway and door between here and the outside," Jessup said. "That witch doctor knew some serious stuff. Breaking in here without first ascertaining what protections were in place… that was a big mistake."

"I checked for guards," Reg said, shaking her head. "But I don't know the first thing about magic."

"But this one does," Jessup nodded to Corvin. "What were you thinking?"

"I was thinking… get in, get the hostages before Uriel and Hawthorne-Rose manage to wriggle free… and get out."

"You got Uriel too?"

"Sure."

"I wish you'd shown some sense! We could have broken this cabal up for good! What's got you so distracted?"

Corvin raised his brows and looked toward Reg.

"Oh, good grief," Jessup grumbled. "Can't you forget your appetite for once and think about the bigger picture? Think about someone other than yourself?"

Anger flashed over Corvin's usually good-natured features. "Why do you think I came here? What do you think is in it for me? If I ever did anything altruistic, this is it!"

"Yeah, sure," Jessup said. "I'm sure the thought of a warehouse full of rare magical ingredients had nothing to do with it."

Corvin laughed and didn't disagree. Reg looked back and forth between the two of them. "So how do you guys know each other? You're friends?"

Jessup snorted. "Adversaries would be more accurate. Enemies doesn't quite catch the essence of it."

"Respected adversaries," Corvin clarified. "Among other things."

"Huh. You wish."

Reg tried to imagine their position inside the building. "So if we tried to go back out the way we came, we would just keep encountering more roadblocks. But what if we went out this way." She indicated the window. It was, as far as Reg could tell, right at the edge of the property line. If they could get out the window, they could get off the property without having to deal with any more traps.

"How are you going to do that?" Jessup demanded. "Those are burglar bars. You can't get through unless you have the ability to shrink yourself down to the size of a coffee cup."

"One problem at a time."

"Unless you can walk through walls…"

That, unfortunately, was not a skill Reg had mastered. It certainly would have made it easier for her to have escaped some of the more abusive homes. Or school. Or interrogation rooms. A quick escape was always better than trying to fight.

Reg examined the window. She touched it, as if she could learn more about it just by being in physical contact with it. Had it been enchanted as well? Maybe there was no point in even trying to escape through the window.

"What do you think?" Corvin asked.

"The grille is over the inside."

"Making it pretty difficult for us to break the glass. Or to get the grille off without any tools."

Reg followed the grille around the edge of the window. At first look, it was attached directly to the wall with concrete screws. Pretty impenetrable. But it wasn't actually. She could see hinges along one side so that it could be swung open away from the window.

"For people to get out if there was a fire," she murmured. She went to the opposite side of the window and gave the bars a tug. There was a clang when they moved and then were stopped. Reg found a padlock through a loop that locked the entire structure in place. That was the weak point.

Close beside her, Corvin reached up and examined the lock. "We still don't have any way to get it open."

"Maybe."

He raised an eyebrow. "Oh?"

She gazed up at the lock. "When you were at my house and you knocked those papers down, and you made a whirlwind that attacked Hawthorne-Rose…"

"Uh-huh…?"

"Was that your power or mine?"

He chuckled. "I haven't ever shown any talent for telekinesis before."

"So it was mine?"

He nodded.

"I didn't know… I never realized I could control objects without touching them. I mean, I've done it before…" She was aware that she sounded like a loon. "But I just brushed it off, you know? Said that it was just a coincidence or my imagination."

He looked up at the padlock. "You think you can work the lock?"

"I don't know. I never tried before."

He shrugged.

Jessup had been listening. "Well, give it a try. What's it going to hurt?"

"I don't know. Could it make something bad happen? I mean… I trigger some spell that starts the room filling up with water? Or snakes?"

Jessup laughed. "I don't think you need to worry about that!"

"You think it's safe to try?"

The police woman hadn't moved from her spot on the floor. She gazed up at the lock, squinting. "I don't think that thing's been touched in years. I doubt if they even saw it. They just thought the grille was installed directly into the wall, like I did."

"Okay." Reg breathed out a puff of air and looked at Corvin. She rubbed her fingers together, limbering them up. "Any tips?"

"It's your power. You know it better than I do. You've been using it your whole life."

"And I gather by the way you got into the building that you're not an expert lock-picker."

Jessup snorted again. Corvin looked at her. "That hurts, woman."

"It's a simple tumbler," Jessup told Reg. "You put a key in, and the points of the key press the pins. When the pins are pushed in, the tumbler can turn and unlock the padlock."

"How do I know which pins to press?"

"Any that are sticking out."

That didn't sound too complicated. If she were trying to insert a tool to find and press the pins, that would be more difficult, but she only had to feel for them with her mind and press them in. No clumsy tools.

Reg thought about the lock. She thought about the parts Jessup described and how they moved. About the purpose of the lock. Its purpose wasn't just to lock, but to unlock. If the people who had installed the bars hadn't had need for them to open, there would have been no need for a lock. They could have just screwed them into the wall.

The purpose of the lock was to allow access, so Reg concentrated on that, talking to the inanimate object in her mind, reminding it of its reason for existing. She felt for the pins and pressed against them, waiting patiently for everything to come together and for the lock to pop open.

Nothing happened.

★ Chapter Twenty-Eight ★

R EG WAS SWEATING. THE room was getting
hotter and her mental work was taxing. She wiped her
forehead and looked at Jessup, shaking her head.

"I can feel it all, but... it's like there's something pushing
back against me. I can't get it to cooperate."

Jessup banged her head back on the wall. "The
protection spells must have included the lock. Good idea, but
it looks like they thought of that."

"So these spells... how do they work? If we cut the
lock... would it prevent us from cutting it? Or would the cut
heal? Or once you cut it, would that get you to the next step,
until you were through all of the layers of protection?"

"If you cut the lock, that protection would fail. But they
didn't leave us anything to work with."

"No," Reg agreed. She stared out into the alley, looking
for anything that they could use out there. If she could call
an object into the room...

But even outside, there didn't seem to be anything useful
to them. The place had been sterilized.

She could hear the calls of birds through the open
window. Sea birds calling to each other. They were very close
to the water. She could picture them circling over the beach,
looking for food.

"Reg?"

Reg startled. She looked at Warren, surprised. He hadn't
shown any inclination to talk to her before that, or even that
he knew her name.

"Yes?"

"Do you think you can get us out of here?" He looked down at Ling, leaning against him with her eyes closed. How much longer was Ling going to last? Reg had failed to help her. She had failed all of them.

She stared out at the sky. Freedom was so close. Just on the other side of the bars and glass. She didn't know whether Hawthorne-Rose expected them to just die of dehydration or whether he planned to come back and kill them when he escaped Reg's house. So far, he had avoided killing anyone outright. Maybe to avoid the bad karma, or maybe he was just a chicken, Reg didn't know which.

She pictured him as a strutting chicken, which lifted her mood a little. She wondered when Sarah would get back from her errands, and if the men would still be in the cottage when she got there. She'd head over to have a heart-to-heart with Reg, and find two strangers there.

Though they probably weren't strangers to her. The magical community wasn't that large. Uriel and Sarah both frequented The Crystal Bowl, so they undoubtedly knew each other.

Or maybe they were working together; Sarah handy to keep Reg from finding out what was going on.

"No," Reg murmured.

"You don't think we can get out?" Warren asked, eyes wide.

Reg ignored him, looking instead to Corvin and Jessup. "Is Sarah involved? Is there any way at all that Sarah's involved in this?"

Corvin frowned and shook his head. "She's the ultimate good witch," he said. "There is no such thing, of course, but... Sarah Bishop would never involve herself in something as dirty as this."

"Sarah helped you to find Warren, didn't she?" Jessup asked, eyes narrow.

Reg was surprised. She had been pretty careful not to tell the police that Sarah and Letticia had been involved, not wanting to get them into trouble. But Jessup had known or guessed it anyway. She nodded, thinking about it.

"Yeah. There wouldn't be any point in helping me to find Warren if she was involved, would there? She'd steer me away. Tell me not to get involved. She wouldn't have offered to help."

"That's right," Jessup agreed.

"Then I might just have an idea…"

Reg had been at it for an hour, and everyone had given up on her, but she wasn't giving in so easily.

"Come here," she said softly through the screen. The pigeon bobbing up and down looked at her blankly, then went on bobbing and scratching away at the pavement.

Reg growled under her breath, frustrated, and the gray pigeon flew away.

"You're better with cats," Corvin said, looking up at her from where he sat on the floor, leaning against the wall. Like the others, he was trying to stay out of the sun and to use as little energy as possible.

"I know I'm better with cats," Reg agreed, "but Sarah doesn't like cats. It needs to be a bird."

"Pigeons are stupid animals," Jessup said. "Talk about your bird brains."

Reg widened her focus, looking for another bird to try to talk to. Jessup was right about pigeons. Reg hadn't felt any connection with the creature, other than that watching it eat made her hungry. She hadn't had anything for breakfast.

She felt pigeons, gulls, other seabirds… none of them seemed like a very good target for Reg's needs. Then a crow. She'd heard that birds in that family could be very intelligent, and they could certainly be associated with witches. Erin's witch friend in Tennessee had befriended a crow. It would come to her and land on her shoulder and talk to her.

Reg focused on the black bird, trying to coax it to come to her. Warren said something, and Corvin shushed him. Reg could feel them watching her, but she forced her thoughts outward, calling to the nearby crow. It was some time before the crow put in an appearance, fluttering down from the sky to land on the open window. He made Reg jump, startled, and she was afraid at first that she had lost her connection with him. But he perched on the edge of the window, looking in at her curiously with glittering, beady black eyes.

Reg tried to project images to him. The cottage. Sarah. The lock that was holding them prisoner.

"Bring her here," Reg told him, concentrating hard. "Bring Sarah here."

There was no way he was going to do it. Crows were smart, and birds had a good sense of direction, but no bird was going to fly from the warehouse to Sarah's house just because Reg told him to. And no bird was going to be able to convince Sarah that Reg was in danger and needed Sarah's immediate attendance. It was a lost cause.

"Don't give up," Corvin said. "You've got its attention. Keep trying."

Reg glanced over at him. He was way too good at reading her. Maybe he'd retained just a little of her extrasensory powers.

She looked back at the bird. She wished she could feed it something or promise it some kind of reward. Animals were very primal creatures. They worked well when rewarded.

She repeated the images, repeated her pleas to bring Sarah to them. Begged the bird to listen.

And then it flew away.

★ Chapter Twenty-Nine ★

REG COLLAPSED ON THE floor beside Corvin. She was slick with sweat, her brain wrung out, and she could think of nothing else that could get them out of their predicament. Why was everyone looking to her for a solution? She was the newcomer. She didn't even know how their community worked, let alone how real magic worked. She didn't know the extent of her own powers. How was she supposed to get them out of a magically locked room?

"You did your best," Corvin said, reaching over and rubbing her back, ignoring the fact that her shirt was soaked with sweat. "You've had a brutal day of it."

"You think so?" Reg returned, impotent anger stirring within her. "Starting with waking up this morning to find that you had stolen my powers from me? What's up with that, by the way? You think there's nothing wrong with sneaking around, stealing other people's gifts away from them?"

Jessup looked over, frowning. Corvin raised his hands in defense. "I did nothing against the law," he insisted. "Everything was by the rules."

"Rules," Reg fumed. "You think you can hide behind some set of rules imposed by this community and that makes what you did okay? You violated me! You got me into a vulnerable position and then took away a part of me! That's not right."

Corvin shrugged. "I can't help my nature. No more than you can help yours."

"Your nature? It's your nature to prey on people?"

"Isn't it a cat's nature to chase a mouse? You don't blame the cat for that. You might not like him bringing you home dead birds and rodents, but you don't expect him to stop."

"You're not a cat."

"When you were a little girl and people told you that you shouldn't see spirits, did that stop you?"

Reg hesitated at that. "No."

"Did you try to stop?"

"Yes. Sometimes. And by the time I was an adult, I was pretty good at keeping it buried."

"But it didn't stay buried, did it?" He smiled. "You decided to become a medium. You decided to come here. You decided to exercise those powers again. And now... everything you buried is coming back up again, isn't it?"

Reg couldn't very well deny it. But there was a difference between her trying to bury her gift for communicating with the dead and his victimizing innocent people, stealing away their gifts. There was no comparison.

"What you did was wrong. It was violent. It was evil!"

"You said you wished to be normal and live without your powers," he reminded her. And despite herself and what she knew about him, she couldn't help but feel Corvin's glamour as he leaned in close. He charmed her even though she knew what kind of a predator hid under that enticing exterior. The scent of roses filled her nostrils, cloying in the closeness of the room.

"It wasn't a wish. It was just... an observation."

"You did everything necessary to allow me into your home. You yielded to me."

"Do you really think I wanted you to take it all away? You knew I didn't. But you did it anyway. You intentionally hid what it was you wanted from me. You tricked me."

"Certainly. There's nothing wrong with that."

"Nothing wrong with it? Deceit and theft? Violation of... of my spirit? How is that not wrong?"

"Because you allowed me to do it." He smiled serenely at her. Reg fought her attraction to him. She slipped into his head. If he could steal what was hers, she could at least have a look around his psyche.

When he had helped her to scan the warehouse, she had been aware of his hunger. It was pushed away so she wouldn't be distracted by it and could just focus on the task at hand, but she had noted it anyway. He was unprepared for her presence this time, and the hunger was almost overwhelming. She backed off, uncertain. For a few minutes, she just observed him, getting used to the strangeness of his mind.

The hunger was like a gnawing in his middle. But it wasn't physical hunger. He'd had tea that morning and little else, so like Reg, he would have liked a good meal. But the hunger in his brain wasn't the same as the hunger in his body. It was much worse, almost crippling in its intensity.

He pushed her out. Reg looked down at Corvin's hand on her arm, warm and friendly.

"You see?" he said softly. "That's my need. And it isn't satisfied by food or other pleasures. Those things won't fill me up. Nothing will. Nothing but… fresh powers. The gifts that others hold."

Reg's mouth was dry. She stared at him, trying to comprehend it. How often could that need in him actually be filled? It wasn't like he could find naive new prey every day. He walked around every day with that gaping hole demanding to be filled, pressing on him during everything he did.

"I'm forced to abide by rules imposed by others. Imagine having to ask for permission for every bite of meat. Not for permission from a parent or teacher or doctor, but leave from the animal itself. Can you imagine?"

Reg nodded. She didn't need to imagine it, she had felt it. A pain that could only be assuaged by taking what he needed from someone else.

"Is it wrong?" Corvin demanded again. "It is my nature."

"I… I don't know," Reg admitted.

Insisting that a carnivore subsist as a herbivore only resulted in the carnivore starving to death. Wasn't it wrong to force a predator to go hungry because you were offended by his table manners?

There was a tapping on the window.

Reg was glad to tear herself away from the discussion with Corvin. She didn't have the answers to their philosophical discussion. She knew how she had felt when he had taken her gifts from her, leaving her feeling naked and vulnerable. But she had also felt his hunger, and she could only imagine what it must feel like to have it satisfied. She had seen that relaxed, satiated expression on his face when she had gotten up in the morning. At peace with himself and with the world. Happy, for however long the new powers would satisfy him.

Reg got up and looked out the window. The crow was back.

"We need help," Reg told the bird again, frustrated. "Can't you bring help? We need—"

She heard screeching tires. Help had arrived.

★ Chapter Thirty ★

SARAH'S VAN SPED INTO sight. It was a good thing that there weren't any guards watching the warehouse, because the witch's approach wasn't exactly covert. She raced into the parking lot of the next property over and slammed on the brakes, screeching to a stop. Corvin and Warren got up to look out the window. Jessup struggled to get her feet under her.

Reg ducked down to the open window. She pressed her hand to the screen.

"Sarah!"

Sarah hurried toward her. "I'm here, I'm here! I'm sorry, it's been such a crazy day…"

"Thank goodness. We need help. I didn't know what to do…"

"I got your message," Sarah said, face wreathed in smiles. She brandished a set of bolt cutters. "I think you were looking for this?"

"Regina, you are a miracle," Corvin breathed reverently.

Sarah used the bolt cutters to bite through the screen, cutting through it like butter. Reg took them, grinning. She went to the side of the window where the padlock was and surveyed it.

"You're taller than me," she said to Corvin. "You want to do the honors?"

"Are you sure?"

"Have at it."

He took the bolt cutters from her, positioned the blades around the shaft of the lock, and snapped the handles together. Despite Reg's worries that the metal of the lock might have been magically strengthened to resist such an attempt, he had no trouble cutting through it. He reached up and lifted the lock out of the loop. Reg swung the bars on the hinge. It creaked loudly in protest. She and Corvin ducked underneath it and faced the large panes of glass. It wouldn't be much longer, and they would be out. Reg looked around for something to break the glass.

"Sarah, is there a rock or something out there that we could use…"

"Just a moment. I've got just the thing."

Sarah went back to the van and opened the back door. She returned with a sledgehammer.

"I thought this might come in handy. Do you think it would do?"

"I think it will do!" Reg agreed.

Sarah passed it through the lower window. Reg lifted the sledgehammer higher. It was heavy and sent lightning bolts of pain through her injured hand. But she gripped it tightly, getting ready to hit one out of the park.

"Better move out of the way."

Sarah withdrew a few steps back and to the side. Reg swung the hammer.

She had been tentative, worried that she would hit some spell or force-field and the sledgehammer would just bounce back harmlessly. But it smashed through the glass with a crash, sending shards of glass scattering.

"We're clear!" Corvin announced, a wide grin on his face. "Let's get out of here!"

They cleared as much glass as they could from the edge and helped Jessup to her feet. Getting up and over the windowsill was not easy, especially for Jessup in her weakened state. Corvin and Warren worked together to get Ling up and over it as well, then laid her on the pavement outside in a patch of shade.

Reg heard cawing and looked up. The bird was above them somewhere, out of sight.

"Thank you," she told it fervently, both aloud and in her mind.

Sarah smiled. "They are very intelligent animals," she informed Reg. "Birds in the crow family are second only to humans in their intelligence." She paused, thinking about it. "Though some birds I know would surpass humans, if you knew what they were thinking."

"We owe our rescue to my namesake," Corvin said. He was the last one to climb through the broken window to freedom.

Reg frowned at him.

"Corvin means raven," he clarified further. "The crow family is called corvid."

"Oh… who knew."

"Maybe that's why Sarah likes me so much." Corvin said with a sly look toward the older woman.

Reg laughed, feeling a bit giddy after their escape.

Sitting on the pavement and leaning against the wall for support, Jessup was patting at her uniform pockets and waist, then finally seemed to realize she didn't have what she was looking for. She looked at Sarah.

"Do you have a phone? Please tell me you're not one of the witches who eschews technology."

Sarah dug into her pocket. "Of course not! I don't know what I would do without my phone!"

They were quiet while Jessup made a call for police backup and ambulances. She hung up.

"Don't tell them you sent a bird to find Sarah," Jessup told Reg, her voice heavy with exhaustion. "Just say… Sarah knew you were coming here."

Reg and Sarah both nodded.

"Did you happen to go by the cottage…?" Corvin asked Sarah.

"Your prisoners are still there," Sarah acknowledged. "I strengthened the bonds a little before coming. Didn't want them following me here."

"Smart old crone," Corvin approved.

"I'll send someone to pick them up," Jessup said. "But you'd better make sure they're physically restrained first. No point in making the police department wonder why they're just sitting there waiting to be arrested."

Corvin chuckled. His eyes were drawn back to the warehouse. "We'll also have to counter the snares here before the police go in."

"I'll tell them we need the bomb squad. It always takes them hours to breach a building. Should be plenty of time for all of us to clear the worst of the snares, if we're working together."

"And what would my payment be for helping out?"

Jessup rolled her eyes. "Hunter, you are the most self-centered warlock—"

"—you've ever had the privilege of meeting," Corvin finished for her. "So? What do we get? You said something about a warehouse full of rare objects…"

"What exactly were they smuggling?" Warren asked. "I thought it must be drugs."

In spite of all he had seen, he obviously still didn't grasp that he really was dealing with paranormal activities. It was amazing how blind a person could choose to be to what he had seen with his own eyes. Reg looked at the others, trying to determine how much it was acceptable to tell Warren. Jessup gave her a warning look. Reg understood they were sanitizing things for the police and it was best to let Warren stay ignorant of the details.

"They were poachers," she told him, "smuggling animal trophies to other countries. Maybe other artifacts as well."

Warren nodded, understanding. "The more endangered an animal is, the more valuable it is to someone. It's really sickening what people will do for profit."

"So…?" Corvin crouched down close to Jessup. "You could afford to let a few items slide in my direction, couldn't you?"

She closed her eyes tiredly. "You help me, Hunter, and we'll see."

He laid his hand on her arm and held it there, watching her face. Jessup's wan face started to pink up. She opened her eyes and looked at him. Their faces were so close together

Corvin would have only have to move a fraction of an inch to kiss her.

"Dial it back, Hunter." Jessup's voice was strained.

Reg waited, holding her breath. Corvin leaned back. He kept his hand on Jessup. Another minute or two passed, then Jessup pulled back from Corvin. She rubbed her eyes as if she'd just woken up, and rose unsteadily to her feet. They could hear approaching sirens.

"I'll see what I can do for you," she promised.

Jessup walked over to meet the emergency vehicles.

"Why do you want any of what they've got in there?" Reg asked Corvin, thinking of the cloud of unhappiness around the objects. "Are they that valuable?"

He stood close to her, keeping his voice low so they wouldn't be overheard. "Some objects carry latent magical power. That's what makes them so valuable for potions and charms. I'd much rather get my power from the living," he met her eyes, "but I will take whatever I can get."

Just looking at him, she felt a portion of that gnawing hunger. Just as a starving person would eat whatever rotting scraps were thrown his way, Corvin would do what he had to for survival.

"Is that why you came? Because you knew what they were storing here?"

He frowned. "I came because of you."

Reg felt herself blush. "Why? I thought you were only interested in me because you wanted my gifts?"

"And having tasted them once, I'm even more enticed." He gave her a long, languid look. "I've never returned a gift before. It has left us... bonded."

"What do you mean?"

"We had an agreement... that you would give me your powers." He raised a finger to silence any arguments. "When you gave them to me—"

"When you took them."

"When I took them, our... *transaction*... was complete. Both sides had fulfilled their covenants." Reg saw the problem before Corvin concluded. "When I gave them back without recompense, that put us on a different footing."

"What does that mean?"

"It means… you owe me something. And that I am duty-bound to protect you, since that is why I returned them to you."

★ Chapter Thirty-One ★

I T W A S S O M E T I M E before they were finished talking to the police and were given permission to head home. Ling and Warren had gone to the hospital, with Jessup drinking copious amounts of water and promising to check in with her doctor later.

Corvin nodded to Reg's hand. "You want me to drive? That looks pretty painful."

Reg had been doing her best to keep the bloody bandage out of sight so that she wouldn't be sent to the hospital as well. She opened and closed her hand experimentally, wincing.

"It's not that bad. I don't think it needs stitches and there's no damage to tendons or anything."

"Merely a flesh wound?"

Reg forced herself to smile back at him. "Yeah. I'll just keep it clean and make sure it's healing okay."

She handed him her keys. There was no reason she had to be the one to drive home. And he was right, it would be painful to hold the steering wheel. Reg sighed as she settled into the passenger seat.

"So we did good. We got some really bad guys off the street."

Corvin shrugged. "For a while. Prison isn't much of a deterrent. In a few years, they'll be back at it again. If they don't just continue to run things from inside."

"What would you do, then? If it were up to you? What would deter them?"

"Perhaps remove the ridiculous stigma attached to trafficking in magical artifacts. Removing the strictures on killing an animal just because it has become rare. Such restrictions just make it more profitable to deal in them."

"So legalization is your answer?"

"There are far too many restrictions placed on our freedom. How does it hurt you if I make use of the gall bladder of a black bear? Or the bones of a tiger? I wouldn't do such a thing frivolously. So why restrict me?"

"Because those animals will die out."

Corvin shook his head. "If it were legal, they could be farmed. We could have thousands of medicine animals available instead of only a handful. There would be no need for this violence."

Reg shook her head. She had to remind herself that his perspective was necessarily different from hers. She could afford to think of the cute furry animals and the need to protect them. Corvin needed objects of power for his survival and couldn't be worried about the consequences of his predation.

"Do you retain all of the gifts you take?" she asked. "Do you just keep getting more and more powerful? Or do they only last for a while?"

He shifted and pushed the gas pedal down. "How long it lasts depends on the carrier. Some are fleeting. Others have stayed with me for many years. If I was in a situation where I could feast whenever I wanted to…"

A smile played over his lips. Reg shuddered to think about how powerful he could become. Maybe the old tales of powerful kings, wizards, and sorcerers had been about people like him, warlocks who had been able to feed as much as they wanted on the populace, growing in power daily.

"But all warlocks aren't like you. They don't all… do what you do."

"No. The curse—or gift—is rare. Tends to run in families, but most of the old lines carrying it have died out… or been exterminated. Those who are left must submit to regulation or be driven from paranormal communities. Either choice leaves us hungry most of the time. It's a wretched way to live one's life."

"I'm sorry."

He glanced over at her, smiling that charming, predatory smile. "How sorry?"

"Not *that* sorry."

He chuckled. "Too bad. I like you, Regina."

Usually, the men who said that to her didn't actually want to consume her. She looked away and focused on the scenery outside, not wanting to be tempted by his mystical charms.

"Norma Jean wants to talk to you," Corvin said.

Reg already knew that. She could feel Norma Jean stirring around the edges of her consciousness, trying to get her attention.

"How do you know that?"

"I…"

"If you gave me back all of my powers, how do you know Norma Jean is trying to reach me?"

"Apparently, there are still some residual powers… like the drops left at the bottom of the milk jug…"

"Or maybe you kept back a swallow or two for yourself," she suggested.

"Norma Jean is your mother. You don't want to talk to her?"

Reg thought about Amy Calvert's reading with her mother. Not every mother was the soft, sweet woman of Hallmark commercials. Reg's mother had been out of her life for a long time, and for good reason. Reg couldn't help it if Norma Jean's spirit still hung around. It didn't mean Reg had to talk to her.

"No. I don't want to talk to her. Besides, aren't there rules about channeling while driving?"

He smiled at her. "I can't make you listen to what she has to say. But mark my words, Reg Rawlins… your adventures here aren't over. Not by a long shot."

Bonus Material

Did you enjoy this book? Reviews and recommendations are vital to making a book successful. Please leave a review at your favorite book store or review site and share it with your friends.

Don't miss the following bonus material:
Sign up for mailing list to get a free ebook
Read a sneak preview chapter
Learn more about the author

Sign up for my mailing list at pdworkman.com and get
Gluten-Free Murder for free!

JOIN MY MAILING LIST AND

Download a sweet
mystery for free

Sneak Preview of
A Psychic with Catitude

"HOW ARE YOU DOING?" the dark, handsome warlock asked in a husky voice, touching the spot on Reg's hand where Hawthorne-Rose had cut her, sending goosebumps all the way up her arms and down her back.

She tried not to let him see her reaction, smiling with unconcern and inching away from his touch and the heady scent of roses that grew stronger whenever he turned on the charm.

Reg ran her hands through her red cornrow braids to gather them together and pushed them back over her shoulders.

"I'm fine," she said airily. "Looking forward to catching up on my sleep now that Warren is all taken care of and won't be disturbing my dreams. How about you? You look…" Reg searched for a word. He wasn't glowing quite as much as he had when he'd stolen her psychic powers, but he was definitely looking… well-fed. "Uh… you look relaxed."

Corvin nodded, leaning against her doorway, his movements languid. Hospitality would normally have dictated Reg invite him in, but she wasn't quite as naive as she had been. It was best to keep her cottage a safe sanctuary and not extend invitations to potentially predatory visitors.

"Marta—Detective Jessup did manage to… share… some of Uriel Hawthorne's hoard with me." Corvin took a deep breath in and let it out again in a sigh. "You don't know how satisfying it is to fill a hunger that is so…" he looked deep into her eyes, stirring a different kind of need in Reg, "so profound and prolonged."

But Reg did have some idea of what he was talking about. He had allowed her to feel that hunger when she had reached out to him. Reg couldn't imagine living with that kind of hole needing to be filled day after day.

"You should probably be getting on your way," she told him.

"Is it getting to be too late?" he teased. "Is it past your bedtime?"

"Yes," Reg agreed, not letting herself be drawn in. "It's time to feed the cat and go to bed. We can talk tomorrow. You can *call.*" She held up her phone to indicate it.

"I'd rather talk to you face to face."

"And I'd rather be able to breathe." Reg again shifted away from him, but the roses and his glamour followed her. She began to close the door. "Good night."

"Good night, Regina. Pleasant dreams." His words reached her as she shut the door on him. Reg shot the bolt and stood there for a few minutes, waiting for the racing of her heart to slow.

She switched off the light, and just as she was turning away from the door, a black shadow streaked across the floor, making her jump and let out a shriek.

It was Starlight, of course, her tuxedo cat. Darting around the room madly, as if tearing after some invisible mouse.

"Regina?" The direction and volume of Corvin's voice suggested he was still standing on the other side of the door. "Are you all right?"

"Yes. It's nothing. Just the cat."

He chuckled. "Goodnight, cat."

Starlight crouched in the shadows under one of the wicker chairs in the living room. Reg heard him hiss a kitty curse at Corvin.

"Now, was that very nice?" she asked him. "He was just wishing you a good night."

Reg went into the kitchen. As she expected, Starlight quickly left his hiding place to join her, letting out a couple of demanding meows and rubbing against the door of the fridge.

"There's food in your dish," Reg pointed out to him, determined that one day he would actually eat the cat food she bought him instead of demanding to be treated like a human being. She had hoped that once Warren's case was solved, he would stop be so demanding and settle into being a normal cat.

But he was anything but normal.

"Other cats eat cat food," she went on.

He didn't even look at his dish, rubbing against the fridge and waiting for her to take the hint and get him his dinner. He must have thought her a particularly stupid human, that he had to keep repeating himself all the time and didn't have her properly trained yet. Sarah, when she had last stopped in for a visit and to make sure that Reg was okay now that all the excitement was over, had automatically walked to the fridge to have a look through the contents and provided Starlight with a couple of tasty morsels, without even asking Reg's permission.

"And Sarah doesn't even like cats," Reg said aloud.

Starlight glared at her, clearly trying to convey to Reg that if someone who didn't like cats could read him well enough to know what it was that he wanted, surely someone with a little bit of telepathy could figure it out.

"I know what you want. I just don't think I should satisfy your ever whim."

He continued to stare at her, his disparate blue and green eyes hypnotic.

Reg sighed. "Fine. But you'd better let me sleep tonight and not keep tearing around here like a Tasmanian devil. Or I'll start locking you in the bathroom at night."

Sarah had suggested earplugs. Reg didn't think she should have to wear them when the cat knew very well that she wanted him to be quiet at night. But she was close to breaking down and buying some.

Reg opened the fridge. She moved slowly as Starlight wound around and between her legs, intent on tripping her up so that he could have a chance at the entire can of tuna instead of just the portion she planned to give him.

She spooned a little on top of his dry kibble, telling herself that if she put it on top of his food, at least there was the chance that he'd eat some of the dry kibble along with the tuna by accident. Even though she knew very well that he was quite adept at eating around it.

"There. Now you've had your supper, so it's time for bed. I'll see you in the morning."

Reg awoke in the morning with cat breath on her face. She opened her eyes, knowing before she did that there was going to be a cat face a whisker away from her own.

"Go away."

Starlight stared back at her, unblinking.

Having had her powers stripped from her for a brief period of time, Reg knew that the feelings that emanated from him, the warmth and intelligence mixed with disappointment and disdain, were part of the psychic energy that Starlight put out. Normal people without any sense of the invisible forces that swirled around him, would just see a cute cat and not feel any of those emotions.

"I need more sleep. I'm still recovering."

She had plenty to recover from, with all that had happened over the previous couple of weeks. But there was no softening of Starlight's gaze. It was light outside. The birds had been singing for hours. Being a nocturnal creature, Starlight had burned off his energy and needed replenishment.

"Just a few more minutes," Reg insisted. She turned her face away from him and closed her eyes again.

Starlight climbed over her and around to her face again. He began to paw at her nose and mouth. Soft paws, no claws. Having felt those claws in the past, Reg was grateful for that, but was not happy with the cat doing his best to wake her up. She reached out and pushed him off the bed.

He went over backward and flopped unceremoniously onto the floor, without a chance to dig his claws into the bedsheets. Reg felt a little bit bad about that.

A little.

Starlight retreated from the bedroom and changed tactics, sitting himself in front of the fridge and yowling mournfully. Reg stuck her fingers in her ears and tried to ignore him; but even with the sound blocked out, she still knew he was complaining and she could feel him calling to her. She pushed herself up and climbed out of bed.

She made the mistake of not shutting the bathroom door tightly, and when she washed her hands and her face with cold water, Starlight had pushed his way in through the door and jumped up on the counter to investigate the running water and dip a paw into the sink. Reg flicked her wet fingers at him, and Starlight went flying off of the counter and skittered out of the room. Served him right for waking her up.

She checked her various social networks and email addresses as she ate breakfast standing at the kitchen island. Starlight chowed down on leftovers from the night before. She knew that Chick-Fil-A was probably not the best choice to keep him healthy, but it at least kept him happy and he wasn't bugging her for anything else while he was at it.

She'd gotten messages from a few new contacts looking for her services as a psychic, some of them through her advertising and some by word of mouth. Her successes over the past few weeks were beginning to be spread around the community. Though she had gone to Florida with the plan of focusing on offering services as a medium, reaching out to the spirits of those who had left the mortal plane, most of the email and direct messages she had received were for other psychic services, and that was okay with Reg. She sipped at her incredibly fresh Florida orange juice while reviewing them. Acting as Warren's medium over the previous couple of weeks had worn her out and she was happy to do some lighter jobs, things that wouldn't suck all of the energy out of her.

"Finding lost objects and predicting the future sounds just fine to me," Reg said aloud to Starlight. "A little palm reading or laying down the tarot cards. That's so much less taxing than channeling spirits."

He looked up from his food for a minute, mouth slightly open as if she had caught him mid-bite. Then he gave his attention to his breakfast once more.

Reg's palm itched, and she scratched it automatically before remembering the cut from Hawthorne-Rose's knife. She yelped in pain. It wasn't deep; nothing that required stitches, but it burned whenever something brushed over it. Starlight looked up at her sharply.

Even though he wasn't yet finished his breakfast, he left it and rubbed up against Reg's legs, looking for reassurance that she was okay.

"It's fine. Just scratched myself."

He continued to rub against her. Reg leaned down and picked him up carefully. "Nothing to worry about. Just a little scratch."

He nosed at her face and sniffed the injured hand she held out to him. He lifted his whiskers into a sort of a cat grimace and sneezed. Reg put him back down on the floor. She did *not* need cat sneezes on her breakfast.

There was a light knock at the door. Sarah opened it and breezed in. Reg had slid back the bolt when she knew she had appointments, figuring that she was safe from intruders during the daylight hours. But she hadn't been expecting a visit from Sarah.

Of course, with the frequency of Sarah's drop-in visits, Reg hadn't *not* expected her, either. Her landlady didn't exactly give her the peace and privacy one would normally expect with a rental property. It didn't help that Reg's summer cottage was right on Sarah's property, in the back yard of the big house.

"You have company," Sarah announced. She was a slightly overweight, grandmotherly woman, who claimed to be both a witch and much older than she looked, which Reg would have put around her late fifties or early sixties. She was wearing a loose-fitting blouse patterned with pink flowers, and rose colored slacks.

Behind her was a young woman, probably just into her twenties, big-eyed and uncertain. She was diminutive, with short, curly brown hair.

"She came to the main house," Sarah said. "I thought I'd just bring her down for you and make sure you have everything you need."

Reg had been taking care of herself for years, but Sarah didn't seem to think she could manage on her own. It *was* nice to have someone who was willing to keep the fridge stocked and steer new customers toward Reg, but at the same time, it could be a little irritating to always have someone in her business.

"You could have just pointed her this way. And yes, I'm fine. I have everything I need."

"You shouldn't be doing so much. You should take a little break and give yourself some time to recover."

"Breaks don't pay the rent. I'm fine. This isn't difficult work." Reg looked toward the young woman, waiting for Sarah to take her cue and leave.

Sarah instead ushered the woman into Reg's living room as if she owned the place—which technically, she did—and bent down to pat Starlight, who was curled on his back on one of the chairs. Sarah wisely petted his head rather than scratching his stomach, which Reg had discovered was a dangerous prospect. Starlight seemed to offer his cute tummy for scratches solely as a means of baiting unsuspecting dupes in order to claw and bite their hands.

"Thank you, Sarah."

Sarah finally got the hint. She smiled and said goodbye to both Reg and her guest, leaving them alone.

"Sorry about that," Reg said. "She means well."

"Oh, no, I am sorry." The young woman's cheeks were pink. "I know you said I should go around back, but I forgot. I should not have bothered her."

"She doesn't mind. Obviously. So…" Reg scooped Starlight up and sat down. Starlight wriggled and squirmed until Reg was forced to let him go, and then he stalked off to one of the bedrooms. Reg looked back at her visitor. "How can I help you today?"

"I hoped you could tell me my future… I have a sister I haven't seen for a long time and I want to find her."

Reg nodded. "Sure, of course. Did you want me to read your palm? Or the cards?" She had recently added a beautiful crystal ball to her props. She motioned to it. "Maybe gaze into the crystal?"

A Psychic with Catitude, book #2 in the *Reg Rawlins, Psychic Detective* series by P.D. Workman is coming soon!

About the Author

For as long as P.D. Workman can remember, the blank page has held an incredible allure. After a number of false starts, she finally wrote her first complete novel at the age of twelve. It was full of fantastic ideas. It was the spring board for many stories over the next few years. Then, forty-some novels later, P.D. Workman finally decided to start publishing. Lots more are on the way!

P.D. Workman is a devout wife and a mother of one, born and raised in Alberta, Canada. She is a homeschooler and an Executive Assistant. She has a passion for art and nature, creative cooking for special diets, and running. She loves to read, to listen to audio books, and to share books out loud with her family. She is a technology geek with a love for all kinds of gadgets and tools to make her writing and work easier and more fun. In person, she is far less well-spoken than on the written page and tends to be shy and reserved with all but those closest to her.

~ ~ ~

Please visit P.D. Workman at pdworkman.com to see what else she is working on, to join her mailing list, and to link to her social networks.

~ ~ ~

If you enjoyed this book, please take the time to recommend it to other purchasers with a review or star rating and share it with your friends!